EARLY MANY A MORNING

There is only one thing which interests me vitally now, and that is the recording of all that which is omitted in books ... only the killers seem to be extracting from life some satisfactory measure of what they are putting into it. The age demands violence, but we are getting only abortive explosions. Revolutions are nipped in the bud, or else succeed too quickly. Passion is quickly exhausted, men fall back on ideas, *comme d'habitude.* Nothing is proposed that can last more than twenty-four hours. We are living a million lives in the space of a generation.

Henry Miller *Tropic of Cancer*

Laeg: You have had no sound sleep
Since you stopped the great táin.
Because there were so few to help
You woke early many a morning.

The Táin (Trans. Thomas Kinsella)

Brandon Originals

Early
Many a Morning

Seán Rooney

BRANDON

First published in 1994 by
Brandon Book Publishers Ltd.
Dingle, Co. Kerry, Ireland

British Library Cataloguing in Publication Data is available for this book.

ISBN 0 86322 181 5

This book is published with the financial assistance of the Arts Council/An Chomhairle Ealaíon, Ireland

For Gerard, Big Tom, Thalia and Lorraine C.

Front cover photograph – the Peaceline,Bombay St. West Belfast – by Mike Abrahams, Network
Cover design by The Graphiconies, Dublin
Typeset by Koinonia Ltd, Bury
Printed by ColourBooks Ltd, Dublin

PREFACE

What we were given, we had to believe.

No matter what was to happen, nor who said otherwise, we had to believe it was possible. The pain, the fear, was penance; was a test, a hardship sent to try us, to push our faith to the limits and finally make us worthy to enter the kingdom.

The kingdom lay beyond the ruins, beyond the gas and smarting smoke, through the ruins of our streets, the ruins of our minds, our hearts, our bodies. Past the prison camps, the filthy alleys with their bloody secrets, the dark green fields of our country; past the concealed wires and traps, further than the watchtowers and checkpoints, beyond villages shrouded in betrayal; through the ruins of our sanity, of what passed for humanity; the kingdom ever beyond our reach, further than hope could carry.

This is not to condemn or to credit. There is no cause to plead; above all, no cause. Also no regret.

For this, this is how it was, how it felt. A shaky recording of an old, unloved melody, the sound of people destroying each other in the struggle to live, the noise of the jail, the party and the wake; the sound of the ruins, which is, ultimately, silence.

CHAPTER ONE

THE PLACE WAS Archer's Tavern (established 1927) in the maw of what the outside world called the ghetto, where we were proud to live. The time was Friday, mid-seventies, just weeks after Claire O'Brien had introduced me to the joys and pains of love. I was hiding from her in Archer's, the pub with an exclusively male clientele, where you had to be under twenty-one to get served.

There was me, Spink Driscoll, Bricks O'Hare and Dingus Grey, who had been drinking all day and was giving out about traditional music.

'Them Clancy Brothers are full of shite. Anyone listens to them wants their heads examined.'

'You looking for a fight, wee lad?' said Spink, mock offence on his pimple-dashed face. 'The Clancys are the best thing to come out of Ireland.'

He proceeded to sing, more with verve than tone.

'What have I now, said yon fine old woman,

'What have I nowww, this fianne ould woman did say ...'

'Quit singing before we're barred,' I said firmly.

'You wouldn't call that singing, for frig sakes!'

'Jealousy, lads. The green-eyed god. I'd give Rod Stewart a run for his money, the hoarse bollocks.'

'At least the hoarse bollocks doesn't sing "The Irish Rover".'

'I take it we're not for O'Toole's tonight?'

'I'm fed up with this traditional shit,' moaned Dingus. 'Let's go down to Dixie's, get some talent for a change.'

'Get your head blown off for a change.'

'Dixie's is safe enough these days. You get the drinks in, Spinkey, then we'll head.'

'Count me out, Dingus. Too much like Indian country for me,' I said.

Spinkey grinned. 'He's only saying that 'cause he's giving Claire O'Brien one tonight. Aren't ye, wee lad?'

'Ye're not, are ye?'

'Dirty rumour.'

'Dirty blurt. Look at his face, lads. What colour's red, then?'

'Claire O'Brien, by Jesus. How did ye manage that?'

'Jammy bastard. Has she any sisters, hi?'

And so it went for an hour or so, until the darts team arrived and we got short of elbow room. Dingus and Bricks set off for the city centre, well tanked up. Myself and Spinkey stayed on a while.

'Why did you open yer mouth about yer woman?' I asked.

'No harm in it. You can't take the slagging when it's coming back at ye. What about the time you grassed me up over Anne Treanor? No word o' that.'

'I never did.'

'Did so, ye bugger. Couldn't put my head out for a month but some bastard was taking the piss, and I only took her out the once.'

'Even-Stevens, then?'

'Evens, but I still owe you one. Ye're not seeing this Claire one anymore, then?'

'She's getting a bit heavy on it.' We were sitting on, our merry band dispersed, the drink becoming laborious.

'The bells are ringing, for me and my gal ...'

'Shut it, Spink. It's just that she asks too many questions.'

'Too intellectual, eh?'

'Too nosy, more like. She's dead on, but I can't get into

anything serious. I'm too young for that.'

'Happens the best of them. Hang in there. Make a man of ye.'

'Do you know who her brother is?'

'I know. I was just wondering when you'd mention it. *The* Joey O'Brien?'

'Sticky Joe. Dead-eye Dick of the non-existent, reformed, law-abiding Official fucking IRA. I can pick the women, can't I?'

'I see how you and Joe might not get along,' said Spinkey. 'You'll look well going down the wedding aisle on crutches, mind.'

Outside Archer's, the traffic ran drunkenly home, car lights jousting in the night, piercing the descending mist. It was Everyslum: lively in a pointless, easy going, weekend way, with shouts and cries from the home-going denizens. Everyone seemed to know everyone else, and were glad to see them out on a raw night, stout and whiskey making friends of enemies and enemies of friends, till the morning brought second thoughts and sore heads. Spinkey and myself rocked up the road to the chipper, regaling each other with opinion and joke until we reached his house.

'We're still on for tomorrow,' I told him.

'I'll fix the gear up tonight, then. The timing is still the same?'

'Nothing's changed. I was over the route again today.'

'Just the two of us?'

'No need for anyone else. Bradley is organising the wheels. We kick off at four. I'll have you back in time for *The Generation Game*.'

'I should hope so, too. Is the rest of this crap on for tomorrow night?'

I grimaced. 'Seems to be. Don't make any plans for the night.'

'For the next ten years, ye mean.'

'Think positive. Make sure ye grab some sleep.'

'Fair enough. See you the 'morrow.'

'God willing. Take it easy, Spink.'

On the way home I thought of Claire O'Brien and how stupid

I'd been to stand her up. I told myself it was for her own good, but deep down I knew I was afraid of her, of letting her too close, into the secret rooms of my life. Despite all the posturing in Archer's I'd become truly fond of her in the past few weeks. I was the one about to get heavy, and there was too much going on to risk attachment.

At night West Belfast takes on a sombre, shifting form. The shadows and the sparse, buttery street lights meld into a gypsy mist that roams and sways from alley to street, a killer's mist to those who don't know it, a familiar cloak to the local.

In and out of the greys and blacks, now lit by a passing car, now smothered in the pitch of a wall. Running, turning, run. Looking back, staring forward. Whispered commands, muttered asides. Hiss and run, rifle ready, mind at once elsewhere but always here, in the black, in the grey, in the in-between which masks the unknown. The radio crackles as they move in a sinister ballet through the killing grounds of the city, their presence a victory of training over fear, hate over love.

Dingus rolls up the street, laughing to himself, poisoned with loneliness and drink at three in the morning. The patrol stops him, but he isn't having any of it. They give up and walk on, chuckling at the state of him, and Dingus, not one to leave well enough alone, stands in the middle of the street, roaring and guldering about their parentage – 'Get home, ye Limey bastards!' – until two of them return and flatten him with fist, boot and rifle butt, then go on about their passage, backs to the walls and hedges, weaving, racing, now walking steadily, now waiting, watching, listening.

Bricks pushes his younger brother over in the bed, grabbing as much space and blanket as he can. The young lad wakes up and curses in the cold of dawn, mutters and reclaims the covers with sleepy kicks and shoves, then lies between sleep and life, listening to the drone of the early traffic on the road.

Spinkey rises when all are fast asleep. Passing his father's room he hears the highs and lows of their snoring selves, sneaks downstairs, and in the scullery spends an hour working, slowly, carefully, with a tin of paint by the light of an unsilvery moon. He has grown used to working in poor light, assisted only by the beam of a pencil torch, but as he has drink taken he makes himself slower, more methodical than ever before. Deep in the morning he hears a voice roar abuse; distant, ugly, alone. He pauses, listening to the dead street beyond the curtains. Satisfied all is well, he goes on about his work while all around are sleeping.

Upon wakening, the morning fears were in my gut, the familiar tightness and tiredness; the low-key anxiety of my being, rubbing up against the day ahead. Slowly relief permeated my consciousness; awakening in my own bed, still free.

My father's cot was empty in the corner, unmade. I hadn't heard him get up, but out on the landing my two brothers were lost in an adolescent squabble about money, punctuated by the clomping interventions of my sister as she fussed from bedroom to bathroom, telling them to be quiet. She brushed past me on the landing and rushed downstairs and out into the greater world. The two boys hushed when they saw me, then dispersed to the lower quarters of the house.

How strange it had become to me. A boarding house, my mother called it, only half jokingly. Each morning was a process of re-introduction, such was the tension and remoteness that had come between us.

That Saturday I came downstairs to find my father warming his feet by the fire. He shifted himself in the chair to holler at my brothers who were carrying on their row in the kitchen, and then wisely took it out to the back garden. Not for the first time I felt like an anthropologist studying his own tribe. We had no time for each other, walking around each other and then off into a world of ever-widening singularity. There was love there, but so physically absent, so tensely formal, as to be irrelevant.

Much of this was my responsibility. The tension, the strain, came from the chasm which had developed between myself and my father. Our emotional separation had run alongside the war, and been more profound because of it. My father had fiercely opposed the civil rights campaign of years before, demeaning it as a 'pantomime'. He did all in his power to keep me away from it. I grew up slightly bemused among my peers, perplexed at my father's antipathy to what was becoming an all-consuming cause among my youthful friends and neighbours. The more determinedly he shielded me, the more bullying restrictions he imposed upon my thought and movement, the more I came to despise him. After the gross insult of internment, he became ever more desperate in his efforts and words as the streets exploded in anger.

It was around this time I got talking to a militant old gentleman, much sought by the authorities. He enquired after my father's health and asked me, 'Is he back with the movement?'

I was sure he'd gotten it wrong, but he went on to admonish me with tales of my father's adventures in a previous drive for freedom. He told me how my father, as a young man, had ferried explosives and bullets from one end of town to the other, spotting targets and generally being up to his neck in pandemonium. I pressed him for more of this stark and startling information, but he realised he had said enough. That meeting left me physically sick, and full of anger.

My father, so culturally nationalist, so publicly correct, playing the tin whistle at local festivals, speaking to his cronies in snatches of bad Gaelic, full of old yarns, but no substance. His now-renounced predilection for armed revolt, a family secret, stank in my sensitive young nose. When I summoned the anger to challenge him about his hypocrisy, he locked me in the bedroom for two days. The rot and disrespect set in between us.

As the aggravation increased, he threw me out of the house, and he only became resigned to the way it was when the soldiery still came charging to the home in pursuit, even though I was no longer resident. His theory was, 'You might as well be lifted here, as shot someplace else.'

So we worked out some ground rules, conventions for a ceasefire. No guns, bombs, components or users thereof on the premises; home before twelve in a sober manner, and chip in for the rent and keep. On the whole, it worked well. My mother (a natural pacifist, against death being dealt in any cause, never mind one she saw as pointless) could manage the illusion of a happy, intact family, and father could feel he was keeping an eye on me. For my part it reduced all manner of risks and discomforts, and it gave me a base both familiar and comparatively safe. As long as I played the game and stayed off the guest list for the Gestapo's dinner dances at Castlereagh barracks, the semblance of family life could resume.

But, oh, it was egg-walkingly difficult. Breakfast was silent, and silence always preceded hostility. He was stuffing his broken shoes with cardboard from a cereal box, glancing over as I scanned the newspaper, weighing me up. I rose decisively, seized my coat and made for the door.

'Where are you going?' said the ould fella.

'I'm going out. Where do you think?'

The indignity of it. Nineteen years old, three inches taller than him, and still so answerable, so weak. But that's how it was.

'Look out for yourself, and stay away from that flaming march that's on.'

Ironically, that day I was guaranteed to look out for myself, and certain not to be near any marches.

The sun was out and about, warming the damp skin of the city, flushing the drab brick into a dozen shades of orange-red, washing the grey and softening the garish graffiti on the gable walls. It leapt across the mounds of rubble, bounced in and out of the alleys, killing the ammoniac odour with its illusory bleach, throwing colour into the curtains, into the clothes of the populace, into their faces.

'Looking well, Mary.'

'So's yerself. How are ye?'

'Grand. What about yer Grandma? Hear she's not well ...'

A warm back and a full belly on a Saturday morning among the great familiar. Everyone restful, communicative. Troubles of home and family being put in perspective, the perspective of the community. West Belfast takes on a beat of its own; infectious, folksy warmth bounds from man to woman, to child, and in the small doing of things – shopping, cleaning the windows, setting off for football, for a curative pint, studying the racing form by the street corner – the community confirms its supremacy, its integrity, its grip. The loyalties of place and people are daily, subtly reasserted in the moil, in the hubbub of the lazily filling streets, while the sinister becomes elusive, then fades to invisible. West Belfast dons its daily finery as soldiers remember the tensions of the previous night. Scanning the shoppers, the travellers, the loungers, following the traffic with watchful, professional attention through slits and gaps in armoured cars; from their foothold forts of corrugate-covered armour now silver in the sun, it could be London, or the Bronx.

More friendly though, as each nods to the other and few go a hundred yards without being hailed, without being inducted into the community. Walking past the local fort, I was trying to figure my Da out, wondering how long we could put up with each other this time. As a child, I had looked up to him. A local celebrity in some ways, he still retained friends and drinking mates throughout the city. As a joiner, he had had no equal according to the men his age, and he was forever doing bits of church work for the pensioners, or taking his place on stage at festival time. His whistle and accordion had been heard all over the city, in many a pub and club in Protestant areas as well as Catholic, if he were to be believed. It all meant nothing to me.

He was a mass-goer and a small 'c' Christian, with no natural enemies. People seemed to like or ignore him, and it was left to me to despise the man. Far above any generational conflict, we seemed locked into perpetual confrontation, founded on a lack of respect for each other.

We lived in silent disagreement about the past and future, finding little in common in the present. Like most families we had been singed by the fires of revolt; less than some, more than others. An uncle, his brother, interned, a cousin of mine killed, others on the run or in the prison camp. A score or more of little incidents, four house raids I could remember, a multitude of small indignities and assaults building into a catalogue of humiliation, eroding the spirit: searches on the street, riots, a shooting witnessed in passing, bombs seen or heard ... we both carried our indexes of grief, yet we'd come to opposite conclusions. Of the same flesh and experience, we were of vastly different mind, and the difference was growing by the death.

While the old fella showed no outward concern, it galled me that we were so far apart and so deep in conflict. He seemed impervious and unmoved by that which was intolerable to me. An average parental gripe, about work, mass, money or friends, that could heal with time, and I wasn't impatient by nature. But this was an unbridgeable disconnection in the very electrics of our lives, a void into which love and respect had toppled, and it threatened to last forever. The man was hopeless. He simply refused to understand. Loping through the weekend shoppers, hands deep in pockets, thus thinking of my old man, I was roused by a slap on the back.

'Jesus, Toto, ye scared the life out of me.'

'Right, wee lad? Ye're in a world of yer own.'

'What got you out of yer coffin? I thought Saturday was yer day of rest?'

'Wasn't working last night. Went on the tear with Barry and Big George. Down at the club, like. You go out last night?'

'We went to Archer's for a few scoops.'

'Dingus with ye?'
'For a while. Him and Bricks headed down town.'
'He ended up fighting with the Brits last night.'
'Not again?' I felt vaguely let down.
'Same old story. Head full o' mad dog's shite, that fella. His Ma was saying she found him on the sofa with his melt knocked out of him.'
'It's getting too regular.'
'Stay away from him, wee lad. The Brits will blow his head off some night.' Toto gave me his 'word to the wise' look. It struck me that I was forever defending Dingus Grey to the world at large, but his drunken crusade against the British empire was getting out of hand.
'Dingus is OK, if he stays off the whiskey.'
'Don't say ye weren't told. Here, where are ye off to?'
'I'm taking a skite down to the club.'
'I'll be down there later, give ye a game of pool. If ye see our Tommy down there, tell him to stay put. I'll be down at half-two.'
'Fair enough, Toto. See ye when I see ye.'
My relief at his departure was short-lived. He stopped, and turned.
'Here! 'Fore I forget. There was a wee girl looking for you last night.'
'For me?'
'Fine looking wee thing, actually. Claire, is that her?'
I tried to hide the rush of anxiety. 'What time was that at?'
'Late last night. Must have been a mistake, though. She was too good looking to be after you. I'll see you later on.'
As I turned the corner to the club, it occurred to me it might have been better to have stayed in bed that day. Toto's brother, Tommy, was at his usual perch by the bar, nursing that essential first pint of the day. The drink was clearly angry at him, for it was hardly touched, and it going on one o'clock.
'Your lad says ye're to stay here till he comes.'

'Bastard's looking for money off me. You having a pint?'

'Get us a coke, or something. I had enough last night to kill a horse.'

'Billy, get the child a coke.'

'Some child that,' hailed the barman. 'There was a big article in here looking for you last night.'

'Really?' I was ready for roasting.

'Awful looking doll. The baby she had was even uglier. Could only a been yours.'

'I claim the fifth amendment.'

'That's a brave man ye have there, Tommy,' said the barman. 'You know Sticky Joe?'

'Joey O'Brien, the people's friend?'

'Yer man's having a crack at his sister.'

'Now, hould on, Billy ...' I rushed to my own, futile defence.

'Safer putting yer dinger in a food mixer, son,' said Tommy.

'Jealous bastards, the pair of ye.'

Tommy feigned innocence. 'We're only looking after yer interests. Imagine Sticky Joe for an in-law.'

'Fucking outlaw,' came Billy.

'Castro doing best man. Five-hour wedding speeches ... Jesus, if they only shot you. It's the torture he'd put you through before it.'

'Spinkey!' I cried out, in relief. 'Over here.'

'What about ye?'

'These two ould farts are giving me a hard time.'

'Youse picking on my mate?'

'He's giving Sticky Joe's sister a hard time,' smirked Billy.

'She was in here hunting for him last night.'

'No?' Spinkey tried to sound incredulous. 'More important, Dingus did a Gary Cooper last night.' He gallantly changed the subject.

'Does he not know the bad guys always win?' said Tommy, disgustedly.

'He should leave them poor wee soldiers alone.'

'Wee fucker hasn't a titter of wit,' Billy concurred.

Tommy looked me in the eye, and intoned, 'He's messing with the wrong boys. You'll always get one that wants a Paddy's head for over his mantelpiece.'

'It must be some sort of death-wish he's got,' I offered.

'He just gets excited when he's had a few,' opined Billy, giving his view as unpaid therapist to the public.

'But he never fights with his own,' I pointed out. 'You can fire beer into him all night, and it would be no bother.'

'I've a dog like that at home,' said Tommy. 'Never bothers the postman; minute it sees a Brit, goes pure berserk.'

'But you've trained it, Tommy,' said Spinkey. 'Dingus is a natural.'

'Fuck it,' I said pointedly, 'I'm not his keeper.'

'Tommy has it right,' said Billy. 'He'll be target practice for them if he doesn't wise up.'

Spinkey grinned. 'Must get them thinking, though. Maybe they reckon we're all sky pilots, fucking kamikazes. Maybe he's got the right approach: baffle the fuckers.'

'Baffles me, anyway,' I said. 'Let's set the balls up and have a game of pool. I'm not making any money talking.'

'Listen to the hustler,' said Tommy, brightening up. 'Set them up and I'll give you a lesson.'

Later, in the club toilets redolent of cheap disinfectant, Spinkey and I got to talking business. In hurried words and nervous laughter, we braced ourselves, needing only our marching orders now. By two thirty, Tommy was four quid down at pool, to my enrichment. Toto came in, and after a fraternal dispute about money, which they settled over a pint, they set about the afternoon's race-card with the relish of two old crusaders seeking the grail, resolving to leave a sum aside for a pint that evening. Spinkey and myself stuck manfully to the soft drinks, despite ourselves, and waited for some action. In the midst of a photo-finish in which the boys had an intense and immediate interest, Dingus appeared among us, like a post-crucifixion spectre, bandaged and be-crutched, with the colour of death firmly on him.

'Looking well, Dingus,' was the best I could offer.

'Kiss my arse,' he replied.

'Mind yer language or I'll get the police,' said Billy. 'Maybe the army as well.'

'Quiet boys,' roared Toto. 'Here comes the result ...'

'Balls. We're bate,' Tommy rounded on Dingus. 'Ye miserable, unlucky fucking jinx, Grey. Coming in here like Long John Silver looking for his parrot.'

'Christ,' I said, in mock sympathy. 'They gave you a right touch, mate.'

'Couldn't move this morning.' He was in real distress.

'Sue the bastards, Dingus. That's brutal, man.' Toto was genuinely moved.

Billy leaned over the counter, taking him in from top to toe, shook his head, and said knowingly, 'A kicking like that could leave serious psychological scars, sunshine. Ye could be left mental.'

'Fuck you too, Billy. Can I have a pint now the cabaret's over?'

The attention turned once more to the afternoon's business, and as I glanced over to the front door, almost instinctively, I caught a fast eye from a passing traveller. Mo, right on time, a real ghost here, a fleeting, chilling presence moving in from the afternoon sunlight, gliding unseen or unremarked down the stairs to the bowels of the club, instantly transmitting urgency and excitement into my heart.

'I'll have a look at that cooler you want fixed, Billy.'

'Fair play. It's down the cellar.'

'I'll give you a hand,' said Spinkey.

'Yeah. I might need a lift with a keg or two. Back shortly, lads.'

Downstairs, the back room smelt powerfully of beer, underlayed by fungus and masked with the same floral disinfectant as the toilets upstairs. It was a sunken, ill-lit midden, where the club records were kept in a set of grey drawers. A small, battered desk took up most of the remaining space, and Mo had draped it in a city map.

'Do they never put the heating on here?' He ran a finger down a poorly glossed wall, dripping condensation. The room was certainly humble, but secure; a bunker, inaccessible to the stranger.

'I can't stay long, chaps. I have to be elsewhere at half-three. You know the routes and there are no changes. Bradley has the transport organised, he'll be here at four, on the dot. Don't talk upstairs. It wouldn't be done to be seen with him too often. Now, is the charge OK?'

'The charge is made up, as recommended. I'll prime it before we leave,' said Spinkey.

'Right. Gather round me. I'll show you what we need.' We stood either side as he ran through the plan. 'Three in the morning, the crack starts. Spinkey, it has to be three sharp, not one minute past, not two seconds before.'

'That's guaranteed. Fireworks at three bells.'

'Right.' He looked at me. 'Give it to three ten at the latest. If the brigade hasn't arrived, or the Brits before them, then we'll know about it, and act accordingly. There's no point making direct contact after three ten.' He paused for this to sink in. 'Now, assuming we get the right response, the firemen will be coming in this way, the Brits will arrive down the road.' He drew spectral lines on the map with his index finger. 'The tricky part comes now. What we need is a major incident. We want them to think World War III has broken out, so we want as much fire put into the area as you can manage, without being captured. Make as much noise, for as long as you feel comfortable, as much as you possibly can. I'm not after a body count on this. Just scare the daylights out of them. We need to get them drawing peelers and Brits from here, from here. The obvious roads will be blocked, but we need more than that. Understood?'

We'd done much of the homework already, and if we weren't deliriously happy about it, we certainly understood.

'You know we'll only have less than three minutes after we open up? Anything more, and the place will be crawling.'

'Sure. Sure.' Mo's gaze held a note of appeal to me, leaking out from behind his normally inscrutable eyes. It was as if he didn't want me talking in front of the child. He was an old hand, Mo. Not given to cross-examination, or having to elaborate. The respect which the community bestowed on him had been earned hard, paid for in the currency of bullets. Despite the miasma of this little room, he could smell my doubt. 'You chaps are the best judges, it's your arses on the line. You'll have all the ammo you can use, just use as much as you can, for as long as you can. Tie them down, do your best, and get home safe. Fair enough? *Slán libh, mo cháirde, agus beannacht Dé oraibh.*'

'*Slán agat*, Maurice.'

'Cheers,' said Spinkey quietly.

Back at the bar, we rubbed our hands to drive off the chill. Dingus was drinking away, rocking uncertainly on his crutch.

'Ye couldn't a been working too hard if ye're cold.' There was a sly look on his face.

'What would you know about work, wee lad,' said Spinkey.

'We're good club members, Dingus,' I intervened. 'We had to tidy up the mess down there. You should take a bit of pride in yer club.'

'Bollocks.'

I saw Mo come quickly, noiselessly up the steps and glide out into the street. I felt relieved. When I looked back, Dingus was staring in his wake. Our eyes met and held. He smiled.

'Throw away that coke and I'll get you a man's drink.'

'I'm saving myself for tonight, Dingus. Saturday night's no fun without money, son.'

'Saturday night's all right for fighting, boy. Eh?'

'Right, Dingus.'

'Right,' he said, and I thought he was about to say more, but he sat silently as we cheered on the next near-winner.

Bradley arrived around four and said 'Hello' to virtually everyone but Spinkey and myself. Toto and Tommy had pulled back a few quid, and were in danger of having a winning day, Dingus was blissfully pissed, and the rest of the reprobates were drinking and joking away. Bradley pottered about, as was his way, and no one paid any heed as we drifted off.

Bradley drove away in his own car, after a muffled conversation with Spinkey beside the commandeered Escort. Spinkey and I drove about the back streets in it, until he was sure of its sturdiness, then we tore off to the top of our street. Leaving me in the car, he walked a hundred crooked yards to his house. He was back minutes later with a carrier bag at his side.

We headed off towards the suburbs. In the bag was a .38 short-arm and an apparently pristine tin of paint. I sat on the gun and studied the tin.

'You would hardly know it was ever opened. Ye fly bastard. Is it set?'

'Set for three in the morning, as requested. Ten and a half hours on the clock. You could hit it with a hammer and it wouldn't go off.' Spinkey sounded tetchy, as if I were impuning his professionalism.

'I take it ye're not impressed with Part B of the plan?' I asked. Spinkey gave a rueful, affirmative smile.

'Sounds like he wants the Magnificent Seven instead of us.'

'As much ammo as we need,' I reminded him.

'Yeah. That makes a change. He's always counting the bullets, Mo. Makes ye wonder he's so generous. Still, could be a bit o' crack.'

'The crack will be getting back to base. That's all that worries me.'

'There's Bradley.'

We pulled up and Bradley drove towards us, having covered the route. He nodded and drove on.

'We're in business, Spink.'

He swung the car out, whistling through pursed lips. We drove in thoughtful silence, vigilant, deliberate, tense.

What would my father have said if he could have seen me? As a child I was taught the proper ways. Honesty over all. If my childhood wasn't idyllic, it was certainly the best that our folks could manage, morally and financially. Essentially it was the same upbringing as any European, working-class child of the time; football, occasionally Gaelic, was the main pursuit of boys: we followed the English league, wore the colours of our favoured teams, and styled ourselves on the main stars, Best, Moore, Law, whoever. Leeds, United, Celtic for some. The records we listened to were the apolitical ones: the Stones, Bowie much later. My father, as all fathers surely did, combatted the more pernicious aspects of the permissive culture which attracted me, but I grew up in the mainstream of Anglo-American influence and cared little for the moribund Celtic legacy which was an accepted, but easily neglected feature of the era. Irish dancing, music, sport, they were all to be had and tasted, but paled in appeal when compared to the brash, magnetic and vibrant culture of the sixties. Who needed Cúchulainn when you could have instant heroes the moment you turned on the box? No Hibernian gunmen we. Groomed to take our places in the Catholic community, future teachers, plumbers, emigrants and unemployed, we grew up oblivious to the sinister undercurrents and the foul potential in the State. We were vaguely aware of the existence of our Protestant rulers, but I for one had no desire to confront them, and had only a confused understanding of the political geography of our savage little nation and our hate/hate relationship with the mother of oppression beyond the docklands.

The feral history of modern Ireland can be found in other books. Suffice to say that the rafts of state so precariously afloat on the high seas of mendacity chose to sink within sight of my adolescence. I was still perturbed over my first wet dreams when the wise and true decided to taunt old demons and bring forth the war, as my father knew they would.

My uncle, a hard and fast Republican, was under orders not to discuss politics in our home. As war progressed his visits became tense affairs and the distance grew between my father and himself. Families creaked, split and found new accommodations within themselves, steeling themselves for the conflagration, and ours was no different from others. My father and I argued about the little things at the start; later we would fight about guns in my room, over strange faces calling, books and pamphlets which spoke of war. We fought ferociously, he against my ignorance, I against what I saw as his naivety, with my mother between us driven to distraction. I had to weigh each action, consider his reaction, and more often than not I shied away from the course which led to his disapproval, his swinging boot and vulgar ultimata that sent the house into shadow for weeks on end. But finally the burden of instinct grew too heavy to resist and I moved to militancy, certain in my heart that he was wrong and I was right.

As Spinkey and myself moved forward on a Saturday afternoon I was as sure as could be in my heart and mind that I was doing what had to be done. At that time, whilst others in nationalist West Belfast might have questioned it, whilst many would call it wrong and my father detest its implications, few would have called into question our motives. We were the children of '69, the incarnation of our fathers' sins, the spawn of British policy, of Irish cowardice, incubated in the fires of supremacist hatred. Whatever could be thought of us, we were the product of all that had gone before, a curse upon our enemies now realised, my father's worst dream come true. Not that I was some 'victim of society'; rather, I felt I was an active part of the solution, that most optimistic and cheerful product of all wars ... a volunteer.

The shopping centre was made up of fourteen small units, punctuated by a large supermarket, a post office and a bank, with a smattering of market stalls interspersed. The units were set on three sides of a square, the fourth side being the main road. Behind the complex was a housing estate where Union flags flapped proudly in the gathering breeze.

The day was turning cold, the morning sun having surrendered to the tempers of autumn. We sat, talking little, covertly anxious, watchful as hawks, waiting for the hardware shop to empty. Across the road was a bank of foot-hardened earth which led to a plateau of waste ground some thirty yards across. This formed a simple vantage point for our later requirements, furnished with a twin set of burnt-out cars which provided the only cover, and overlooked by a huddle of Catholic houses, siege written all over them. Their gable ends stared blankly out at the road, defaced and windowless, removing any hope of a conventional snipe. We would attack from the waste ground, retreat through the knot of Catholic homes to transport and thus to safety. Mo would have to do without his frills, but with luck a few hasty rounds would draw in enough Huns to keep him happy. My reservations about the attack became bleakly reinforced on inspection, and I could feel Spinkey wasn't any more impressed than myself. He prodded me on the shoulder.

'Shop's ready to close, mucker. It's show time.'

I entered the shop, striving for nonchalance, with the tin of paint in its carrier bag. Butter would not melt in my mouth. The owner's wife was behind the counter as I walked in, and that put the confidence on me.

'Sorry to trouble you, love. My girlfriend was in here yesterday and got this paint, but it's the wrong colour. Is there any chance of changing it?'

She gave the tin a cursory inspection.

'That's no trouble, love. What colour were ye after?'

'Primrose yellow, if you have it.'

'Ye know,' she glowed, 'that's what I thought she was looking for yesterday. That was the first tin I showed her. Primrose yellow, where are ye now? Ah! Here it is.'

Her husband was up beside me now. A small, wiry man, hard looking.

'Right, Rhoda?' he asked.

'I've just to change this paint for the young gentleman, then we're ready.'

'Did ye get the wrong one, then?'

'Sent the girlfriend for it. I knew I should have got it myself.'

He nodded in male solidarity, but I felt him sizing me up; a strange face in days when you couldn't be too careful.

'Funny ould weather, isn't it?'

'Aye. There's a drop of rain in it somewhere.'

'Shaping up that way, aye.'

'Here ye are, son,' his wife said. 'Primrose yellow. I had it on the floor, I did.'

'Awful woman.'

'Get away, you. You'd be lost without me.'

I grinned at their *badinage.*

'Do I owe you any money, missus?'

'Not a bit of it. Glad you got here before we closed, that's all.'

'God, am I keeping ye open?'

'Not a bit of it, son. Any time,' said the man.

I walked out, straight across the road, paint in bag. Spinkey sat in the car, looking bored. In the corner of his eye he watched the shop front, the counter with the tin of paint on it. The man was about to knock off the lights and she had one arm in her overcoat when she walked back to the counter, took the paint, paused, then put it in its rightful place among the creams and yellows. Spinkey was a methodical man himself, and was drawn to neatness, to order. A place for everything and everything in its place. He drove out and swung the car round, catching me in its beam.

'Come on to fuck. *The Generation Game* will be starting.'

'That old guy did everything but take my photograph,' I commented. 'And the old dear remembered whatever bird bought the paint yesterday.' Spinkey was well used to my paranoia. 'Slow down,' I barked. 'This isn't a fucking race.'

'Jesus, relax. When that thing goes up they'll be able to put the shop in a matchbox. They probably won't know how it was done.'

'They'll guess,' I replied.

'Let them fucking guess. If ye're that worried, grow a beard.'

'I don't want to spoil my image.'

'Jesus,' said Spinkey. 'What image? Ye're just a faceless wee bastard no one would look twice at. Spoil yer image ... fuck ... what's this?'

We were on the last stretch home, convinced of our safety, when a roadblock reared in front of us. Spinkey frantically recited the car registration number scribbled on his hand. When satisfied, he put his hand to his mouth and gave the figures a discreet lick, wiping his hand on the seat cover. I sat tight, at my feet the carrier bag, pistol inside beneath a gallon tin of primrose poxy yellow. After a dozen cars we reached the head buck cat, a gaunt refugee from Oxbridge, studying and processing the lane of captive travellers. Responding to his imperious nod, the corporal gave us a flat palm up, and Spinkey wound the window down to its limit.

'Where are you going, sir?'

'Woodvale.'

'Where have you been?'

'Dundonald. Working down there.'

The corporal was about to go further when a car behind pulled out of the queue and tried to make a slow, clumsy turn. The captain stepped forward, a squaddie raced to the offending vehicle, and the corporal, fingers gripping the rifle a fraction tighter, looked again at us and waved us irritably through before walking to the more suspicious car. We drove around the Saracens, carefully, precisely, breathlessly, and pushed on up the road, gradually picking up speed, still speechless and shocked.

'I think,' said I, 'I've done something childish.'

Spinkey exhaled, very carefully.

'If ye mean all the shite on the floor isn't mine, I'm delighted. Where the hell did they come from?'

The streets became short of traffic as we neared home, but knots of pedestrians gradually turned into crowds heading up the road.

'The march!' I decided. 'The wankers rerouted it.'

Spinkey looked at me, the tension in his face dissipating, the sly bravado sneaking back beneath the sheen of sweat.

'Maybe you should do something with that mug of yours. They wouldn't have stopped someone with an honest face like mine.'

Claire O'Brien had been working that day in a cloud of anger and boredom. The security man, who saw her to the door, tried to cheer her up with a joke, and she afforded him a polite laugh, but inside she was raging at herself for having fallen into a signposted trap. All day she had felt used and foolish, dying to get home, if not to cry then to replan her emotional life. On the bus out of the city centre, she was bitterly formulating a life without men. She was lost in her thoughts and didn't notice as the bus began to be driven in cautious fits and starts and the other women began to fidget. The march had disintegrated into a series of running skirmishes between the young bloods and the Crown forces, and the bus she was on had crept to the edge of a dangerous carnival. Outside the swimming baths, a youth forced his way on and called, 'This is as far as it goes. Everyone off.'

As she and a group of elderly women rushed and hobbled to a safe distance, the prepubescent arsonist splashed petrol from a Rosses lemonade bottle down the aisles, then set the yoke alight, running away to join his mates with a maniacal laugh and his gutties smoking. She stood a moment beside the bus driver, who was shaking his head in disgust. An old woman commiserated with him.

'Don't worry, son. There'll be another along any minute.'

He strode off manfully, ignoring the jeers. Taking her cue from him, Claire marched on, her mood of confusion and doubt over her love life compounded by the vagaries of life in the war zone, and as Spinkey and myself were dumping the motor at the agreed spot, she turned the corner some yards away, approaching at ramming speed. Spinkey had an almighty grin of recognition on his face, but fought the urge to chuckle. Heart pounding, I leaned against the nearest wall, knowing I'd been spotted and that there was no escape, desperately trying to get my excuses in order. Three yards from us, Claire did a ninety-degree pivot into the next street.

'Doesn't look as if she's talking to you,' Spinkey pointed out.

'You'd think I stood her up or something,' I replied lamely. 'Call in and tell my ones I'll be late for tea, will ye? I'll head her off at the pass.'

'Is this the one that's taking things too seriously?' he asked.

'That's an order, ye blurt. I'll see you in Luby's at ten.'

'Right ye are, general. Before ye rush off, do you wanna leave me something.'

It took me a moment to realise I was dashing off with a .38 pistol and a redundant tin of paint. Sum total equals ten years of misery. Spinkey was quietly beaming at my discomfort.

'Calm down, Casanova. I'll drop the shooter off at Bradleys' on the way home. You go crawling to yer one.'

I thought the better of replying.

Spinkey got home as *The Generation Game* was oozing on to the television. He was addicted to the show, and sat beguiled eating his tea. His father rambled on about the march that afternoon; he enjoyed his marches, and had followed the flag of discontent in every nationalist town over the years. His wife was in the kitchen, dutifully pretending to listen as she did the dishes. When Spinkey let out a roar at some colourful piece of inanity that tickled him, she looked at him thoughtfully. He was like a big baby sometimes, an eejit. He'd never lost his acne, indeed he hadn't changed a fidge since he left school. Was it really four years ago? Now he was almost qualified as an electrician, but he was working well below his station, fixing up broken TV sets for the Rogue Maguire. He was like most lads in the street, drifting in a vacuum of grief and mayhem, striving for identity and happiness in the middle of crisis. Her big hope was to get him away to England where his brother was, to peace and good money. She would miss him badly, miss the laugh and the smiling way he would set about the housework. Though he didn't have any time for his father, he would do what it took to please her. Shop, clean the windows, polish the lino. But he was a perpetual worry.

She knew he was in the movement, despite his denials, but she blocked out the thought that he might be in the firing line, just as firmly as she blocked out the idea of him killing someone. Years of storm and passion had eroded any respect or trust she had for outsiders, and her loyalty was solely to the family. Spinkey had chosen his path, as thousands before, and she knew how pointless it would be to challenge any further. Already they'd had the raids, the heart-flattening days and nights of waiting for her son to come home, the screeching fear that he might not, not for years. She was realistic enough to know that he showed all the signs of ending up doing time, or worse. His life was like a case study, a history which repeated itself up and down West Belfast, year in, year out.

'That Bruce Forsythe, Ma,' she heard him call. 'He wants locking up!' Mrs Driscoll smiled.

As the last shops closed, their lights going out one by one in salute to the oncoming night, as the workers threw farewell to each other for what was left of the weekend, a tin of paint sat snugly in its proper place, with a coiled and sleeping snake waiting in its belly.

Dingus Grey had found his way to Archer's pub, and sat immersed in anger and remorse, the pain of last night's indiscretions shining through the alcohol. The barmaid cast a cold eye upon him as he hooked himself up on his crutch and propelled himself to the counter.

'You've enough drink in ye. It's time you were home for yer tea.'

'Right, right. No problem, love. Just one for the road.'

He was blitzed on cider, and the painkillers were exhausted. Dingus had the constitution of an ox, despite being a small, weasely man who looked much older than his twenty years. My sister once remarked, 'He might clean up well,' but Dingus lived for the next bit of crack, stumbling from one emergency to the next. He had no time for the war. Of all my friends, he was the least complicated, least involved. There were no corners on Dingus. What you saw was what you got; an outrageous rebel, restless and good natured in even parts. He drove his family to distraction, and most viewed him with caution due to his unpredictable mouth, but he grew on you, like a benign fungus.

His real troubles had begun months earlier as he sat one morning in Archer's. There was a royal wedding on the television, and the rest of the clientele were calling for *Sesame Street* on the other channel, but Dingus was irresistible when he got into one of his Bolshie moods.

'Ye'll watch this, ye disloyal bastards, and ye'll like it.'

So he got his way, and was watching the proceedings with bogus interest, ignoring the gripes of the old boys behind.

Just as the joke was wearing thin, a passing patrol of Her Majesty's best called in on a 'getting to know you' visit. The piano stopped playing. No one spoke, but studied the optics and newspapers with intense and sudden interest. Nor indeed did the soldiers say a word. There was no urgency about them, nor animosity. These guys were not out for trouble, simply familiarising themselves with the interior of the place, asserting their presence. There were no issues at stake for either side, so none of the regulars were getting excited by the incursion. They passed through the bar, down into the lounge and came back, three on patrol, one at the door. The guy at the door sidled up to Dingus and, nodding at the television, made an attempt at friendliness.

'How's it going?'

Dingus glanced up at the clock. 'It's a bollocks. Bomb should have gone off an hour ago.'

The barman covered his lip to forestall a laugh, and a ripple of acute embarrassment went around the bar. The sergeant returned from the lounge in time to catch the remark.

'Smart boy, is it?' came his singing, Welsh tones. 'What's your name, sir? Date of birth?'

Having noted this, the Brits proceeded to leave, and the bar collapsed in rasping laughter. The sergeant stopped in the doorway, and a shutter of silence fell once more. He was like an out-gunned teacher who leaves the room, reluctant to turn his back lest the children sneer and jibe.

'Smart boy, is it?' mimicked the barman when the coast was clear.

The consensus was that Dingus had put one over on the wet-eared Welsh boys, and the story went around, a bit added here and there to join the million anecdotes of verbal resistance. A week later, as he was coming home in the early hours, a foot patrol stopped him. He answered the usual 'P' check questions, more interested in getting home to bed than giving cheek to the enemy. As his clearance came through on the radio he was set to leave, when a voice behind him sang.

'That bomb, it never went off then, boy?'

He took a hammering that night, and I've always felt he never fully recovered. Getting a digging from the Brits is an environmentally induced certainty over a boyhood in West Belfast. You always run across the odd, mad bastard once, but usually you get a slap or a kick, a thump with a rifle or suchlike, and it might never happen again. Only the unlucky or the lippy ones got the regular stick, apart from well-known players in the game, and even then the Brits were circumspect in whom they clobbered. Usually they settled for harassing and hounding a face, stopping him every time, surprising him with personal details, letting them know who was boss.

For some reason they began to take Dingus apart, switching

from his body to his brain and back. After that night he couldn't get past a patrol without a whispered threat, a rifle stroking his neck, a damaged shin as his legs were kicked apart for a body search. By the time the Welsh regiment left, he was a nervous wreck. What he didn't know was that they'd left his name with the incoming troops.

A week into their tour and Dingus was getting the same shit as before.

Until he snapped.

Bricks and myself had told him to go to the papers, or the movement. Get this vendetta out into the open, as the Brits never liked the oxygen of publicity. But Dingus just went along with it, then began to respond, going out looking for the soldiers when he'd had a few. Come and get me, lads. I'm fit and I'm able, and spoiling for a fight. Just as the Brits were losing interest in him, he was going cuckoo looking to take them on.

But tonight there would be no trouble. He half-hopped and half-swung out of Archer's big double doors. He hadn't eaten since the day before. Alcoholism had killed off his appetite many moons ago, and he could run on booze for up to three days. Two years before he'd picked up a nice few thousand after a car crash, but that was long drunk, and he survived by foostering about with motors and claiming the dole, as well as operating as a small-scale fence on the side, selling on gear for some of the hoods he used to run with. Dingus was the man to see if you wanted a cheap radio or a fan heater, but he could only operate if he could duck and dive. From hard experience he knew that his smashed toes and numerous abrasions would have him crippled for the week. Once the anaesthetic of drink and tabs wore off, the injuries would flex themselves with a vengeance. All he had to look forward to was a wickedly long week with no dollars, sitting in a home he loathed, listening to the Ma and Da giving out at each other and at him. As he hobbled up the road, Dingus was a wee man full of hurt and apple juice, inwardly losing the battle against the relentless isolation of his heart.

A mile away Bricks sat in his darkening room, a cigarette burnt out between his fingers, staring at a spot on the wall, now invisible in the gloom, but clear as a diamond to himself. A spot only he could see. The door opened and his young brother turned on the light. He jumped in surprise.

'Jesus, I thought you were out.'

'Well, I'm in,' said Bricks, stirring.

'I can see that. What are you doing, sitting in the dark?'

'I'm thinking.'

'That's bad for ye. I had a thought once. Took me weeks to get back to normal.'

'Did you want something?'

'This is my room, too, don't forget. I was coming in for a think as well.'

'For a wank, more like. Get rid of those dirty books you have in the cupboard before yer Ma finds them.'

Suitably humbled and flushed, the young lad didn't even deny it. On the basis that changing the subject removes danger, he asked, 'Is this a bad time to put the bite on you?'

'Anytime's bad. How much?'

'Two quid?'

'I'll give you a pound, but ye'll have to work for it. Go over to Spinkey's house and tell him to call over later.'

When the cub had gone, Bricks lit up another smoke, switched off the light, and settled back into his reflection.

Claire O'Brien was walking a mile a minute, ignoring my breathless cry of 'Hold up, there!'

When I finally caught up with her, she was in no mood to talk, at least not in a civilised manner. She rounded on me.

'Do I know you?'

'We've met once or twice.'

'Were you the wee shit who was to call for me last night?'

It was the first time I'd heard her use profanity. Strangely, it seemed to hurt me.

'I got tied up.'

'You can go get strung up. God, you're one waste of time.'

'If I said sorry?'

'Sorry? Sorry? I'm sorry I ever ran across you.'

'Listen till I explain.'

She stopped, just a few yards short of her home.

'I had business to take care of last night, and it went on till ten. I swear, there was no way I could get out of it. I'll get down on my knees if you like. I ballsed it up, and I'm sorry.'

'I suppose you were busy planning that carry-on today?'

My life flashed in front of me.

'What carry-on? I was planning no carry-on.'

'That fiasco down the road. Bloody heroes, burning people off their buses. Scaring old-age pensioners and the like, that would be your level.'

'Hang on, here. I was working today, and I never burnt a bus in me life. You would think I was Public Enemy Number One to listen to you.'

'You are in my book. I stayed in for two hours waiting for you last night! I'll never do that again, for no man.'

'You won't have to. Scout's honour. I'm sorry as hell.'

She was gazing thoughtfully at her shoes, the rage resolving itself, outwardly oblivious to my apparent distress. Finally, she raised her head and I could see her looks were softer, more resigned. 'So, where do we stand then?'

I didn't hesitate.

'Way I see it, we either see a lot less of each other, or a lot more.'

'Which is it?'

'Much more, Claire, if you agree.'

She smiled, looked away from me, then back, eyes narrowing in joyful suspicion. 'Nine o'clock sharp tonight. You've a lot to make up for.'

'Nine on the dot.'

Three months earlier, Dingus and myself had fallen into the Eagle's Rest, seeking female company. Normally when it comes to women the shyness overwhelms me, the excruciating legacy of separate schooling. The gums tighten and the mind slows to bottom gear as clumsiness intervenes. The fostered ignorance of early years told us women were another species, an alien culture. Everything around us fastened this attitude, the macho ethos murdering you for any open expression of admiration of feminine values. You never really had women friends. You always had to be looking for something, and if you weren't there was something the matter with you. That night I was after as much action as I could get my arms around. Drink and hormones had my tongue hanging out, and the shyness was overcome by desperation. Dingus rapidly paired off with the first woman who thought he was sober, and I slowly began to get the familiar old feeling of rejection. It seemed I wasn't destined to be a conversationalist, so I settled for a poseur's role at the side of the dance floor.

She was sitting on her own, watching her friend dance, studying the table before her, looking around, musing, hoping to see someone she could talk to. Her mate was clearly getting off with the bloke she was dancing with, and it might turn out a lonely night, or, worse, she could end up spoiling it for her friend. Our eyes made contact and, swallowing deeply, I went across and asked her to dance.

We'd seen each other many times before in the street. It hadn't occurred to me she was fanciable. Undoubtedly, it was the same for her. There was an element of 'different sides of the track' in all this. She went around with a different gang: trainee teachers, office workers and such, mostly from out of the area. Also, there was the little matter of her brother, one of the major ex-hard men of the area, who belonged to a nominally Republican organisation. The variables of politics and power in the street had left us sworn enemies, although I'd never so much as spoken to the man, and he was barely aware of my existence.

Generality Rules, OK?

A family was known through the actions of its members. So there were quiet families, criminal families, Provie families, Sticky families (the O'Briens), and families whose allegiances were split, or who couldn't control a member. Much to my father's chagrin, my own activities had given our crowd the reputation of leaning towards the Provies, and the young brothers were getting the resistance bug, being treated by neighbours and Huns alike as potential revolutionaries. Once labelled, never to lose it.

Other families had been riven asunder in the war, one son going to the British army overseas, another to the revolt. The streets abounded with stories of broken homes, fractured in the maelstrom. Rancour and bitterness, unremitting and abiding hatred, brother to brother, sister to sister ... all the stuff of high tragedy was to be found there if you went looking for it. Feuds had left great ugly holes in too many people's hearts for there to be easy alliances. The best you hoped for was truce, and that was built on silence and demarcation; ley lines which ran beneath the surface determined who you spoke to, where you socialised, which part of a pub you drank in, where you did your shopping, even where you sat in church and who you sat beside at any time. Hatred had its etiquette. It was important you went out with the right partner. Imperative. Taking out the wife of some guy doing a life sentence in the Kesh could end you up in the graveyard; taking out the sister of some semi-retired psychopath working for a different cause came roughly into the same terminal bracket.

Nevertheless, there are times when it all seems so safe, so simple. That night was one of them, paranoia diluted by attraction, by need. Talking away to her, I noticed Dingus at the door, searching for me. Hanging on his arm was a half-fluthered girl who appeared up to his requirements, and after a while she dragged him off.

Claire's mucker and the fellow she was dancing with came

down and sat with us. He was a prospective solicitor from down-country, and her mate Angela was studying at Queen's. Drink being a great leveller, there were none of the awkward silences you sometimes get when one of the company has nothing much in common with the others. Claire was clever at directing the conversation away from topics that would have left me out, and by the time I'd left her home, kissed her goodnight and arranged a date, I was hooked. Looking back on it, she had picked me up.

By half past eight I was watered and fed, relieved at the restoration of our faltered romance, and deep-down anxious at the promise of the night's action. My home was the fulcrum of the great balancing act. My father was ruminating over a documentary on the television, one of those pointless debates on 'the Province' which enjoyed brief popularity in the seventies. David Frost was guiding a host of acceptable faces, hand-wringers, sin-eaters and professional egotists through the angst of desperation politics, and my old man was gorging himself on it, feeding his own reaction. For a man who professed no politics, he could be seduced by the media. All I ever got on the airwaves was distortion and hypocrisy in even, angering doses. I knew from experience that watching such programmes put the old man's blood pressure up a fair few notches. I went into the kitchen and casually got my jacket.

'Ma, me and Spinkey have a do to go to over at Queen's tonight.'

'Next ye're gonna tell me you won't be home tonight, is that it?'

'Ye're a mind reader, Ma.'

'So's yer father. If you're up to something he'll smell it a mile off. I'm having no more rows in this house, do ye hear? No more trouble brought to this door. Is that clear to ye?'

'Clear as mud. It's only a dance I'm going to.'

'What's the problem here?' It was the old man's usual refrain, uttered always when he was about to invoke a problem where none had previously existed.

'I'm away to a do tonight, and I won't be back till the 'morrow.'

'Are ye now? What sort of do?'

'A fecking do, that's what sort. What's the big deal?'

'Where is it, what's keeping you out all night; that's deal enough for me, ye pup.'

'It's over at the university, and me and Spinkey have bought the tickets for it. It'll be over too late for us to go traipsing back here. Are ye satisfied?'

'I will be when I see the tickets.'

'Spinkey has them.'

'He has, my arse. Don't be pulling the wool over my eyes. Some bloody do. You and that latchico are out for trouble, and you won't be leaving this house tonight, not if ye want back into it.'

'Ye reckon ye can stop me?'

'I'm wise to you, boy. Leaving here to bring trouble on us. Do you not think I've had enough with ye?'

'I'll see yez tomorrow. Listen, Ma, is it all right if I take someone home for lunch tomorrow?' Divide and conquer. Offer something to one to split them up.

My mother was baffled, my father momentarily derailed.

'Who is it?'

'It's a girl I know. I haven't asked her yet, but if she says "yes", will it be all right?'

'Sure, I've only the food in for us. Why didn't you tell me earlier?'

'Because he's just after thinking of it, woman. Are ye blind, or what?'

'Shush, you. Who is this girl?'

'She's just someone I know. Don't be embarrassing me with yer questions.'

'Wonders never cease. It'll be nothing fancy for her. She'll get what we all get.'

'That's sound, Ma.'

I knew we'd now be having caviar for dinner, once the old dear knew she was entertaining her young lad's first guest. My father was less enamoured of the prospect, smelling tactics. He stood directly in my way, rising to his full height. I could feel myself shrinking to meet him. He always had a way of diminishing me, no matter how dismissive I was of him.

'If you're up to yer tricks, boy, and them bastards come to this door after you again ...'

'That's enough,' my mother demanded. 'No more. I can't be putting up with you two no more. What time will you be bringing this one for dinner?'

'Half-one, I suppose?'

'You suppose? And no name to her?'

'If I told you all about her you'd have nothing to quiz her about, Ma. I'll see ye around half-one, and nothing fancy.'

My Da turned away for a split second as my sister came in, and I was through the door like a light. The old dear caught his sleeve as he set off in pursuit of me.

'Enough. No more of this fighting, please. In the name of God, no more.'

'Fighting? Do you think he's being straight, woman? He's going to be hooring around all night with the other commeedjan, and they won't be up to trouble?'

'I don't know any more. I don't know anything any more. Ye have me bate out, the pair of ye, and all I want is a bit o' peace. Is that too much to ask?'

'You'll have peace enough when them fuckers hit the door looking for the skitter. Ye'll have peace in the mental ward, ye bitch ye, and don't say I didn't try to stop it. Do ye hear me? Don't say it ...'

That was my father, reduced to an angry, impotent little tyrant in a three-bedroom kingdom. Exiled to his own home, deposed by the reality of the seething, traduced streets. The shout from a passing jeep at my sister on her way to convent school:

'Oi, Mary. Any 'airs on your cunt yet?'

My father's face contorting.

'Pretend you don't hear them. Keep walking. Don't give them the pleasure.'

Pretend. Pretend.

There was no pretend when they stopped us on the way to my cousin's funeral. The black trooper, pushed to the front and made honorary white man for the day, thick grin on his face, playing up to his mates. 'My sergeant reckons you're a fucking terrorist. What you say to that?'

'I don't take sides.'

'You calling my sergeant a liar? Sarge, this Mick says you're a liar ...'

He let them push him, grabbed me when I went to kick one of them, thrust me behind him as the boots came in; he let them shove him, rip the buttons off his only suit, spitting at me, 'Stay still, stay still.' The fear in his eyes. And afterwards he never spoke about it. As if it had never happened. As if there were no debt to pay, no pride to salvage. They could do what they liked on our streets, and we could do nothing. That was the turning point for me, fifteen years old, breathless with fear and rage, left with a devalued father I couldn't understand. I had done with pretence.

Dandering up to *chez* O'Brien, the only thing I needed was a posy to complete the picture. Best shoes and jacket, and I'd even changed my socks. By any standards, things were getting serious.

An obsessive drive in all of us informs our greatest triumphs and costliest defeats. Not fate or a deity, but some phantom genes, a portion of the brain yet undiscovered which holds a synopsis of our lives. The start of the story, the highlights leading to the end. A synopsis which cues our finer moments, our worst decisions. Some type of genetically triggered device which makes us act against all current information. Philosophy was not my forte, and I didn't let it guide my life, but when I'd seen Claire juke out of sight, not wanting to talk to me, I suddenly, intuitively, knew what had to be done. All logic had told me to let her go. It would have been hard, but sensible. There was nothing I could give the woman but the same ointment of love and pain I gave my mother. I was sure that my days were chosen and numbered, by me or for me, whatever; but running after her I knew it was impossible to do other than grab at whatever happiness was on offer. It might last a week, or a lifetime, but I was certain that this was one of the big moments, the grand decisions. My mind implored me to leave it, but selfishly and against logic I had wheedled my way back into her affections, and now, approaching the uncertain welcome which lay behind her door, I was no longer sure it was the best decision.

Sticky Joe stood in the hallway, a mangled sandwich in his hand.

'Are you lost?'

'I was supposed to see Claire.'

'Wonder she never said anything.'

I was about to get drawn in when yer woman came bouncing down the stairs. Joe turned on his heel and went into the sitting room.

'The butler wasn't going to let me in.'

'Pass no remarks. Joe's in a bad mood.'

I gave a fake wobble of the knees, and she laughed, fixing an ear-ring diligently into place at the same time.

'Are you ready to go?' I asked hopefully.

'I am not indeed. Come in.' In the sittingroom Joe was finishing off his sandwich in front of a barren grate.

'You two know each other?' We nodded in mutual recognition, like two funeral directors finding themselves at the same accident. She was setting in the other ear-ring.

'You two chat away and I'll be down in a minute.'

She scooted off, leaving Joe and myself sitting by the empty grate, with enough silence and suspicion between us to fill every coal bucket in the city.

'You work down the timber yard?'

'That's right, aye.'

'I can't place you. Would you be a nephew of Patsy the Crab?'

'Patsy's my uncle, all right.'

'I knew Patsy. He wasn't the worst of them.'

'He's living down in Newry now. Took the family down last year.'

'Is that where he is?' He knew damn well where Patsy was, who I was, where I worked. We weren't on different planets. We were part of the same community, like it or not. Joe was sussing me out, and I was trying to be cool, but there was no point to it. He came to the same conclusion.

'Are you still operating?'

There she blows. Out in the open, big and bad as you like. The etiquette book was out the window.

'I'm not, as it happens. Are you standing in the next elections?'

'Would you vote for me?'

Would any of the two hundred suckers who voted for you before, I wondered.

'I'm open to persuasion,' I replied.

'A reasonable man, then.' He smiled, the smile of a man who had had his suspicions suitably confirmed.

'Will you have a beer?'

'Not at the moment, thanks.'

'You drink in O'Toole's, don't you?'

'The odd time.'

'With yer man Driscoll and wee Bricks O'Hare?'

'Nothing escapes you, Joe.'

He leaned forward and pointed a finger, all controlled anger.

'Nobody likes a smart arse, fella. The last wee fella she fell for did a runner to England. Are you going anywhere by any chance?'

'Sorry to disappoint ye, Joe. I'm going to Sligo for the *fleadh* next month, but that's the height of me travelling plans.'

He raised his eyebrows and sat back, trying to look enigmatic and dangerous. It worked a treat. As the frosty silence set in, broken only by the noises of the preparations upstairs, I could feel the truth of our enmity sour in my guts. He was a man to be afraid of.

She was coming down the stairs. I made a last attempt at compromise.

'You've nothing to worry from me, Joe.'

He held my gaze, then broke fluidly into smiles as she came in.

'Are you ready, kind sir?'

She was simply dressed in jeans and white shirt with a blue floral pattern and a navy-blue jacket, but her face was so radiant and carefully tended that my stomach twisted further. She was worth it. At that moment I had an inkling of Joe's concern. You had to feel loving and protective of one so fine.

'I've been ready ages, madam. Lead the way.'

'I might see you lovebirds later!' proffered Joe, false warmth in his voice. I felt his eyes burn into my back as we walked down the road, only feeling relief as we turned the corner.

'Well?' she said. 'He's not as bad as he's painted.'

'Nor was Cromwell.'

'You're on probation, remember. He was raging you stood me up last night.'

'Do you tell him everything?'

'When you're sitting in the house for two hours, done up to the nines, waiting for the phone to ring? It's hard for him not to notice.'

She didn't mention her trawl of the club, seeking my whereabouts. There were many things she didn't mention.

'What about this cowboy who did a runner to England?'

She blushed, and I was instantly sorry I had mentioned it.

'Joe told you?'

'Was it serious?'

'Not at all. I bought the wedding dress for a laugh.'

'Bad as that?'

'That bad.'

'All I can say, the fella was an imbecile.'

'Is that so?' she said gaily.

'Certainly. The money's far better in America.'

She gave me a playful dig and a laugh, and we walked on painlessly, easy in each other's company. The endless streets were tarted up in incongruous neon threaded through their dark, dirty fabric, the evening given over to sinful colour and noise leaking from the doorways, the scarred face of the slum packed deep with dark foundation and highlighted with harps and shamrocks glowing behind defensive corrals of steel mesh. The 'ghetto' had money in its handbag and its feet were itching to dance. On the fringes, in quiet shade, was a shop with a Trojan tin of paint which contained a charge of plastic explosive six hours from detonation.

By the time we got to Luby's the crack was well under way. The three-piece band was launching into 'Hotel California'. The benches and the barstools were mainly full, even though it was early. The noise and smoke soon got me going. Most of my best times had been in such noisy, sweaty dens, but tonight there was the niggling thought of what was to come. Perspiring crowds, swirling, trapped smoke, good beer and music: the hallmarks of defiantly unadvanced civilisation – frenetic, decadent, thoroughly shameless. Dingus was propped up at the bar, drawn like a moth to the light, burning up a borrowed tenner. Big George sat with Tommy's wife, Helen, and her fiercely attractive sister. I copped Barry Quinn at the bar.

'Barry, grab a barman for me,' I said, leaning through the crush.

He called a pint for me and a vodka and orange for Claire.

'How come you're not drinking with George tonight?' I asked him.

George and Barry were normally inseparable. Dingus figured they were 'queer for each other'.

Barry's face broke into a broad, knowing grin.

'Big George is out to shift. Yer mates Tommy and Toto are off on the piss, by the sounds of it. Helen's out on the tear.'

I shook my head. George had always fancied Tommy's wife, something I put down to perversity, for Helen was a notorious 'badger' who would go through you for a short cut. She was by no means physically repulsive, but whatever love at first sight is, she and I shared the opposite. The only reason she waved us over that night was to give Claire the 'once over' and to keep Big George from licking behind her ear in public. The man was infatuated, and not best pleased at having to shove over to make room for us.

'Have you seen that husband of mine?' she asked, directly.

'I haven't run across him today.'

'You would say that. All you wee boys stick together. If he can go on the piss, then so can I. Good for the goose, good for the gander.'

Brenda, her sister, was her antithesis. She had a sexy sort of listlessness about her, a slow, soft voice and manner which hid an incisive brain and will of steel, and she was able to exude the impression of a slow-thinking, easy-going goddess in a crowd. The perfect male-destroying act which left a man reduced to slavering dross. She threw out heat with a mere flick of her eyelash, and busted hearts with a regularity that would seem ruthless in another. In the litany of those shot down in the battle for her affections, my name ranked highly. Brenda was devoted to her work at the hospital, sold on a vocation, unconvinced of the need for a man in her life. All in all, if I hadn't known the score, and I'd been free to embarrass myself, Big George and I would have made a prize pair, champing at the bit.

The drink flowed freely, but I was careful not to get involved, missing out on every other round, sipping it instead of throwing it back. Claire seemed to take a lead from me, and as the evening wore on we got mellow and amused beneath the noise. Helen was pumping Claire for information, Brenda doing her sex-goddess from next door routine, and poor George continued to abase himself and spend a fortune trying to get into Helen's affections and underwear.

We danced and drank and smiled, merrymakers and sots, lost in our own hopes, dreams, lusts; angling for love, for attention, concealing hurt, seeking recognition, diversion.

At the bar Helen said, 'She's a lovely girl. Too good for you.'

'I know, Helen. But I'm a lucky sort of bastard.'

'Does she know you're involved?'

'Helen, you're my friend's wife. But you've some nose and mouth on you, and I'd be glad if you kept out of my business.'

'She has a right to know, before she gets too far in.'

She was looking down at Claire, who was noting our conversation while talking away to the buxom Brenda, not letting me out of her sight.

'I'll tell you for free,' said Helen. 'That wee girl's gone on you.'

'You can fair alarm a man, Helen. I'm worried now.'

'Men never worry. They cause worry. You look after that wee girl.'

As I collected the drinks, the thought came to my head: 'Fucking women.'

'Fucking men,' said Helen as she walked away.

At that Spinkey came in and fought his way to the bar, returning with a coke. Bradley appeared shortly afterwards, and I left the company to join them.

'Where's he gone?' said Claire.

'He's at a business meeting, love,' Helen said quietly. 'You have to get used to the business meetings.'

'How's it cutting, fellas.'

'You watch the drinking tonight.' Bradley was a stickler for rules.

'Just a pint or two, Bradley. Everything's under control.'

'In that case I'll leave yez to it. No changes in orders, according to Mo. Ten-to-One is your driver. He knows where to meet you.'

'Fair enough. He can't do much harm behind the wheel.'

Bradley didn't comment, but put his half finished glass down and left, seeming to say 'hello' to everyone in the place as he went. Spinkey was looking around, appearing unconcerned as he spoke.

'I was down with Bricks earlier on. He says he'll meet us there. He was doing that spooky shit, that meditating. He's not the full shilling.'

I repressed a laugh.

'If it keeps him happy, pass no remarks. I'll get back to this woman 'fore she thinks I'm lost. Two o'clock sharp, right?'

'Cheers.' There was a hint of resignation in his voice.

On my way back to the company, Dingus grabbed my arm.

'How are you fixed?'

'I'm broke, Dingus. This woman has me bled dry.' He didn't answer back, but turned to the bar in a truculent huff and stared at the pint in front of him.

'Dingus looks rough,' said Brenda. 'I remember he was a lovely fella.'

'The demon drink,' I responded.

'The demon dope, you mean,' she confided in me lowly. 'He's been turning up at the hospital pharmacy with all kinds of dodgy prescriptions. There are a lot of stolen ones floating about.'

She startled me, but I took the hint. I resolved to catch Dingus sober and have a word with him. A young lad in the bordering area had had his knees blown off for raiding a doctor's surgery, and word had it that there were a lot of prescription pads missing. I didn't enjoy the thought of Dingus falling foul of the robust and ugly policing the community generated within itself. He was a mate, after all.

Claire was feeling a bit giddy by around eleven o'clock.

'Come on then, sir. It's time to go, or you'll be carrying me over your shoulder.'

'Why the rush? The night's still young.'

'That's what I'm thinking. You can leave me home.'

'I thought you were enjoying yourself?'

'I am. We can enjoy ourselves just as well down in my house.'

'Fair enough.' I was well pleased. The thought of going on for a Chinese or a late drink was troubling me. I would be cutting it fine to be at the starting post at two, and I wouldn't have time to let the drink settle. Still, I'd only had three pints, and that presented no problem.

We said our goodbyes and pushed out through the crowd, just as the band began another set, out into the car park which was being doused in a fine autumn mizzle, and we kissed as we had been dying to all night, kissed with a slow and gentle ease that built into passion, deep and damp, then set off for home, holding each other snugly.

'Boy, you know some funny people.'

'They're all OK, even Helen. A little eccentric, maybe.'

'Who were the boys over at the door?'

'You know Spinkey, don't ye?'

'And the other fella?'

'Ye're fishing, O'Brien. You know who Bradley is as well as anyone, and if ye didn't know I'm sure Helen would've told ye.'

'Will you never give it up?'

'Give up what?'

'Them that asks no questions don't get told no lies, is that it?'

'Something like that. Are we going to have this conversation every night? You knew the score when we started going out, and we've been through this twice before. There's nothing to worry about, or to talk about. I'm not involved. I've only done small stuff, and none of that in ages.'

'I believe you, but there's thousands wouldn't.'

'Bradley is just someone I know. You're reading too much into gossip. He retired ages ago.'

'You forget I was through all this with Joe. He would swear to my mother that he wasn't at it. Next thing you would meet him on a roadblock with a rifle up his coat, or find a pile of ammunition in the pantry. I know you're telling lies, so don't think I'm a fool. I believe you because I want to. First sign of trouble though, and I'm gone. I've seen enough hassle in my own house without taking on any more. I won't be one of those daft ones who sit and wait for their man to finish a twenty-year stretch, just to swan about and say they've done their time for their country, or some poor cow like my mother who thinks her boy can do no wrong. You get into that kind of trouble and you're on your lonesome.'

'How come everyone's talking like we're engaged or something?'

'Maybe you need taking in hand. Or are we just knocking about, then?'

'I guess not. You know I wouldn't hurt you for the world, O'Brien. But ease off on the third degree. I'm just a peace-loving man.'

'Until Bradley or those boys whistle for you. Then you remember what I said. You won't see me for dust.'

I felt suddenly empty and alone. There was nowhere for my anger to go, no way to argue, to explain, just the long night stretching ahead.

'Did you ever take Brenda out?' She interrupted my musing.

'What's she got to do with anything?'

'You fancy her. You were like a wee puppy-dog every time she talked.'

'She's good looking. Not my cup of tea, mind.'

'What's your 'cup of tea', then?'

'I guess I kinda like you. I wouldn't be walking you home and taking all this abuse if I didn't.'

'Ach, God help ye. Tell me, why are men such awful liars?'

'I'm a good liar. And it's only 'cause ye make us that way.'

'Be careful, boy, or you'll be standing on the doorstep tonight.'

Spinkey sat in Rusty Joe's mulling over a plate of chips that had been cooked in a mixture of blood and grease. Business was slow, for the pubs were still full, but this was the only late-opening, sit-down chipper in the area. Spinkey watched the drunks pass by outside. He was glad he was sober. Saturday was the night for rowing over girlfriends and wives, over money and children, over someone looking sideways at you. Friday night rows were for the hell of it, but Saturday brought out the tensions for real, with a full, dull day ahead to recover and make up. West Belfast always had a peculiar, dangerous buzz at this time, as if it were holding its breath.

Spinkey was just taking in the scene, killing time and letting his nerves gather for what was ahead. Over three and a half hours to go. Ten-to-One weighed in eventually, and chanced a beefburger. He'd heard somewhere it was best to operate on an empty stomach, better for any gut wounds you might pick up, but he was famished after running Mo from one end of town to the other all day. He didn't say anything to Spinkey but he knew the job at hand was part of something major. Mo had made four visits that evening, ranging from the north of the city, through the city centre and out to the flashy suburbs.

As Rusty's filled, Spinkey nodded to a tall fella he knew who was glancing around as if he'd lost something.

'Right, Toss? What about ye?'

'Hello, Spinkey.' He came over and asked quietly, 'Did you see Lar Morgan or any of his boys on yer travels?'

'No sign, Toss. You could try Archer's. He sometimes shows up there late.'

'No. I've been there. Anyway, not to worry. Behave yourself, Spinkey.'

'Who was that?' asked Ten-to-One as the guy left.

'Just someone,' Spinkey replied. Just Toss O'Reilly, one of the lads from the next company area. Spinkey had a feeling of dim apprehension; a creeping, intangible suspicion worming into his thinking. Something was up. O'Reilly wasn't looking for his unit leader at this time of night for a game of cards. Spinkey and myself would be at large in their territory tonight, and if those guys were out as well it could get a tad cramped. Mo's valediction of the afternoon came back to him: 'all the ammo you can use'. Spinkey smelt a rat. This whole operation insulted his methodical streak: a place for everything and everything in its place.

Bricks came in, calm, relaxed, and found Ten-to-One with his legs stretched out beneath the table, eyes closed and gently snoring in the midst of the greasy anarchy which Rusty Joe's had become. Spinkey was sitting over an untouched plate of chips, deep in thought.

In the low light of her living room we played out the timeless game, though neither had the courage to call it love. There was passion, and power, kindness I had never felt before. No fumbling, no pushing. Stroking and feeling, exploring, touching, reaching, laughing with quiet delight and trepidation, as people not quite aware of what was happening, yet more than aware, senses electrified, unable to stop the overwhelming assault of sentiment.

Suddenly we were together, one, moving in unity unknown to us. All was so damned right, so powerful and obvious until our needs became a strangled roar from her, a surprised, uncontrollable rush through me which drove a long pleasure-teased gasp from my throat, and we fell to the floor as the last thrusts and shoves sent us over the top, and her legs viced me to her, as I squeezed her for dear life, as I emptied, as she flushed, as we kissed and rose, as we fixed our clothes, as she turned away, as I waited in the hot silence for my heart to slow. When she looked at me her face was damp and intense.

'I wasn't counting on that.' Her voice was trembling.

'It happens.'

'What happens after?'

'No difference.'

'Until you get tired of me.'

'Not a possibility.'

'You say that now.'

'You're stuck with me.'

'How often have you done it?'

'Never like that. Never so good.'

For once I wasn't lying about sex. This was no lumbering, mechanical thing. It was caring, and correct.

A key turned in the front door. Sticky Joe peered into the half-lit room. His breathing was laboured, his eyes vainly trying to focus.

'Behaving yourselves, children?'

'Fine, Joseph,' she said. 'Go on you to bed.'

'I will. It's time you were away home, chief.'

'He's going in a minute, Joe.'

'Can't have the neighbours talking.'

'Goodnight, Joseph.' Her voice was firm. He lurched off, up the stairs.

'I meant to ask you ... will you come to our house for dinner tomorrow?'

'So your Ma can have a look at me?'

'Something like that. I cleared it with her tonight. She's expecting ye now.'

'Can't let her down, then, can I?'

She was so pleased. We were building bridges. Then she asked it, brought the word up first.

'Do you love me?'

'I might do.'

'Might you now? Are you sure?'

'I'm sure I might.'

'That's a start, I suppose.'

It was one thirty when I left. The streets were empty, cold and drenched, the wind whipping low and hard, carrying stinging flecks of rain. By the time I reached the alley behind Bricks's house, she was a confused warm memory buried deep in my heart, but now a monumental tiredness was on me. I stood for a gloomy moment across from the alley, aware of the unholy darkness and deathly silence. When I was sure no one could see, I strode across the street and into the dank, uninviting hole where the boys were waiting.

The rifles were stored a few doors down from the alley by an elderly sympathiser, a ghost of a man, long widowed, quietly doing his bit for his beliefs. The risen people; a mythical constituency which provided the backbone of the struggle, disaffected and brutalised by the State, silently working away in the shadows of the gutted nationalist psyche. Their views ranged from semi-pacifism to mad-doggery, socialists and super-fenians all united by a common thread of seeking self-respect in the midst of cynicism and corruption. Their loyalty was transient, conditional, but vital. Their dependability was determined by results and the extent to which they felt outrage and threat from the Orange State. But they were always there, finally, the wisest collection of political malcontents that Ireland had ever seen. Such was this wee man, quiet, unremarkable, but astute.

Days before, I'd stood in his kitchen behind drawn curtains, patiently waiting for him to retrieve the rifles which were cached in a false window-sill upstairs. I checked them for cleaning, for smooth and regular action, loaded the clips and taped them, finally wiping all the equipment for dabs and rolling them up again in their blanketing. It was only after he'd let me out the back door as he would a cat that I realised he had spoken not a word nor responded in any way to a single word I'd said.

Everything in his life was deniable. Now the same weapons were standing against the alley wall, and Spinkey stood guard with a pump-action resting across his arms.

'Nice night for it,' he murmured. 'How did you get rid of the quare one?'

'I left her home, simple as that.'

'The way you two were eyeing each other, I didn't expect to see you at all tonight.'

'Grow up, fella.' I was always ratty before a job, just as Spinkey got the shakes and Bricks, well, he just went off to a different plane. He was standing in the darkness beyond, and I could just make out Ten-to-One by his side. Bricks handed me a jacket, took my own wet coat and went up into the house. In the jacket were gloves and balaclava.

'All you fellas got rid of your ID? Let's get the show on the road, so.'

Ten-to-One went out into the street, glanced around, then nipped off to get the car; Spinkey put the shotgun under his jacket, while I handed Bricks his Armalite.

'Take the safety off, and try not to point it at me.'

'Cheers.'

'You're very quiet, Bricks. Are you OK?'

'I'm never right till the crack starts. You know me.'

'Well, take it easy. We've nearly an hour to go. Spinkey clue you up?'

'How the fuck do we get out of this place?'

'We run like shite the minute I tell ye, that's how. No frigging about. And whatever happens, don't get split up. There's only two dozen Catholic houses over there. Nowhere to go if ye're stuck, just a mile of Prods and Brits between there and here. So, in and out, full automatic and away.'

'Full automatic it is. I get the picture.'

We each put a spare clip in our jackets, just as the car rolled quietly to the alley's mouth. Spinkey held the door while we skipped into the back. As we drove off he wound down the front window and placed the shotgun over his knees ...

Dulce et decorum est ... certainly so. Less for those with no say. Barely three-quarters of a year before, Spinkey and myself had been sitting on a bus going into the city centre from a base in the university area. We were avoiding the security gates which protected the main commercial area from nationalist West Belfast; going in by the back door. As we neared our target, an electrical goods shop, Spinkey reached into his bag, set the last wire to the timer, putting the bomb in motion. This on a half-filled bus, mind. Over-confident, cocky, inexperienced. We had walked over to the store, casually checked the area for security, and entered. As I held the revolver on the shop assistant, two astounded customers and a trembling manageress, Spinkey put the charge at the back of the premises. We gave them a ten minute warning, walked out around the corner, then jogged up to the broadest street in town to a waiting car which was idly ticking over by a bookshop. The driver gunned it up, and we were quickly around City Hall, seeking to get lost in the flow of traffic.

We'd been half-way to base when the car pulsated, filled with the wake of a dull, mid-distance thud. You could see the tight worry on the faces of the other motorists, the sudden interest in their driving, windows winding down, looking out for smoke or sign. The processes of fear and preservation setting in. Traffic had slowed as the sirens rang. A military patrol careened past us, rapidly followed by the first ambulance. Not one of us spoke, lost in anxiety.

The driver had taken the car off the main road, swung it down a series of unfamiliar streets, populated by the students and bohemians of the city. This was as near to a demilitarised zone as we had, and the car was easily dumped, along with the revolver. It was too far to go carrying a piece, with the enemy on full alert and my face on the 'wanted for questioning' list. So we had split up to make our way back to home ground in a patient, controlled manner, picking up bits of the horror as we went.

A snatch on the radio in Peoples' pub, a remark between two pensioners on the bus, a comment by an arcade owner in the small streets near the Falls. The first television reports as I walked into Archer's. Two dead, fourteen injured, some seriously, reported over footage of panic, of terror, strained dumb faces of police and firemen; prone, twisted bodies beneath blankets, fixated, shaken expressions of the onlookers. Wreckage on the smoking street: human, plastic, wood and glass. Fused into a montage of pain, destruction, dismay.

It was all so purely distant, so second-hand. Something I was detached from, knew nothing about, yet knew all about. Ours was another bomb, not yet gone off. Same street, same premises, but not ours, surely?

I was watching a play, but waiting for a different production. Of all the people watching those bulletins that day, I had been the one least affected, the most removed. I'd been able to commiserate. I could nod when someone said, 'That's getting us nowhere.' I actually replied, 'God help them. That was a lousy operation.'

The girl in the tobacconists, who knew my sympathies, said, 'The boys who did that have a lot to answer for, if not in this life, then the next.'

I had agreed with her. After I'd gone, I guess she must have thought I wasn't such a bad fella. Not as hard-hearted as some. I wasn't trying to deceive her. I was just gripped by a huge feeling of unreality, frantically removing myself physically and mentally from the equation, struggling to get home. For that first day I kept myself busy, talking, drinking, laughing, hyperactive, doing anything but thinking. Above all, I avoided Spinkey like the plague. That night, I fought myself to sleep, and in the morning came down to find the ghost of Spinkey standing at the door, gaunt and hunched, his eyes flicking like snakes'.

I knew instantly what had happened. I had blown the life out of a load of civilians. Personally. No one else to blame, not another time or place, not another bomb. Mine, my operation; no fiction, play or dream. Nowhere to run. In a sheet of red wind and fire I'd blasted them into elastic and blood – not one, but many. A whole cast list scrapped and deformed for my politics, for my sins.

We'd walked without talking. Talked without saying much. He broke first, passing through the children's playground at the back of the park where we once played. By the broken swings he talked, slow and ill came the words, the anger and hate welling up, the fear, the disbelief, the horror ripping at his tight, fearful features. He was desperately looking for excuses, for parallels, for comparisons. Then on to the cause, and he was reaching out to me, his eyes pleading for agreement, as if his very salvation was in my hands. What comfort was in me, sick to the soul?

'Spinkey, we fucked up, and now we have to live with it. These things happen. They'll always happen. It's the price of war. You just get on with it, or get out. We followed orders, and it happened; now we have to put it behind us, somehow. If we weren't occupied, yesterday would never have occurred. If you don't see that, you've had it. You did your duty as a soldier, and that is all you need worry about.'

I'd been angry at his weakness, for it was too close to me. I gave him the full party line with both barrels, no punches pulled and not a trace of doubt on my face or manner. Spinkey had nodded his head and reeled my words in like a man realising some finer truth for the first time. Shit, he would nearly have gone out and done it all again. Even as I said it, as I offered him our absolution in political, historical communion, I didn't believe a word of it myself.

It had taken weeks to get back to normal. After a fortnight of a slowly increasing, escapist binge, Mo found me wrapped up in myself in O'Toole's bar at the crack of opening. I'd gone out of my way to avoid him, and any movement people come to that. I'd been running scared, sleeping rough for the most part, if I slept at all, tapping old mates for money and a bed.

The peelers were still after me for a blast-bomb attack on the local barracks, which I had nothing to do with, and I only stayed at home the odd night when I was stuck and the old man took pity on me. I had a mortal dread of interrogation, too weak from the slaughter. So I was juking around corners, physically and in my head, frightened of what I might meet.

Mo pulled me from the bar and ordered me into his car. The driver was my comrade from the bombing, and we whizzed up the coast road in polite deferential distrust. Shame, I learned, brings defiance.

The small-talk ceased when we pulled into a lay-by near the polytechnic. Mo and I got out and walked to the wall above the sea, where the driver couldn't hear.

'I was expecting to give you a debriefing, but you haven't been available.'

'What do you want to hear, Maurice. We put the charge in, gave a warning and cleared off. It went off. Worse things happen at sea.'

'No they don't. Be flippant with anyone else but me, chap. I see you're taking it well. Hit the bottle and hide, is that the plan?'

'Best I can come up with. I'm fucking destroyed. I'm jacking it in.'

'That figures. When it happened to me I felt that way too. Four-year-old kid. We were on a snipe, near the meat factory, ye know? I could never work out if it was a lousy shot or a ricochet. The inquest didn't say. Missed the Brits by a mile, either way, scalped a child further down the road. That's a war story for ye, all right. One of the ones you don't want to hear repeated. Outside, they want it all crack and gallantry. We both knew it isn't like that, never was.'

'Mo, I feel so dirty inside. Like it'll always be so. It wasn't right, man. I can't feel it was right.'

'Of course it wasn't right, you fool. But you did it for the right reasons. The question is, are the reasons still right for you, even if the result was a mess? The reasons are still there. The Brits are still here. In the long run, what you did was a matter of bad luck, just a faulty timer. It's only a speck of dust between a good operation and a calamity.

'Believe me, I know. What happened those people, what you did to them under my orders, my responsibility, will never be forgotten. That's conscience. Sometimes it's the only thing keeps you going. Take me. I still believe there's no other way to justice. I still believe this is a war that will have to be fought. I can't palm it off to the next generation, the way it was done to us. My conscience won't let me.'

'I don't know if I'm that committed, Mo.'

'You believed when you came to me. I think beneath this guilt-trip you still believe. If not, you'd have been screaming to get out. Spinkey told me what you said to him. You owe him better than what you're doing to yourself.'

'I'm not his keeper. Don't saddle me with that.'

'He's your friend, your comrade. Listen, I've fifty quid to give you from funds, and a score of my own. Take a run across the border for a few weeks, get yer head sorted out. If you still feel the same way, I'll stand you down. Just remember, it was bad luck. But it could happen any time, any operation. You knew that when you came forward. This isn't kiddies' games. It's a filthy political war. If you've not taken that in, then turn yer back on it, for ye're no good to me, or the struggle, and those people have died for nothing, nothing at all. You're either a soldier or a common criminal. Nothing in between. And I'm not having you moping around pubs feeling sorry for yourself. That way you're a liability. Dangerous to yourself, and dangerous to me. Is that plain?'

'I could do with a holiday.'

'Good man. Just remember, I've no answer to give you. No one has. Go away and work it out for yourself.'

Now, some nine months later, I was in the back of a car, heavily armed and moving to an appointment with a tin of paint.

Big George had his wicked way that night. To his astonishment, Helen pulled him into a drapery's doorway and turned a few years of flirtation and empty promise into a few moments of grossness. He was drunk and delighted; she was suddenly sober and disgusted with herself, but bitterly blamed it on her husband, the years of neglect and being taken for granted. Her sister, Brenda, took a cab to the nurses' home, and came back to an orderly, empty room.

Joey O'Brien slept a drunken, noisy sleep, as his sister in the next room lay awake, hugging a pillow, wondering what the future might bring.

All over, the streets slept or lay on the fringes of sleep, but in pockets, in dark places, young men and women were alert, were moving, in a black mime of cowboys and Indians.

We bailed out of the car a hundred yards from the hospital's flank, and while we trotted through the estate, Ten-to-One drove on and around to the pick-up point. We moved hastily, quietly, eyes and ears straining to control the increasingly unfamiliar environment. No troops, no traffic. Moving the quarter mile till we reached the wedge of homes which stood across from the shopping centre. By the time we arrived, Ten-to-One was in place at the rear of the block, slumped down in the driver's seat. We walked past in file, down between the houses which lay in slumber, to the edge of the waste ground which ran down to the main road. As we waited, all we could hear was the sound of our own excited breathing and the odd shuffling of position.

'Five to three,' Spinkey whispered.

He walked back into the estate, shotgun directly at his side. In a crouch, Bricks and I ran forward to the two wrecked cars mounted at the foot of the plateau. Bricks moved to the left, I to the right. We both had a clear field of fire on to the road, and squatted tensely, breathing deep and heavy until the night was sent reeling. A huge thump, carried on the wind, broke the stillness, and the darkness was jerked into relief as a blinding flare tore like a clenched fist from the shopping centre. For what seemed minutes the debris fluttered and fell down into the square as the eruption receded and the fire took hold. Rolls of black smoke came tumbling out, broken by vivid orange sheets of flame. The square and road were lit up, but we lay in darkness, grim, ready, dry-throated and fearful. A wailing of alarms began, each shop responding to the assault on its family, alarms vying in the night to outdo each other in outrage.

Bricks muttered in the darkness to himself: 'Nice one, Spinkey,' as the fire began to rage in earnest.

CHAPTER TWO

SPINKEY DRISCOLL WATCHED the flames climb and claim the air above the rooftops. He fought to keep his stomach from turning, savagely defying his instinct to run or to fold. In an instant his mind was back at the electrical shop, back at the turmoil of months before. Since then, he had woken many times to the sound of his own whimpering. Then he would bite down deeply, force resolve back into himself, rise and stick a smile on, lightly shouldering the burden of self-hatred.

Where I had resorted to denial and drink, Spinkey had secretly turned into his own worst enemy. I'd had the benefit of a month in the South: dances, amusement arcades, relaxed surroundings. More importantly, Mo and another old hand had come to meet me after the third week. In a house hard by the Dublin road, Mo let his hair down, and the three of us talked into the early hours; we argued and listened, the doubting volunteer, the army fixer and the old-timer seeking election to the local council in some rural backwater. That night had been a turning-point for me. Up to then, my politics had all been of the negative. I knew what I hated: British gall, Orange fascism. That night I got an inkling of what I was fighting for. I came back, rested, determined and interested.

I was rapidly arrested and spent four rough days of grilling. The peelers questioned me about everything bar the passion of Christ, but they missed out on the bombing of seven weeks before. To my sly gratitude, they had marked down the slaughter to a north city unit. All in all, I got to sleep well, but Spinkey changed in subtle ways. Outwardly, he was more militant than ever, unperturbed after the initial crisis, but often I would catch him staring into the distance, just a shade more thoughtful, occasionally agitated. He'd grown up thinking it was all crack. He was one of the inherent believers, joining his father on civil rights marches, goggle-eyed to be a child among men, marching peacefully, asking for a share of the Northern cake. Spinkey hadn't benefited from my father's cynicism. All he saw was glamour and righteousness. He didn't look beneath the skin to see the workers and the unemployed being led by the feckless down a road to confrontation. My old man knew that Catholic workers were naturally at the bottom of the political food chain, and suspected they were being used to further the ends of the 'respectable' people, the Catholics who had done all right out of partition, who just wanted a little more power, a little more recognition. Spinkey had inherited his father's unquestioning idealism.

While I came to the struggle infected and weakened by my father's perspective, Spinkey had answered a noble calling. I was too confused and ambivalent to be an idealist, but Spinkey was a natural. He was a victim. The shock would always be greater to him, to find that gallantry and nobility don't count for much when you are cutting pieces out of families. He was learning the hard lesson. What had started as political mobilisation for a recognition of Catholic respectability had turned into bloody repression and even bloodier revolution, where only the ruthless triumph. In conflict with my father, at least I had picked up on a bit of sour knowledge. Spinkey wanted to come up smelling of roses. Now he was desperately holding his mind together, determined to get on with the job at hand, gripping his shotgun in the thundering dark, choking down apprehension, every sense fiercely heightened. He had started his war as if it were some social service, but now he was tied down in a street full of sheepish civilians peeping from their bedroom windows into the smoke-dyed night, trying to ascertain the source of the uproar; embarked on a mission he was suddenly, completely suspicious of. He knew it was a wrong one, from the start. As bedroom lights came on, he strode into the street, stroked a shell up into the shotgun, and stood where he could be seen.

'Stay inside, ye fuckers!' he shouted. Then, to himself, 'I've enough to worry about.'

Less than a mile away, in a dim hospital canteen, a British officer called his men to action.

'Bomb down the road. Mount up!'

'And I thought it was some Paddy farting!' joked his corporal, to the chuckles of the hurrying troops. Leaving behind tables cluttered with unfinished snacks, discarded magazines and brimming ashtrays, the eight soldiers rushed to the call of a muted bugle, stretching over generations, young men caught in historical inevitability. As the noise of their jeeps receded in the night, Toss O'Reilly, Lar Morgan and two others moved timidly out of the shadows, their silent steps becoming more assured as the sound of the jeeps faded in the distance. The evacuation of the soldiers had left the military wing of the hospital half-protected. In the car-park there remained a civilian guard. Three soldiers stood in a sanger fronting the main road, and up on the third floor two policemen guarded a private room, one at the patient's bedside, the other outside the door. The men pushed through the tall privet hedge separating military from civilian wings, and walked across the car-park in Indian file. The civilian guard stood looking out to the orange glow which was playing on the horizon. He was baffled by the sudden company of four strangers, but he realised the import of the jabbing hand at his stomach. Glancing down, he could make out the outline of a pistol pushing tight to his belly.

He stammered: 'No trouble, lads ... no trouble ...'

They forced the security guard back into the hospital foyer. As one man watched him and the duty nurse, who was on the verge of screaming panic, another took his place in the car-park, positioning himself in full but distant view of the soldiers in the gateway sanger.

Morgan and O'Reilly took the lift to the third floor, shedding their overcoats. The policeman at the end of the corridor rose to the sound of the lift. Two men emerged in doctor's white and came towards him. From four feet Morgan cut loose with a silenced pistol, hitting the young officer square in the face. As he crashed to the floor O'Reilly leapt over him and burst into the room beyond, firing as he went. The officer standing by the patient's bed had barely time to clear gun from holster when the first shot hit him, picked and pitched him up, to crash against the patient's locker.

O'Reilly leaned across the bed and fired again, leaving the injured officer for dead. Between them, Morgan and O'Reilly hustled the half-conscious man off the bed and dragged him down to the lift, past the prone corpse of the first fallen policemen.

As the lift doors closed, the injured man focused on O'Reilly's face. 'What fucking kept ye?'

'Here comes the posse.'

Four minutes after the explosion, a fire-engine came hammering down the road, siren fit to wake the dead, blue light spinning crazily on its head. It swung over, only yards from us, then made a lazy arc on the road and crept into the square, now lit by angry yellow light from the hardware shop. As the firemen disembarked, the first Brit mobile appeared. A single jeep with an outrider flew past the incident. Down the road its companion slewed in tight to a garden wall, disgorging the soldiers in orderly panic, rushing to take over. The one I singled out was fractionally slower than the rest; for a second he remained on the road, turned briskly and began to move back as if this were a normal road-check. I raised myself and squeezed the trigger, more nervously than I would have liked. The muzzle flash obscured the target, but after the initial burst I dropped my aim to chest height and brought the rifle around in a spitting fan of ammo, ranging both sides of the street. To my right, Bricks was battering away, and with the sound of exploding paint cans and screams of fear from the scrambling firemen, I guess we didn't hear Spinkey roaring at us from behind. One of the soldiers on Bricks's side had got our position and was banging back at us. The rusted tin barriers of the cars whined as a stream of lead poured through from boot to front. Bricks was flat to the ground, rifle to cheek, blasting on. As the soldiers on my side began to return fire I spun back and down.

'Change clips and out to fuck!' He sounded off two more rounds and crawled back. Side by side, we ejected clips and turned them around, putting in full loads. We heard an almighty report from the houses, a blast which could only have come from Spinkey's shotgun.

'Out!'

Bricks bolted in a zig-zagging crouch across the muddy patch as I threw a burst to the right. Behind came the flat plop of bullets tearing into the mud.

'Out!'

Bricks roared and fired at the same time, and I ran back to the comfort of his rifle flash, ran like a demented hare frightened for its life. I raced past Bricks into the nest of sheltering houses, filled with fearful, praying families. I paused to allow him to catch up, loosing off a futile round down to the road.

'Shite!'

Spinkey was squatting by a car, pointing the shotgun in the direction of an abandoned grey Land Rover which was parked precisely on the spot where I wanted to see Ten-to-One. He fired off a massive charge from the gun, which rang through the estate. A policeman who had been tempted to glance around the corner flung himself back as a charge of pellets kicked the wall by his head.

'What fuckin' kept ye? Did ye not hear me calling?'

'Where is the fucking car?'

'He let a roar out, and tore off. Next thing these bastards landed on me.'

'We're fucked.'

'We have to go through these houses and out. Come on.'

Bricks rose to follow me. The shot spat past where he had been, and struck Spinkey clean in the side of the head. All I knew of it was the rifle flash from the corner of the waste ground, and the deathly noise that Spinkey made, a noise so bestial, part howl, part hiss. A strangled gasp tied to a low, offended scream. It was the sound of a wounded creature, done to death in dumb incomprehension, trying to yelp. When his head stopped jerking he keeled over, his feet shot out and under the parked car, and we watched stupefied as his body shook and wrung its way into death.

When I had enlisted, I had been more aware of the dangers than of any possible rewards. The forts and fleets of a foreign nation were parked on our backs. West Belfast was besieged. We had to fight, or so I felt. But not even I was prepared for the calamity to come, the fear and awe of early resistance gradually wearing off to be replaced with unthinking disdain for the British and their surrogates, leading right to this, the explosive payback they wrought on us. In an instant, the game was over, the price demanded, *realpolitik* Irish-style. We'd bought in, boyhood friends, and the debt demanded by our fathers' failure was about to be collected.

No amount of training or hard experience could have prepared me for that second. Only the facility to deny, to blank and blot. In the midst of life, death goes on. I watched in disbelief as he went, friend down the years, keeper of my secrets, and there was no time to weep. We live, for there is no other way. Survival. If it were only myself to worry about, I fancy I may have stood there and waited for execution, as there appeared no way out, and no reason. But Bricks was my responsibility, the remains of my command, my piss-poor, shot-up, buggered-off unit. I cancelled the deadly second, anger surging to my rescue, anger and hatred of the enemy coming like a warm, energising flood to my chest, and it pulled me back from collapse, from fatal resignation. Some bastard would live to regret all this. I seized Bricks by the arm and dragged him further into the shadows, into the garden. The soldiers fortunately failed to press their advantage home. A healthy spray into the general area would have sliced us to pieces, but they had spotted the police vehicle lying in the line of fire. Both sections were immediately wary of each other, and radio communication began. As they paused to confirm each other's identity, we rushed through some innocent's back garden, desperately trying to find a route to safety.

Further away, Ten-to-One was pinned to the roof of a stolen car. As the shooting had begun he'd started up the motor and moved it over to the top of the street. Spinkey was standing in the middle of the road with the shotgun on full display, like some bandit from a bad Western, and the few people who ventured to their doors and windows to investigate the blast rapidly changed their minds at the first sight of this masked desperado patrolling the street. The moments ticked by. The night was alive with gunfire and his throat was as dry as hell. Looking in the rear view mirror he saw the dark, unmistakable form of a police Land Rover beetling up the estate towards them. Ten-to-One jumped from the car and bawled a warning to Spinkey; then, using a discretion I'd always suspected of him, he jumped back in and flew off like the proverbial bat out of hell.

Spinkey was left to warn us and pin the peelers down at the same time. Ten-to-One hadn't got far when British reinforcements spotted his speed and flung their jeeps across the road. When they found the unused pistol in his pocket, he was frog-marched to a Saracen and given the greatest hiding of his miserable life. Just then, if I'd been with them, I would have joined in.

As it was I was racing frantically over creosote fencing and through bullwire, working a hasty way from the centre of operations. We clambered together over a chest-high, concrete wall and dropped to the road just fifty yards from the police position. We hared across the road and almost got to the opposite side unnoticed when an alert peeler spotted us, called, and fired. The bullet passed perilously close to my head, but we made the cover of the houses before they could nail us. It was here that it became every man for himself. We were in unknown territory, in the middle of a loyalist estate, pursued, it seemed, by half the Crown forces in Ireland. Whatever hope there was for one, there was no hope for two. By a low wall we crouched, gasping, both operating on fear and desperation, completely lost. Bricks looked in my eyes.

'See ye in jail.'

'Take care, big fella. And keep your head down.'

Bricks went east, I went straight north, facing low and strong with the Armalite pointing forward, willing to shoot the first thing that came in front of me.

As Spinkey died, two men bundled a third into a hedgerow gap. A nurse screamed and bashed in the fire alarm nearest to her. A soldier stepped from the sanger, and Lar Morgan took a parting pot-shot at him with his silenced pistol. The bullet flew innocuously over his unsuspecting head, and Morgan joined the push as the rescue unit stumbled and fell through the hedge into the adjacent civilian wing. In moments they were burning rubber, making for the motorway, laughing frantically and nervously among themselves.

Behind, they left a doctor trying in vain to staunch the wounds of a dying policeman as the resident military came to their senses and tried to rally and pursue, but they were breaking for the countryside. With every rapid yard gained they toasted Mo and his ingenuity, each of them professing their confidence in hindsight. As they fled the scowling city with their liberated patient, they were unknowingly assisted by a set of bomb scares which had to be dealt with in West Belfast itself, a pair of sniping incidents to the west, and a bombing in the city centre. Their escape was made providential by a set of noisy and co-ordinated diversions, of which our operation was one. They were given a clear run to the motorway and beyond, scurrying off to a farmyard retreat far from the urban furore in which Bricks and myself were caught up.

The hunter hunted. We had crossed into a strange land, only a mile or more from home. I knew my own streets, my own turf. Trapped there, I would know whose door could be knocked on, whose hall I could slide through, who would force open an attic and let me hide, let me lick my wounds. For they were near mortal that night, the wounds I carried. Spinkey, topped in the gutter. There seemed little point in carrying on. The distinctive whine of the Saracens arriving, the sound of running boots, of Cockney calls and radio static carrying from the street to the garden where I lay, tight to a wet wall; it all spoke of hopelessness, despair. Capture seemed almost welcome, an end to the torturous tension. Again, it was a rush of hatred which pushed me on, provided the adrenaline which sent me crawling flat into the next garden, then the next. Behind I could hear gravel being crushed softly underfoot, and I slithered faster and faster, knees, elbows, belly, further on, further on. A shape of black speed flashed in front of my face, and I held back a scream. The cat squealed at this invasion of its territory, then raced off into the gloom. On cue, a dog barked, maybe three or four doors away. There could be no further progress in that direction. If the Brits were on the ball, they would be moving in towards the noise. I was already convinced that one was behind me, prowling on my trail, hunting.

The back door of the house had a plain glass panel, and when I crawled over to it I discovered that the lower half of the door was made up of a roughly nailed-on piece of hardboard. It took a shaky second to prise out a nail from the top. The damp board almost peeled away. It left a hole just big enough for a fist to pass. Fumbling inside, my fingers finally located the door bolt, and I worked it across, eyes fixed on the garden, expecting discovery at any moment. With the bolt drawn it was a simple operation to lever the door handle down. With the weight of my shoulder, the door swung open. I recovered my fist and arsed my way into the scullery, rapidly closing the door behind me.

As I sat on the cold linoleum, the sweat began to dry. A profound chill set in, right to the bone. Terror and exertion left me a shivering wreck, heart thumping, hands shaking, but at least there was a door between myself and the coming hunters. A footfall in the garden sent a paralysing jolt into my frame. Stock still, I listened. The silence from outside took on a life of its own. The sound of life before man, the forest before the stranger. Autonomous, omnipotent energy, a beat alone in space.

Beyond the door was the void, and in the void a man was walking, hunting. His footfall touched the patch of cement by the scullery window, stayed, hesitated, then passed on. There was the sound of another, then a third, following their leader in brisk, careful procession. I breathed again.

Even in such shallow safety as a busted door, there can be tremendous comfort. The world demanding blood could not reach beyond a few inches of wood.

As children we had played up and down our streets, hiding from our elders, looking out to a world that couldn't see in. Then the growing up, the anger, the mutation into fighters. The State attacked my community with inexplicable venom, a descent into anarchy which troubled my childish vision. Then the learning began, the same learning as my father, most ways. Expect unemployment, expect poverty, expect to emigrate. If the State hadn't called in its markers and sent the British against us, tooth and nail, I would have evaporated into the norm of life in the community, having no more to fight for than my father. But they shocked and insulted us, put our backs to the wall. Spinkey was my classmate, Bricks was in the same year, different form. By sixteen we were old men, battle-hardened, resigned to a life of distrust and struggle, single-minded but of a mind. It was our fight, our generation. We knew just enough to glean that the division of Ireland, and the supremacist doctrine of Unionism, were a personal challenge to us, a personal insult encountered daily on the streets. Years later I came to see that it was in the interests of all parties that the country be divided, that beyond the show was economic 'reality', that we were the party poopers in this carnival of reaction. Corruption and hopelessness were enshrined in the South, and whatever accommodation was reached, short of freedom, would be reached at the cost of perpetual humiliation of the Catholic workers. They had no power, no army. That was where we came in. We dealt out death. We gave them a war they never got in Aden or Cyprus, we gave the Unionists the embodiment of all their bad dreams, the self-fulfilled prophecy that came with the State. 'Ireland unfree shall never be at peace.'

Out in the gutter was the proof. Spinkey Driscoll, topped and tailed, seldom knowing anything of peace. Damn it. What war had he started? Or those that killed him? The big boys sat in clubs and bars, in London, in Dublin, and devised a thousand ways to postpone the inevitable. They were getting a whole Ireland, whether they liked it or not, because enough of the kidnapped people of the North, the political hostages, were no longer playing games, no longer content to leave the field to the respectable ones. They'd had it for decades, decades of avoidance, of sentimental chicanery, of conning my father and his like. Possessed of the narrow view of youth, the one that brings change, unable and downright unwilling to compromise, we seized the only protest weapon that was left. War. Not 'troubles'. Troubles are when someone knocks your pint over and you haven't the money for another one. War is when someone tells you he'll kill you and all belonging to you if you seek to change him.

God, was it tough going. There's no more efficient laxative in science or nature than a trip in a car reeking of gelignite and mix. My first operations were such short runs, part of the commercial bombing campaign designed to raise the cost for Her Majesty's government. Ground-to-ground bombardment, unseen in Europe since the Second World War.

After one such delivery, a three-hundred-pound charge, myself and a colleague revisited the scene. I was astonished at the extent of our attack. It created an outlandish effect on the city landscape. The entire area of offices and shops was smashed to pieces in a giant's footfall. People still shopped and chatted in the destroyed acres, windows for half a mile boarded up. Smoking ruins, greasy streets, broken wall stumps where once a proud office block stood. Democratic destruction. Massive bombing, running out of steam and purpose, the civilian casualty rate giving the State spurious morality. The romantic integrity attached to the cause took a knocking in the televised carnage, those same cameras studiously avoiding British and Unionist excesses, but racing to bring the results of faulty timers and broken telephone boxes to the screen. Hearts hardened on all sides, romance was the casualty of this war. It was our tailored vocation.

In '72 I joined in. I'd done with looking anxiously on. I'd become heady on the potent cocktail of West Belfast, drunk from the cup my father feared. It was an intense mixture of pressure, pain, excitement and hope. Next year, victory. It was the time of greatest fear. Right-wing Unionist squads were cutting swathes through the Catholic population in a genocidal drive to quell the revolt. There were more reasons to stay uninvolved than to sign up, but my patience eventually snapped. Bricks joined a month after me. He was a natural joiner, in the library, in the youth club, in the Christmas club for all I knew. He was a thinker, an enquirer. A quiet, assured young man at school; pensive, disciplined, but capable of getting carried away in a fight. I knew him as a boy not to get annoyed. Spinkey had an indelible reputation as an eejit. He was good with his hands, and played goal for the school. For some reason, we'd always been mates, running around from the time we were in short trousers. He knew me better than I knew myself. Spinkey was able to cheer me up when the old man was hounding me, and forever taking my part in arguments. His father being solid nationalist, it was a fair bet he would go one better. For ages, I thought he was involved. As it turned out, he enrolled around the same time as myself, and was astonished when my cynical, fickle self took the field. We trained apart, and initially worked apart, until Mo teamed us up with Bricks and two other guys, Ten-to-One being a roving operator. Through it all, Spinkey and myself grew ever closer, perpetually watching each other's back.

Now he was gone, gone for good. Bricks was lost to me. All I had for comfort was this strange refuge, a door between myself and the world, sealed into a trap, unable to move, stripped of the power of choice, frightened and so terribly alone.

Bricks used his rifle-butt to smash the side glass on a Volvo. He'd waited for the quietest moment before taking a chance. Once inside, he blindly hunted out the bonnet lever, finally reaching it and wrenching it open. As the bonnet popped he heard a slow, wavering voice behind him.

'One move, ye cunt, and ye're dead. De ye hear me? One move and ye're dead.'

In seconds they were all around him. He was lying across the front seat of the car, awkwardly stranded, belly-down with the rifle underneath him.

'I've a rifle under me.'

'Where is it?' Another voice, less shaky, less Ulster.

'I'm lying on it.'

'Crawl over it slowly. Get out the other side of the car.'

'Make a false move, and ye're a dead man.'

And that was how they did it. He opened the other door and crawled on his stomach and elbows until they were sure his hands were free, then they grabbed him by his arms and dragged him onto the street.

Mo was sitting on a settee, nursing a cup of tea, long gone cold. He had given up drink years before, but at times like this he could feel a little demon nudging the back of his throat. Upstairs, the house owner was monitoring the police and army frequencies, rushing in occasionally to report some inane piece of information in low, portentous tones. It was clear that all hell had broken loose around the shopping centre, but barring the odd detail of movements and shots reported, there was nothing to give Mo an overall picture. It just boiled down to waiting for the telephone.

At ten to four the phone rang, five times, then off. It was the country man reporting success. Cargo delivered with four others intact. The patient was sprung, and Mo felt a gush of relief pass through him. He picked up the phone and rang Bradley.

'Any signs?'

'No signs.'

'Ring if it changes.'

He replaced the receiver. Mo knew he'd given us the shitty end of the stick. It was the downside of the night's work. He had a lot of time for our unit. We had operated under difficult circumstances with a reasonable strike rate, drawing little enemy attention to ourselves, and this at a time of high attrition, infiltration and lax security. In the year past we'd had only minor personnel changes, when the operational lifespan of a volunteer was a little under six months and often less than that. Mo knew we were crafty, and that I could be over-cautious, but we usually got the job done.

From the start he probably had me figured as a faint-heart, for I wouldn't come forward like the others, but he soon got to know that I wasn't prepared to let myself or anyone with me become cannon-fodder. We developed a huge respect for each other, which grew with the triumphs and the tragedies, but back of it all, it was me on the spot and him with the orders, so there was a healthy, silent distrust. I was no 'reluctant terrorist', no dupe. I certainly didn't operate through fear. No army can run on fear, and there was no room for conscription. The revolt had always had more volunteers than rifles, otherwise it would have been over years ago. But once in, I was determined to look after myself, and that meant looking after the interests of those around me.

He had run us through the plan the day before, through it for the third time. I'd taken a back seat and studied him for a sign, but only the words 'all the ammo you can use', and that fleeting look of appeal had slipped past his tired features. Mo was old and venerable to us. He was somewhere in his thirties, with a legend pinned to him. He wore it heavily, aware of what was expected of him. He gave off the air of a doleful, studious man, slightly cultured, gentle and composed. But when he switched it on, the cold passion at the bottom his soul, he could torture and alarm you with a glance. He wasn't in his job for nothing. He'd been a ruthless operator and a conscientious officer, worldly wise, pragmatic. He'd survived, and more. He had applied himself to his beliefs and experiences with iron determination. In the normal run of things, he could ill afford to lose a decent unit like ours. It was one thing letting us have a go at equivalent forces in our own area; it was another dispatching us to attack superior forces, better trained, better equipped, motorised and with radios, and this in an alien environment. They had the armour and electronics, always. The only thing we had was surprise and local knowledge. Shoot and scoot was the name of the game.

But he had his orders, his priorities.

He knew as well as I did that the moment the hardware store went up the place would be crawling with the enemy, but he needed us to clear the way to safety for the real operational target, the bit we didn't need to know about. The big picture, that made our lives and liberty a secondary consideration. He'd been there himself, and lived not to talk about it. So he sat by the phone, hopeful and calm, until five o'clock came and went, with no word from Bradley at our base.

The householder came down the stairs, nervousness on his

face. He'd been monitoring the wavebands all evening, listening for word. Now he had it.

'The Brits are talking one dead and two arrests. They're fairly chirpy about it.'

Mo sighed, and closed his eyes.

'Shut that lamp off, till I get some sleep.'

He stretched out on the settee. For Mo, it was a night of mixed fortunes.

For me it was the culmination of years of wrestling with anger, with indignation, with myself. Born into a time of hope masking cancer, I'd been moving to this point of despair seemingly from birth. The suits and the dog collars had brought it about, corruption, nepotism, self-delusion their guiding principles on every side. Only the people at the sharp end had a clarity of vision and a purpose which made sense to me.

Easily sold as a religious conflict, an inexplicable *mélange* of Irish bigotry and national psychopathy, in fact it was about jobs and houses, about power and who got to wield it. It was about British self-absorbtion and Catholic Irish infidelity, a sickly opera playing over the generations to a correctly uninterested world, only punctuated by occasional pogrom and atrocity. When my people finally sanctioned violence, in this, the last Irish war; when Mo and his like answered fire with fire; then the funk set in and the desperate twisting and turning to find peace, but all too late, for the war was ready-made for us.

'What better way for man to die,
Than fighting fearful odds,
For the ashes of his fathers,
And the temples of his Gods.'

What indeed. A bit of training, endless lectures. Then welcome to the war of the flea. Political war. The sneak attack. Ugly chameleon of wars, where your next-door neighbour can be the next target, where the State must pay an extravagant price for its respectability. Where it becomes exposed, naked and hideous, seething with bigotry and reaction. The guerrilla lies within the community; without the silence or help of those around, he is without substance, defeated in his own terms. Others come and go, with their fancy ideas, but Ireland still produces the goods after centuries; still, from the first invasion, holding a legitimised legacy of political 'crime' as Britain as ever cries 'foul'. At the bare bone, only one rule to cherish. Look after Number One. That's the key. You do your best by your comrades but when the chips are down you are no use to anyone in jail, less than worthless dead. The important thing is to prolong your liberty and life for as long as you possibly can, to stay in the game. You only give up hope when hope itself is hopeless, when you are disarmed or disabled. You realise the possibility, the probability, of your destruction, but you work to postpone that outcome. You are part of a cadre; on your own you are pure cadre. You carry the future of the revolt in your heart, and your heart must beat free for as long as the revolution needs you. There is no disgrace in flight, if it isn't desertion, and there is no profit in martyrdom. You attack, you run, until your back is pressed against a wall, and there are no further options save surrender or death. Then you decide.

How often did I tell myself I would never be taken alive? Juvenile bravado. Sitting on the cold linoleum, I studied the options. The last thing I was going to do was go out in a blaze of glory. They had had their chance to kill; so had I. That was enough excitement for one night. When they came in the morning it would be surrender, with all the complications. The first Brit I'd fired at had gone down, so the sentence would be anything from sixteen to twenty-five. Not bad for a first offence. It was now unlikely they would show up before daybreak. That would mean getting hundreds out of bed in the midst of darkness; it would be imprecise, provocative. They had the area sealed, the problem contained. It would be a sweep at first light, then house-calls. By that time, the game would be up.

The house was in silence, as if deserted. That would have been too much to hope for. I peeled the soaking balaclava away from my face and gently raised myself from the floor. Using my sleeve, I wiped the night-damp from the rifle stock, switching the action to single shot, and set about exploring.

The scullery was much smaller than I'd thought. A table, a fridge, an alcove for coats. I felt around and made out what I took to be a parka jacket, male. Bits and pieces, a schoolbag resting on the floor, a furled umbrella ... my foot hit a broom lying against the wall. Before I could seize it, it toppled over and hit the floor with a wooden rattle which seemed to reverberate in the little room. I frantically scanned the garden outside through the least misty patches in the window. There was no sound, no movement. Just the eerie quiet, as if the hunter had heard a twig snap in the forest, and was poised silently to strike.

A full two minutes elapsed with the weight of an hour in them. The game would go on. No response. As I turned the handle to the kitchen there came a noise from above which threw fear into my heart, froze my hand, froze my mind. In blind apprehension, I heard the sound of a floorboard groaning at the pressure of a foot. The noise went along the ceiling overhead, as someone rose and crossed the bedroom floor.

None of the three detectives had been able to put a name to Spinkey's bruised, ill-coloured face. One of them thought it was familiar, but try as he might, the name wouldn't come. So when the perfunctory forensics had been done, they fingerprinted his rocky hands and sent two uniforms racing off to the station. They needed to launch whatever house raids were required before the dawn light. After that it would be a matter of raiding a wake-house in daylight, and once word leaked out the place would be clean as a whistle. If they failed to get swift identification, whatever raids followed would be made to exemplify police insensitivity at a time of grief, disrupting mourners in pursuit of wild geese.

At six o'clock, as the dark of night tamed into a dirty grey wash, they gave the word, and three soldiers raised and hustled his corpse into a Saracen which had a huge red cross painted on its flank. The grey-haired priest who had been summoned an hour before called, 'Gently. Gently does it there!' as the soldiers dragged the body into the vehicle. They kept their thoughts to themselves, in deference to their officer standing beside the cleric, but inside they were boiling. One of their own was lying in hospital with two rounds in his back, and the padre expected them to be gentle with this stiff scum. Fuck him for dead meat.

At six ten the detectives followed the military ambulance to the hospital, still expecting confirmation of the deceased's identity, growing more impatient as the dim morning began to assert itself. At the entrance to the military wing, a dozen troops were staked out, in and around the sanger, lying by the perimeter fence and behind the overgrown shrubbery. The police car continued to follow the Saracen on into the civilian complex. The driver looked back at the face-blackened troops.

'Talk about shutting the stable door after the horse has bolted!'

The other bulls murmured in agreement.

Ten-to-One had been lucky to make it to the barracks conscious. In the forecourt two more soldiers joined in the pasting, and he was pushed and kicked into the custody of a solitary police duty officer. Eventually he was processed and examined by a doctor. His injuries were recorded, cuts disinfected, and complaints noted; then he was rapidly exhumed from the bowels of the station and rushed into the interview room. He was in a state of physical and mental exhaustion, but dug deep into his reserves and refused to give any name other than his own. At six twenty the shift changed, and two large Branch men (one of whose faces was known to every Provo in the city) took over the interrogation. The famous one sat down in front of the prisoner. He grabbed him under the chin, as if testing an apple before purchase, and stared into his face, into the panic-stricken, tired eyes. It was an inflexible, penetrating gaze, and try as he might, the prisoner was transfixed.

'You know all about the "two ways of doing this", don't ye, son? Well, you make your mind up damn quick about which way you want. Now, I'm going out to get a cup of tea and a sandwich. That's my breakfast. You got me out of bed early, boy. I had to rush here just to talk to a prick like you. Now, wee cunt, when I come back I want full co-operation. You get your filthy little mind straight, and get ready to tell me the lot. Is that clear?'

When he left, Ten-to-One stared at the other peeler in shock and fear.

'Ye wouldn't have a cigarette on ye, mister, would ye?'

His words seemed to belong to someone else, to some schoolkid with a stammer, waiting for the playground bully to approach, seeking friendship, alliance.

'I never use them.'

'Neither do I.'

'You being smart, boy? You should know something, shit-for-brains.' He rose and came over to Ten-to-One. 'We've no time to be screwing around with you. Yer man who left? He was the nice part of the routine. Ye know? The good policeman? That was him. When he's finished with ye, I get to have a go. And I'm going to tear your Fenian balls off; get the picture?'

Ten-to-One got the picture all right. Fifteen minutes later he was letting go. He rapidly admitted his part, and the reconstruction of events began, but he managed to keep out names and addresses. Half-way through the second interview, much later in the morning, they dropped Bricks's name, and he gave a 'no comment'. Then Spinkey. It became a treacherous two-way channel he was swimming in, as his nerves collected themselves, as his wits regrouped. He was trying to find out how much they knew, how little he had to tell them. When they got to the operation at the hospital, of which he knew nothing concrete, the interview turned around on itself, and as they landed back to square one, the promised torture began.

Brenda, bleary-eyed and head thumping from drink, fumbled in the dark for the hysterical alarm clock. She swore fiercely to herself, and stretched like a cat in the bed. By the time she had showered and made up, caught the first taxi and made the short trip to the hospital, by the time she walked into casualty for her shift, it was seven o'clock dead. She walked past reception to the children's ward, passing a short-haired guy using the reception phone. He was talking about some 'Noel Driscoll'. Wasn't that Spinkey's name?

'Did you hear about the carry-on last night, Brenda?' The night nurse was gathering her belongings, glad to be going home. She filled Brenda in with the details of the previous night's events in the nearby military wing, the hundreds of shots, the piles of bodies and wounded. Brenda listened aghast.

'Did you not see the police as you came in? They took in the body of that wee terrorist boy that was shot ...'

Brenda left her in place and marched apprehensively out and over to the mortuary, an instinctive, sickly excitement rising in her mind. She cajoled the attendant into giving her a look at the body of the latest addition to his stock. He warned her it wasn't a pretty sight, but she had seen them before. As long as you dehumanised the product, saw it for what it was, deceased flesh and bone, a shell, then it held no horror. Far more affecting was a sick child, a wasting life. Brenda was unprepared to view Noel Driscoll laid out on his gurney, awaiting the pathologist's ministrations, the undertaker's grip. She tottered from the room, fighting the desire to throw up. She remembered his grinning face from eight hours ago, the wink and the puckered lips he'd offered her in the pub the night before. She had known him from childhood, from sharing the same street games, the dances, the drinking, the laughs.

Brenda was sick in the staff toilets. When she straightened herself up, she went to the phone and rang her sister.

The kitchen door opened slowly. A woman's voice came from the hallway.

'Is there someone there? Is there?'

What did she expect? 'Yes, love. It's the local battalion. Go back to bed.'

She came into the kitchen before switching on the light, and, as her eyes adjusted to the sudden glare, I stepped out from behind the door and brought the rifle-butt fair and square into her face. She didn't go down, but staggered back, mouth open in stunned silence, giving me the chance to bring the gun back for another drive, which caught her in the mouth. As she fell she began to screech, so I brought the weapon back and struck down into her head. She lay still on the floor, blood flooding from her lips on to the carpet. In a mad bound I was racing up the stairs, three at a time, stumbling on the last and falling back, finally reaching the landing. The man of the house was standing in the bedroom doorway in full pyjamas, dreaming of a gunman racing up the stairs towards him while his wife had vanished. I levelled the rifle from the shoulder, the muzzle pressed firmly to his mouth.

'Back into the bedroom, squire. Back in now or you're history.'

In a trance, he obeyed, stumbling into the room with dead eyes and shaking head. 'What is this? What is it?'

'On the floor, face down. Hands on the back of yer head. If you want yer wife alive you stay that way. Right?'

'There's childer in the house. Don't go near the childer, for God's sake.'

'No one's going to be hurt if you do what ye're told. Now, if you move, my mate will blow your head off. Understand?'

By the time I got back down the stairs, the woman was trying to regain her feet. She was confused, and seemed fascinated with her blood, which soaked the nightshirt. I grabbed her by the arm and pulled her to the stairs, telling her not to shout, and pushed her, protesting, up the stairs.

She too was going on about the children, don't touch the children, but her voice was little more than a frightful gurgle of noise pouring over smashed teeth and split flesh. Suddenly she bolted up the stairs, making for the children's room, frantic, moaning. I caught her on the landing and flung her in to her husband. They lay on the floor, her squealing in terror, he comforting her, holding her face and talking to her, trying to calm her down and analyse her injuries. The other bedroom door opened and a child appeared, sleepy-eyed, a boy of about seven. Without hesitation he rushed into his parents' room where his father caught him and held him close.

'Who else is there?'

'A wee girl. She'll be sleeping. Is Annie asleep, son? Is Annie asleep? She's asleep. Don't go in there. We're what you want. Just leave the childer.'

I levelled the gun once more on all three of them.

'I don't want to hurt you or the kiddies, squire. But if there's any more fuss, I'll blow the crap out of ye all. And don't think I won't, right?'

The woman settled into a sobbing lament, clutching the young boy's arm as the husband soothed her. The child stared into my eyes, unconcealed defiance and hatred in him, his lower lip jutting out in rage, his eyes red and sparkling with anger. It was a look I knew from my own life. It was the rape of innocence, the end of his joy forever.

In those first, ghastly moments I was to all intents and purposes their jailor. In fact I was prisoner to them, if only they could see it. They were blinded by the rifle, by the brutality, the threats, by their conditioning. Only the child, with the eyes of bruised innocence and unaware of the power of the gun, only he could feel my weakness, my fear. Only he knew how pathetic I was, behind the mask, the gloves and the gun. How uncertain, how out of control. He could smell it a mile off.

Bricks refused to speak. A uniform in the barracks identified him, remembering him from a spot-check some weeks before, but Bricks refused to confirm his name. He had been remarkably well-treated by the peelers: a kick, a shove, a lot of verbals. It was hardly unknown for a captured operator to be plugged in possession, summary justice if you like. It was an acceptable hazard for any revolutionary. The only people to complain about 'shoot to kill' were the liberals, the constitutionalists. It nullified their attempts to portray the war as a police v. criminals situation. The Provos freely accepted it as a facet of the conflict. What they sought was recognition of the facts, the reality, that the Brits state publicly that such methods were necessary for the upkeep of the State. They sought to have the war declared; the British to keep it off the world's record books.

At the start Britain had painted itself into a military corner. To deploy troops on the grand scale, to intern, torture and gun down sections of a community supposedly British, that was pure enough colonialism, but this was a televisual, European war, against an enemy which could trace its resistance back eight centuries. The government had moved rapidly to put press and TV in the shackles of 'responsibility', but the problem had remained of explaining the prison camps and the fortifications to a suspicious world. Thus began the process of criminalisation. The struggle was a perversion, a distortion of history, an abnegation of the wishes of Irish people, North and South; those who indulged in violence were the criminal and psychotic dregs, fat with hatred and local power. But the central reality was the reality of nationalist West Belfast, where the people, rightly or wrongly, perceived themselves to be under an oppressive, predatory occupation by foreigners.

Bricks, caught bang to rights, had to consider himself among the lucky. Many others had died for much less. He did not consider himself a criminal; quite the reverse. As the Branch got down to interviewing him, they found he was made of proud, strong material. He simply repeated the phrase: 'I will answer any questions that you may have in the company of a solicitor.' Each word lazy and thoughtful, always the same deliberate mantra as he avoided their eye contact and stared at a selected spot behind their heads, a spot on the wall which only he could see. And his mind was back at home, back in the bedroom, back with his family, his brother, back, back ...

The detectives had enough to deal with in the 'hospital fiasco' as it had become known. They were stretched, and the call-up had begun to drag in bad-tempered reinforcements who had been expecting a good drunken Saturday night followed by a quiet Sunday. They had all week to work on Bricks. See how smart he would be when he was facing twenty years and a roomful of professionals working on him. See how smart he was after three or four days of the special treatment...

Brenda rang her sister Helen, who woke her husband Tommy, who rang Gerry Barron, who gave him Tommy Farrell's number, who rang Bradley's sister, who went across the road to her brother's house, but he was out scouting at first light, hoping to run across one of us on the way, and gauging as he went the enemy disposition and deployment. All on his milk float. So his sister went to our house first, and went with my Da to the Driscolls' house, where they roused the family and the crack in the street began. By eight, the place was buzzing.

It was ten past four by the clock on the bedside cabinet. The woman was lapsing into shock, rocking the young boy as he stood staring at me. The husband was facing me, his thoughts finally coming together. I ordered him to face his family with his legs stretched on the floor. He would have no chance to spring up and perform; he'd be dead before he got a leg off the ground. I got the child to switch on the bedside light, and turned off the main light, so all was dark to the outside. There was no activity, no enquiries at the door, so I figure the noise of my invasion hadn't extended to the outer world. I slid down to the floor, back against the banister railings, rifle aimed from the stomach.

It was cold and strange. An air of unreality descended on the house. What had started as a complicated but by no means impossible mission had turned into a bloody, unpredictable disaster. There was no reason to be here, to be here particularly. I had no wish to throw this family into chaos, into danger. It wasn't expected or planned. The whole thing was a sick joke. A dodgy back door had brought me here, had brought terror to these people, had changed their lives in the most extreme and subtle ways. I had no idea what might happen next, no plan.

'Have you got a car?'

'What?'

'Have you got a car?'

'I've a van. Flatbed Ford. I use it for work.'

'What's your job?'

'I work in the quarry. Masterson's quarry.'

Enough of the personal stuff. It would have been my luck to get to like him.

'This is what's going to happen, squire. First light, you and me are going for a spin. You're going to drop me off in the nearest Catholic area; you come back here, wait an hour and report this crack to the police. Do you correspond?'

'What if we're stopped?'

'Don't even think about it. If ye all stay calm – no heroics, no hysterics – we all come out alive. Any fucking about and there'll be bodies. So cover yourselves with a blanket, and we'll wait for first light, all right?'

He clawed the clothes off the bed and the three of them huddled on the floor beneath them, the woman's heavy breathing and swallowing the only sound left in the world.

Time dragged on in the bedroom, each moment a painful burden on the three hostages squatting on the floor, a dead weight on my heart. Even beneath my gloves my fingers grew stiff and cold. Tiredness set in rapidly, and it was a struggle to keep my mind on the matter at hand. I was drifting into lethargy, away from the fear and responsibility, out into the other world of the night, the world of Claire, and her brother Joe, of drink and laughter, of my mother, of those brothers and sister I never talked to. Other times, other places, that might never have existed now.

Sentiment is the great killer. Emotion is weakness in the crucible of death. I forced my mind back down, down into the room with the three huddled captives whose lives I was controlling. The clock hand dragged itself pitifully, inexorably towards five o'clock.

In the late autumn mist, the policeman drove down the boreen, jostled by the hard humps of the track. His heart was heavy and his body tired. No longer a young man, he had been woken in the middle of the night and had lain awake till daybreak, thinking of the local lad he had known for years. A big red-faced boy in his memory, a rangy, rural lad with an infectious laugh and a bounce in his step, who had come to him years ago and asked about a career in the police. The sergeant had known his family for years. Quiet, respectable folk, firm Christians and fair dealers, and now he was going to tell them their only boy was dead, died in a bloody hospital, for pity's sake. Shot in hospital and couldn't be saved. Things were going from bad to worse in this flaming country. The sergeant would have given his pension not to be here, to be appearing on their doorstep like a messenger from hell, breaking the news that breaks all around it. He felt he was a pariah, carrier of disaster. This was the part of the job you never quite got used to, no matter what you told yourself. It didn't get easier, and with the times in it, this bearing of bad tidings had become a grim routine.

The farmer was walking down the lane when he saw the car approaching, and he instantly recognised the grey, bull head of the policeman. He was a long way from town and it was too early in the morning for the news to be good. He took his cap off and fixed the lining, letting the soft rain cool his pate, and he gently drew in the cold air as his heart began to pound. The sergeant stopped his vehicle and got out.

'Morning, Mr Patterson.'

'Good morning, George.'

'Raw morning.'

'Raw, indeed.'

The sergeant came over, rubbing his hands together.

'Is it bad news then?'

'I'm afraid it is. The young fella's been killed, Mr Patterson.'

'Killed?' He looked out over the fields, up to the smoking chimney of the farmhouse, where his wife would be dressing for the early trip to church. 'Well, I suppose ye may come up for a cup of tea.'

'I could do with a cup, all right.'

'Aye. That's what we'll do.' They left the car in the lane and strolled up to the house. The farmer paused by the door, momentarily shaking. 'She's going to take this awful bad. She'll certainly take it bad.'

Forty miles away, Spinkey's father and my own were on their way to the hospital. They had had a fierce row in the hallway of Driscolls' house, my old man having gone off his head with worry and run down Spinkey for having led me astray, forgetting that their son was believed to be in the morgue. My mother had rushed to Mrs Driscoll's side, and between them they had calmed the two men down and packed them off in a taxi.

Mrs Driscoll then sat at the kitchen table, instantly aged by the morning's events, weak and shaking like a leaf, while my Ma made the tea and the neighbours came in and out, seeking news. Little knots of people began to assemble on the doorsteps, frowning and shivering in the cold, returning to their kitchens at each bulletin on the radio.

At eight thirty-five a cry went up of 'Brits!' An expeditionary force had driven in to inspect local opinion, and was duly met by a barrage of noise and stones. Immediately a helicopter moved overhead, circling and photographing. The estate erupted just before nine, as the army raided Bricks's house. They had left the whole thing too late, and met the full anger of the local youth, petrol bombs and all. Those bound for mass found themselves ducking missiles, and the calm and tedium of a normal Sunday morning gave way to the sound of rubber bullets and stone clanking upon steel. The initial raiding party withdrew, having discovered nothing.

At the morgue, my father and Mr Driscoll made up, as the worst was confirmed, and they left the hospital, one in grief and torrents of tears, and the other impaled upon a spike of fear as he wondered what had become of me. As Driscoll went home, my father took to the side-streets and went looking for an old friend.

Finally dawn broke. I was sitting stiff with cramp and just about overwhelmed with tiredness. The woman asked to use the toilet in shy, bruised tones. She kissed the young boy who had crawled onto the bed and finally fallen to sleep, while giving me the evil eye. I used the opportunity of her exit to limber up, and by the time she came back, a little heat was re-entering my bones. A sudden spasm of pins and needles didn't help matters. With the coming of the light, slowly filtering into the room, the tension inside me eased a little. It was approaching decision time. The long night was finally drawing to a close. Standing on the landing with my guard down, pumping each leg into feeling itself, things didn't seem so bad. I had survived thus far and was still in good shape. The circumstances weren't ideal, but things could have been worse.

'Are you going to kill us?'

It was the husband, standing in the room, fists clenched at his side, with the face of a man who had come to a momentous decision.

'What are ye talking about?'

He had flipped.

'Put that fucking gun down and ye'll find out.'

The woman jumped back up and grabbed him by the arm. He was quivering with anger. The wee boy on the bed began to stir. I spoke quietly, summoning all the gravity I could find.

'You take a deep breath, chief, and count to ten, and if you haven't settled down by then I will blow you away, and then her, and then the child.'

The woman was about to go into a fit. Her head was bobbing on her shoulders, her breathing strained and shallow, shaking from top to toe, and slowly he came down from the mountain of his anger, his gaze wavered, and his breathing calmed. He stood open-mouthed, his face filled with hatred. The hands unclenched and he turned his attention to his wife and his fascinated, terrified child. I began to realise the quiet desperation which the night had engendered. It had all gone too well, and ended up an inch off a bloodbath. If he had come forward I would surely have shot him, then her if she had screamed, and maybe the child, or the kid in the other room. Maybe I couldn't have stopped. Beneath the cover of the gun I was as much in trauma as they were. The whole situation was transforming, changing into an unpredictable morass, where all was possible. It was time to move, before it got further out of hand. We had sat in a pressure-cooker of emotion for almost three hours, three hours of torture and fear – I the afflicter, they the victims. Three hours of agonised silence and uncertainty, of evaporating sanity and undiluted fear.

'Get yourself dressed, chief. It's time we were gone.'

He drew on a pullover and trousers, over his pyjamas, telling his wife continuously not to worry, it would be all right, stay calm and wait. She was imploring him not to go, not to leave, but she knew it was the only way to get this monster out of her house, away from her children. I stood on the landing and let them get on with it. They kissed and held each other, a proud wee man and his battered wife, under the worst of pressure.

On the landing, he paused. 'Can I go in and see the wee one? Just for a minute?'

I put the rifle into his side. 'You can see her all you like when you get back. Get down those stairs and follow everything to the letter.'

He drew himself together and set off down the stairs.

'The keys are in the front room.'

We went into the living room. He picked the keys off the

mantelpiece, and his hands began to rattle at the thought of what might come. I nudged him out, into the dawn.

He looked around. 'There's no one about.'

He was a barrel length away as we walked down the short path, went left and walked two doors down to where the van was parked. He was guiding me as much as I directed him, leading me away from his loved ones. I got him to open the passenger side and get in, sliding over to the driver's seat. The van was like an ice-box, the upholstery damp and ripped and most of the accessories taken out. It was just a runaround, a worker's vehicle that had been gutted of ashtrays, radio, heater and any sign of comfort.

'Does this thing go?'

'The engine's all right. Maybe ye should have called a taxi.'

He started up the motor without prompting and put the wipers on. They swiped away the night mist and the dirt. Through the arch of clear windscreen I caught sight of a soldier walking across the top of the street.

'Turn it off.'

He turned off the ignition. We watched the soldiers trot across the street: I counted them: two, four, six and the last two walking backwards – a full patrol.

We sat breathing deeply, the driver looking down at the rifle driven tightly into his side, then back up at the passing soldiers. I counted off their progress, imagined how far they would have gone.

'Drive slowly, drive carefully.'

He drove the van to the top of the street and swung left.

'Away you go.'

He gunned up the vehicle and raced up the street.

'Slow and easy, squire. You're a Sunday driver.'

He began to get the idea. We slid through the first few streets easily enough, not fast, not slow; trying not to draw attention or waken the neighbours. I took the chance and rolled the balaclava back from my face, and we looked like two guys going out to do a spot of Sunday overtime.

'This road takes us out onto the main road, then I'll go left and take you up to your part of the country.'

'As long as we go the shortest way, and you don't cross me.'

Just at that, we turned onto the main road. Directly ahead was a roadblock, a Saracen and two jeeps blocking both road and pavement, only allowing access by crooked, single file in either direction. The driver exploded into a sweat-drenched spasm and my finger tightened on the trigger.

'Stay calm and drive slowly towards them. Don't panic.'

I heard myself say it, but it bore no relation to my thoughts. We could have reversed and driven off, but that was sure to draw fire. I could hardly rely on my hostage to get us out when the shooting started. The evening before, Spinkey and myself had slipped through a check, but that had been the product of fortune. There was no getting out of this. My heart seemed to leap out of its sling and came banging against the wall of my chest like a bird trying to escape a cage. Darkness flooded my soul. It was over.

CHAPTER THREE

MY FATHER KNOCKED on a door he had thought he would never knock on again in his life. He was desperate, and cared not what welcome he would get. Betty McGinn was frying sausages and bacon in the tiny kitchen. She cursed at the sound of the door, but when she opened it her irritation gave way to wonder as the leathery, nervous features of the caller swam in her mind.

'It's not you, is it?'

'I need your help, Betty.'

'Any time I ever saw you, you were looking for something. Come in.'

'Who is it, Betty?' The broad voice came down the stairs.

'You may come down, Billy. Someone to see ye.'

In the awkward silence memories rebelled, struggling to be recognised, expressed and exorcised.

'Will you take a cup of tea?'

'Don't trouble yourself. I wouldn't be able to take it.'

The great bulk of Bill McGinn came through the doorway. He was a formidable sight, over six foot and seventeen stone in his greasy vest with its one empty sleeve where an arm had once hung. He had the look of a pirate who had come ashore, with his small, sly eyes and wealth of iron-grey stubble.

He nodded to my father. 'I thought I'd see you at my funeral. To what do we owe the honour?'

'I've nowhere else to go, Billy.'

Bill and Betty McGinn looked at each other with the

knowledge and memories of an age between them.

'As long as you don't make a habit of this,' said Bill. 'Ye can't be rolling in here every ten years and getting me out of my scratcher.'

Betty thought out loud. 'More like sixteen years. Sixteen years and not a cheep out of ye.'

My father started. 'My oldest one was out last night. He was up at that shooting and hasn't come back.'

'Jesus help us,' said Betty.

'The young lad with him is dead in the hospital.'

Bill McGinn exhaled. 'Aye. Ye can hardly go to the peelers. They wouldn't tell ye if they had him anyway. But, sure, we've nothing to do with it nowadays. Betty just collects for the prisoners, and I've no say in it.'

'You could find out where he is, Billy. Just so I can tell his Ma.'

'You could ask some of the boys up your way,' Betty suggested.

'They've no time for me, nor I them.'

'Have you tried?'

'I don't need to try to know what the answer will be. Will ye help me?' His presence in the little house was token enough of his desperation.

Betty and Bill communed in their telepathic way. Betty spoke decisively. 'Young Bradley will know what the score is. Do you know his number, Billy?'

'I know where he lives,' interjected my father. 'But I would need you to talk to him.'

'Betty will go with you. Sure, he lived here for a year, near enough. He was better fed than in his own home. Bradley would be the boy to see.'

'I'll get my coat. There's sausages in the pan, Billy.'

As she fetched her coat, my Da dropped his head into his hands, the tension tearing through his mind like a wild horse, his thoughts racing into the dread-filled realm of conclusions without knowledge.

Billy took a picture off the mantelpiece, a six-by-ten snap in a gold frame. He handed it to my father, diverting his thoughts. It was the photograph of a stern-faced youth of sixteen or seventeen. He was drawn to attention, hands at his sides, wearing a beret and webbing. He was painfully correct in his posture, but from the black and white image shone youth and hope. My father held the photograph in faintly trembling fingers, and remembered.

'I'd forgotten what he looked like.'

'Ah, sure that was years ago.' Bill relieved him of the photograph. 'Your boy will be all right. Strange it took that to get ye to come and see us.'

At the door, Billy extended his hand to the ould fella. 'I hope everything works out for ye. It's probably just a false alarm.'

My father didn't answer, but gave the big man a nod of the head. He and Betty set off to the taxi rank.

Further up the Falls, Mrs Driscoll was roaring the house down. The doctor and the priest arrived, as her husband cried in the scullery and the neighbours rallied around to comfort and assist. Relations had to be informed, funeral arrangements made, and the waking had to be organised. Bradley was one of the first to call, and with him a politico from the area. For the next few days the Driscolls would want for nothing save their son.

Outside, the local youths took the riot down onto the main road, but the Brits pulled out. There was no percentage in escalating the trouble, so they simply left out a few mobile patrols and monitored the activity from the air. If they felt serious about it, the rioters would come to the barracks to perform, but they estimated the aggro would peter out. It was Sunday, after all, and the weather was poor. The invisible rules of West Belfast would apply; the real aggro would come during the week, after the funeral, when the anger would consolidate and turn to the search for revenge. For now it was enough that the young lads had made their point, asserting their territorial rights and venting their anger. Around midday, the Provo scouts arrived and gave the word for the rioting to end, so that people could get to the last mass and planning could be done for the funeral. The action fizzled out after another half-hour, leaving an Ulsterbus and a handful of cars blazing on the road, a few boys in hospital with injuries, and having given the film reporters a surfeit of footage for the national news.

Claire O'Brien stood on her garden pathway, listening to the primeval echoes pouring over the rooftops. A neighbour came bustling past in her Sunday best, face red and worried.

'God, Claire, don't go up there. They've gone berserk, they have.'

'What's up with them now, Mrs McShane?'

'Did ye not hear? They shot a wee lad.' She whispered conspiratorially. 'That wee fella, Driscoll, ye know, him that's got a sister married to yer man McCabe, him that left the wife that time.'

Claire was none the wiser. 'Ye know him rightly. He works with the Rogue Maguire, the TV boyo ...'

'That's yer wee man "Spinkey".' Joe O'Brien was standing beside her at the doorstep, drawn out by the sense of trouble.

'Ye're right, Joseph. I heard that's his name. Spinkey Driscoll, that's who's dead.'

In the house, Joe put the kettle on. Claire looked into the empty grate, hands deep in trouser pockets, chewing her lower lip.

'What time did lover boy leave last night?'

'Mind your own business, Joe.'

'He left at half-one.'

'I take it you don't approve?'

'You know I don't. He's lying through his teeth.'

'Takes one to know one, eh?'

'I know the crack, better than you ever will. That Spinkey fella was running around with a shooter at last night. Pound to a penny says your mate has something to do with it.'

'Catch yourself on, Joseph. Of all people, you should know not to talk like that.'

'I'd only say it to you. I'm worried about you, not anyone else. Can ye not see where this is leading. Have ye learned nothing from my mistakes, or from the last wee shite that took ye up the garden path?' His voice was loud, boiling with frustration.

'You know where to put the boot in, Joseph. You always know.'

'Go on. Tell me he's different. This time we all get to live happy ever fucking after. Fool yerself, but not me. That wee bozo will get what he's looking for and ye won't see him for smoke. He's a bad lot, Claire. They all are.'

'Are you finished?'

'No, I'm not. But maybe you've heard enough? Is the truth that sore? Listen, pet. I watch you come and go, I see what's happening. Ever since ye started with this cowboy, ye've been on cloud nine, but, believe me, he's a bad risk.'

'He must remind you of yourself then, you nosy bastard.'

'Jesus, Lady Muck, where are ye? Is this the real you, swearing and spitting. Maybe he taught ye? You listen to me, girl, and listen good. You finish off with the wee shite, or I'll be taking a hand in it, for he's no fucking good for you.'

'Ye're not my Da, Joseph O'Brien, and ye're not fit to lick my father's boots; you never could. I have my own life to lead, and you stay out of it.'

'I may not be Da, but by Christ I'm the man in this house, and I will not, I will not, have you whoring about with some no-hope fly boy.'

'Joe, go and fuck yourself.'

He hit her with an open-handed slap that sent her teetering back on her heels.

'You always have the answer, Joe. Always in your hands. That's the last time you'll ever hit me.'

She charged from the room in tears, and Joe stood blankly staring at the slammed door, trying to think what to say, what to do. He was close to tears himself, tears of frustration. He had seen and done many hard things. When they had buried his mother by his father's side, he had tried to change. He had given them a dog's life, sent his Da to an early grave. But then came the time to knuckle down, and to raise his young sister as they would have wanted.

He had striven to give her as much freedom as was possible, counting on her smartness, her intelligence. She could move in any company she chose, she had the looks and the personality; their aunt had given her all the womanly lore that Joseph couldn't, and for many years it had seemed to work, with no secrets and no questions. Then came the Brogan lad, and things changed. Ever since he'd done a flit to England and left her with a wedding planned and a broken heart, it had been Joe who had picked up the pieces of her life and handed them back to her to fix. He'd nursed her through it, taking her to clubs and dances, forcing her to make new friends, seldom dictating, but being watchful. He was determined to see her happy, if it killed him.

It didn't take a genius to work out the political relationships in West Belfast. There was a verbal and signified code which governed our lives, an ethereal system of semaphore which gave the initiated a fair idea of who was who, and who was not what they appeared. Body language and associations, things said and unsaid, gaps and dashes in the social fabric. A man talks to another man, changes subject when a third arrives. Your uncle is friends with that man's cousin, but they never speak on the street. Who is related to whom, why are they together, or not ... the nefarious relationships of a threatened society, only to be interpreted by someone born into it, someone who couldn't be surprised. Joey O'Brien could smell a chancer a mile away. They had that entrenched look about them, wearing their secrets like a shroud, quietly powerful. They spoke when spoken to, but said nothing. They were the ones who didn't look long in one direction, but took it all in. They talked past you, not to you. They walked slow, a business saunter, casual but coiled, always going somewhere. Apart from the odd bow-legged, plank-thick shithead they had among them, Joe could spot an operator just by the way he looked at his watch.

At that time, the whole command was common knowledge in West Belfast, and most people had a fair idea of the structure and often the content of their local forces. If they didn't know who was actually operating at any one time, they knew who might be. It didn't take Joey O'Brien a great effort to find out the SP on his sister's new beau, and he knew for sure I wasn't in line for a New Year's honour from the Queen. All credit to him, he hadn't dunged me out of the house at first meeting. Joe was smart enough to know that what is prohibited is most attractive.

But Spinkey's demise had altered things considerably. Every time he'd heard my name, Spinkey's name had come up. In the web of local relationships, we were inseparable. Joe wasn't about to take a back seat and watch his sister take another emotional pounding. Now, it had come to this. Violence and anger back in the house, thumping the only person who meant anything to him.

He hadn't been a great ladies' man. He carried an exaggerated reputation as a hard man, a knee-breaker, and the type of girl he sought wasn't drawn to that. Plenty of the other sort, mind. Years before, when his military commitments ceased, he had tried to mellow. There had still been a few about who had it in for Joey O'Brien, friends and relations of those he'd done in in the past, so Joey kept himself reasonably fit and watchful, living the life of the retired gunslinger, wary of the up-and-coming hard men who wouldn't mind scalping him. He had to exude an air of potential menace, and he did it well. But it had involved lots of drinking with old comrades while boringly regurgitating the past. He had missed his chance to find the woman who would appreciate him for the mellow, considerate man he felt he was, and so his sister had come to represent all femininity, for it was all he knew of it. For her he held the deepest love of all; she had become his life, in many ways, and he loved her in a manner too deep for words, for showing of it.

Hitting her was a relic of years gone by, times when he had been unable to leave the violence on the doorstep, when savage depression would overtake him and he would smash the house into matchwood, his mother wailing in the background as he spat invective at his father, who trembled with rage and love, trying to calm him down. A legion of old demons had now come marching back to trouble his mind, all trumpeting past sins. He sat down and tried to organise his thoughts. Upstairs he could hear her rushing back and forth, making a point of banging doors, throwing things out of her way. He climbed the stairs, suppressing his anger, slowing down his thoughts, and knocked on her bedroom door.

'What are you packing for?' She had a suitcase on the bed and was drowning it in shoes and clothes.

'Fuck off.'

'Charming. Now what's the case for?'

'I'm moving to Aunt Sheila's if you must know, you ... bastard.'

'For how long?'

'I'm not coming back here to be a punchbag for you or any other fucker.'

'I'm sorry about that.'

'Sorry is too late.'

'There's no way I can stop ye. Are ye not forgetting something, though?'

'I'm taking everything I need.'

'I thought you had somewhere to go for dinner, that's all.'

'It's none of your business where I go.'

'That's what I was thinking. Look, if you want to screw your life up there's no way I can prevent you. Stop that packing stuff. Just be careful from now on. Go and get yer dinner, and I hope it chokes yez both.'

'You don't mind?'

'I do mind. We'll not fall out over it though. Go get yer Brussels sprouts with lover boy. Tell him I was asking.'

'It *is* different this time, Joe. I wish you could see that.'

'Tell it to the Royal Marines.'

'It is, really.'

'Get on with ye.'

She crossed the room and hugged him. He squeezed her in a bear hug, then put her down and stood her back, a firm hand on each shoulder.

'I'm sorry I belted ye. Maybe I didn't hit ye hard enough, though. Maybe ye want some sense knocked into ye, but it's not my place. You tell lover boy for me to get out of whatever he's into. If he thinks that much of you, he will. And you tell him this, tell him from me: if he hurts ye, he'll have me to answer to.'

She nodded her head uncertainly, not fully understanding his mood. He rubbed her shoulders and released her. 'You tell him that. Tell him I'll kill him, stone dead.'

The seriousness left his face, and he gave a broad smile.

'Enjoy yer dinner.'

Paranoia rules. OK? The Unionists inherit 'the siege mentality'. We get alienation for our birthright.

The persecution complex: never sit with your back to the door, always keep to the inside of the pavement; measures to counter the Unionist pub bombers and drive-by killer squads. People jostled for seats and danced down streets trying to keep close to the hedges, open to every urban scare story going, every hideous rumour. Catholic found dead last night: the Shankill butchers got him. By dinner time everyone knew for certain what part of his anatomy had been mutilated. You could never relax, regardless of the outward banter and machismo. Unless you were like Dingus Grey, who professed not to give a toss, and meant it. 'When yer number's up, yer number's up.'

I had all the dark cynicism and distrust which leaked into the Catholic soul in the late sixties, multiplied by ten. Getting into the war had made it worse. Conscious of the obvious dangers of police or British army; rushing around deceiving family and friends; lying, cheating, living in limbo; always fearing that people knew more about me than I did about them, fearing informants, thinking every bugger had a plan for me, a plan to do me down or do me in. I dripped of paranoia, but tried not to show it. Paranoid society in which there were never enough couches to rest the fearful on. So integral to me, a constant dangerous edge to my nerves. And it cut all ways. Seeing conspiracy in every face.

A peeler once said to me, in interrogation, 'You don't like us because we're British.' There was genuine sulk in his tone. It occurred to me then that the Prods took it all personally, that they were really wanting to be liked. If our war was one based on indignation, on anger, maybe they were just crying out for help, for acceptance. But they always wanted to take the ball home if they were losing, they always wanted to own the ball and make the rules. Try telling that policeman that to the Brits on 'the mainland' he was just another 'bog wog'. At some level, he knew it. They all did. Their paranoia involved continuous overestimation of the nationalist 'threat'. Ours was that we always rated their potency and intelligence services too highly. As a rule, they were so glutted on their prejudice that they seldom got to know as much about us as they might have; if they could have seen how badly set up we were, they would have felt more secure. But their British, self-righteous blindness had left them unable to tailor any settlement which would have undermined the struggle. If our imagination had gotten the better of us, then fear had gotten the better of them. Result: stalemate.

The average Tommy, unhindered by personal involvement or political education, was more interested in doing his tour and getting out in one piece. He stood with less than enthusiasm out in front of all the political rhetoric of his London masters, resigned to being a target in this interminable, demeaning little war, an endless Paddy curse of which he knew little and cared less. His job was to keep us quiet, to allow the London establishment to get on with running their enterprise, their great, liberal 'world power'. That was how it seemed to us, and perhaps that's to underestimate British motivation. As long as the echoes of imperial mistakes couldn't reach into the daily lives of the 'mainland' community, as long as there was no challenge to their beliefs about themselves, then all was rosy. An acceptable level of violence, a reasonable price. And now I was playing out a street production of my worst fears, brilliantly realised: paranoia incarnate, the stage set, the auditorium awaiting.

The driver stopped the van twenty feet from the blockade on the outskirts of the pale. We stared straight ahead at the inquisitive troops, at their raised rifles. The cold had kept them alert. There were no slouchers. You always looked for a drongo, the one you might have a chance of using. In this case there was only one twat, and that was me. Their guns were trained from behind walls, behind armour, trained on the van which had turned the corner, then paused, like a bull scratching the ground with its hoof before the charge, but had not stopped dead. To reverse was to die. A few feet backwards was to invite a fusillade, a few feet forward, capture. Nor could I summon the strength to bale out. It would only be two steps before they had me. Instinct had played a part in getting me thus far, but its influence was exhausted. What was there told me to surrender or flee, but there was no survival in either, not on an empty road, in a strange place, in the quiet of the morning.

I spoke to the driver in soft, firm tones.

'Wind your window down and call one of them over.'

He looked at me, a mixture of horror and incomprehension on him. A soldier was approaching. The driver wound the window down. I rolled down my balaclava, as if it were the most natural thing to do, and slid to the floor of the van in a single, fluid action, drawing the rifle up so that the muzzle slid to beneath the driver's chin, so that they could see it clearly and consider. There were shouts and roars outside, to which I was oblivious. I had my back to the enemy, and was fully awaiting the gunfire. It didn't come. Seconds passed. The driver was breathing great clouds of steam, his hands welded in terror to the steering wheel.

'Call one of them over.' His voice had left him. I let out a 'Hi' which I hoped would carry to them. He moved his head away from the rifle, ever so slightly.

'Stay with it, chief; if you want to get home, just stay with it.'

From below him, I could see his mind working overtime, trying to flee from the reality, going into possibilities. This guy was being swamped with instinct.

'This is an M16 rifle. I have only to hit you once and it will blow your head into shite. Now, stay calm.'

A soldier was standing near the driver's window, incredibly unperturbed. Plummy, educated tones came through.

'Step out of the van, please.'

'I can't,' the driver muttered.

'I want you both out of the van immediately.'

He was looking at a guy with a rifle stuck under his chin, and speaking to him as he would to a naughty child. I called to him.

'Are you in charge?'

Tentatively, he moved closer to the window. I caught my first good look of him. A tall man, pale, thin beneath thick wrapping, de Valera minus the glasses, aesthetic, professional, totally untrustworthy for my purposes. I liked him about as much as he liked me. A Paddy toe-rag in a mask, pretending to be John Wayne. If he could have got a clear shot at me it would have made his year. That much was in his eyes.

'I am the commanding officer of this unit, and I want you both out of this vehicle immediately. Lay down your weapon and step out.'

'Fuck off.'

The driver's eyes were following our conversation; for him it was becoming a terrifying game of tennis.

'How do you suggest we play this?'

'No problem. We are just going to drive around your roadblock, drive up the road, no interference. Then I let this man go. Ye follow that?'

'Who is this "hostage".'

'Tell him yer name.'

The driver murmured his name and address as if it were a prayer.

'I'll have to check this out.'

'You have two minutes, then we drive past ye, no hassle, no one following us. Any grief, and he comes with me.'

The officer walked away, back to the barrier, and consulted hastily with his NCO. 'What's happening, sir?'

'One terrorist, one hostage, I'm afraid.'

'Are they not in it together then, sir?'

'No. The driver is a civilian, a petrified one at that.'

The radio operator waddled over and the officer used his back-pack to phone in the driver's details.

'What does the bastard want, sir?'

'Free passage into Provoland.'

'And a plane to Cuba, I shouldn't wonder.'

'The trouble is, sergeant, we may have to let him pass.'

'Really, sir?' He could hear the derision in his subordinate's reply.

'Pass the word, sergeant. Return fire only. That is a strict order. Return fire only.'

The officer thought long and hard. To allow shit like this past him was distasteful, but the alternative was a dead civilian. The driver checked out as clean on the radio. Politics, bloody publicity and politics. He got on to his barracks. As he was doing that, the van started up.

He drove it with the enthusiasm of a man mounting the gallows. He carefully took the handbrake off and started the motor, forever aware of the pressure of the gun beneath his face. The van moved as if by will-power, the engine throbbing to a delicate attention it hadn't known before, purring as we crept towards the block. I began to feel an awful tightness in my head, my breath refusing to rise from my chest.

The movement forward, the creeping, seemed sickeningly slow. The officer was in the process of relaying the full situation to his base and spat down a demand for reinforcements, anger welling in him. He was stranded, his sang-froid collapsing at this challenge to authority. He walked briskly to the oncoming van.

'Hold it, hold it.'

'Drive on.'

The driver's eyes were misty, but fixed on the road ahead. He was on the brink of tears, but responded to my orders, to my control; helpless, in too far. The officer was in a tizzy; he covered it well, but the initiative had gone. His men were perfectly placed to turn the vehicle into a colander at his command, but in front of him was the terrified face of a man with a rifle poised to blow his brains through the top of his skull. He walked back and loudly reiterated his orders, instructing a soldier to move the Saracen further onto the pavement to provide a straighter route through. Overhead, a helicopter appeared. Walking to the tail end of our van, the officer pointed our registration to the spotter overhead, reduced to the role of an angry traffic warden. The helicopter passenger gave a thumbs-up, then the machine swooped away.

Listening to the sound of the flapping rotors, I began to doubt. I was hit by the enormity of what was to come, what I was asking of myself. From here to home ground would be pursuit and ambush. I struggled to suppress my anxiety, the fear which was prowling around my mind. I raised myself and chanced a peek out of the side window. We were creeping past the Saracen, a soldier was but two feet away, hatred stamped firmly on his features as he watched the enemy glide by. Beneath the mask, I couldn't resist a grin. I felt as if a fit of hilarity was about to overcome me. It was the surreal nature of the occasion, the nonsense of it, surrounded by the might of the murder machine – the technology, the training, the philosophy of centuries. And me being carried through it, taxied. I felt like giving that soldier a little regal wave in passing. I was positively giddy.

'We're getting there, squire.'

'Listen, mister. When we get past this and up the road, I'm getting out of this van, and I'm walking away. You can shoot me all you like, but I'm doing no more for ye.'

His voice was shaky, fearful and tired. He was cornered by a nutter, and the options were becoming clear to him. I realised he could see no funny side to it, that he was concerned that I was going to waste him, that I was capable of breaking any promise, of carrying out any threat. He couldn't see it as a game, an enactment, a bluff. Every inch I gained, every second, was relief. For him, it was torture. I decided to mollify him. We were between the two juxtaposed jeeps, clearing the block, and all it took was for him to turn turtle and we were both dead. I talked to him gravely.

'When we clear shooting range, ye're a free man. You can go walkabout then, but only then.'

The van seemed to falter. He was considering my magnanimity, hesitating. I applied pressure to the rifle, boring it deeper into his flesh.

'You're the first to get it, remember. All I have to do is squeeze.'

We turned past the second Land Rover, and he put his foot down on the accelerator. Amazingly, in my oppressed perception, the thing lifted off the road and soared crazily over the tar. In a second I was up. The troops behind were frantically piling into their vehicles. Above the racket of the van's engine, I strained to hear the flapping, thrilling sound of the helicopter. All around West Belfast a ring of armed steel was alerted, was waiting, but now there was a chance.

The driver swung off the road and braked, throwing me off balance. He yanked down the door handle, shaking with anger and distraction, the same anger he had shown hours before in his bedroom prison. I was momentarily shocked.

'Ye're on yer own.'

He climbed out of the cab. He stood looking at me, challenging me, strain etched clearly on him. He had reached the end of the road. Finished, nerves shattered. I could have killed him there, but that was of no use. Dead civilians, bad politics.

As he slammed the door and staggered away, I jumped across and started the engine.

Out ahead, and then to the left, lay home. There also lay the guns of the enemy. I carried on straight into the loyalist estate, into the heartland, past walls of alien slogans, red, white and blue kerbs, through streets and past avenues I had never seen before and never wished to see. Overhead was the helicopter, the pilot calmly detailing my progress. If there was any way out, it involved ditching the van, seizing other transport, or getting lost on foot. Traffic would have helped me, but anyone with sense was abed on this forlorn Sunday morning. For the first time since this farrago had begun, I was gripped by panic. Nothing was familiar, nothing to relate to. Yet this landscape would be familiar to my pursuers. They would know it from their maps as a route into the Falls. They would live here, have relations in the community. They would visit it in safety, know the connections and the arteries, know where I was bound to end up, where to wait, where to cut me off. I was surrounded by a phantom array of hostile forces, besieging me in this tomb of a van racing to God-knew-where. In blind fear, I parked the van at the corner of a main road, leapt out and ran, leaving the rifle behind. I stripped off my gloves and mask in mid-flight and threw them into a garden hedge, and ran, ran till the fatigue hit me, thumped me in the chest and side, and threw me sick into the doorway of a supermarket.

Doubled up, I retched and slobbered until my senses calmed and the blood thundering in my head subsided. I was riddled with stiffness and pain, tired and frightened, and Spinkey came to mind. Spinkey, lying with the life knocked out of him, with his daft head flopping onto his shoulder as he fell over, a big divot taken out of it in the dark. Hatred rose again, and cunning. 'Fuck it man,' I heard my anger say. 'You got this far, you can go further.'

Across the road, a man was staring at me from the newsagent's. I straightened up, swept my hair back with my fingers and squared up my clothes. I left the doorway and walked firmly on, purposeful in appearance, making like I owned the town, like the Lord Mayor's bastard son. I could feel his attention go off me. Like I belonged. On down towards the main junction, pretending to be oblivious to the oncoming Land Rovers racing up the road; jacket pulled up tight to the neck, passing the odd pedestrian, looking for all the world like a straggler from some drinking party, half-foundered and heading with certain direction homewards.

The grey police vehicles did a one-eighty and came crawling back. My brain scrambled to assess my position. By this time they would have reached the abandoned van, but the helicopter had failed to follow my chaotic and panic-inspired retreat. It was nowhere overhead. But the cops were certain to be looking for a single man on foot. I walked into a pokey newsagents and took a long time selecting a paper. The elderly man behind the counter was serenely opening the parcels of paper, and took no notice as he made up the orders for his young carriers who would be arriving shortly. It took me a little longer to purchase cigarettes, before returning to the counter for matches. I didn't smoke.

The patrol snailed past, missing me through the dirty windows of the shop, driving on down to the junction. I came out, and retraced my steps, back up the road. They parked at the junction, and two peelers got out to study the lower end of the street. I promptly turned off into a side-street, and took shelter in the doorway of a derelict Baptist church, shivering under its big red eaves. The street was draped with rows of faintly coloured bunting, hung from house to house, a remnant of the July festivities.

'Are ye lost, son?' An old woman was staring up at me, her eyes hooded in suspicion, or perhaps concern.

'I'm a wee bit baffled, love. Is there not a bus station up here?'

'Not up here, son. There's a bus stop down the road.'

'That's the very thing I want, is a bus stop. Is it far down the road?

'Come on round the corner and I'll show ye. I'm going down that way anyroads. Isn't the weather cat?'

'Cat melodeon, love.'

'Cat melodeon, indeed. It's years since I heard that. Are ye from the country?'

'County Armagh. I'm up here at college, but I was over here at a party last night.'

'God, you students has the times of it. It's well for ye has the brains. I used to have the brains, but sure we never got the chances you young ones have. Aye, we had the brains. Brains doesn't butter bread though.'

'You're right there, missus.'

We were walking straight to the junction and into the face of the police patrol moving slowly towards us. They slowed even further and passed, the young lad leaving his granny to church being quite acceptable. Even the combat jacket was fitting to the weather. When she left me at the junction and pointed out the bus stop, I could have hugged her and asked her home to meet my people. Angels come in many sizes, and this one came in the form of a wrinkled bundle of tiny bones that delivered me from mine enemy, and then pottered off about her business, unsuspecting. I loved her dearly, for she was luck. Lady Luck. In this game you needed luck. For the most part the luck you got was bad, and your bad luck was another's fortune. Your gun jammed: bad luck for you, good for someone else. I felt I made my own luck.

This was our only advantage, that we could blend in at times of crisis, lay low, integrate, disappear. They had all the force, all the big cards; they had the churches and the media, the unions and the businessmen. All we had was a grim determination to harry and provoke them, and a native cunning in a war where each side felt free to change the conventions without warning. I wasn't bound by some officer code, like the politically strapped soldier at the roadblock. The only people I was answerable to were the people I sprang from, theirs the only rebuff to my actions, but today I was alone, adrift, and mine were the rules. As the little old lady soldiered away on her Sunday routine, I felt she had left me strong, protected. But deep down I suspected I would get my come-uppance. I had to get back to my own, and the only way was to be brazen.

I was standing at the bus stop when two children came along in the company of a rosy-faced young girl of about my sister's age.

'Have ye been waiting long, mister?'

'Five minutes.'

'It'll be along in a minute, then. I thought we missed it.'

As she said this, an Ulsterbus came trundling into view. The little girl of the two children looked up into my face.

'You're funny, mister.'

'Karen, don't be annoying that man. I'm sorry, mister. That one has a mouth would disgrace ye.'

'Have not. He's funny looking.'

'Karen.'

'It's all right, love. I'm not as funny as you, Karen.'

'How'd you know my name?'

'It's written on yer forehead. See? Right on yer forehead.'

As we boarded the bus, the kid was rubbing her head and twisting her eyes to see the name on her brow, and the young girl was grinning as she manhandled the pair on board.

'You go to the city centre, driver? I'll have a single.'

'Single it is. Did ye have a rough night?'

'Ye're not the first to notice.' He laughed.

As we drove off, I lumbered to a seat beside the wee girl and her two kids, and fell to talking with her. She was an amber-eyed girl of about seventeen, with a smile and giggle most fetching. All the time I was looking out the windows on either side, seeking a landmark or an omen. I was fly enough to take off my jacket and drape it over the seat in front. We were nattering away, fooling with the kids, me telling her about the mad party I was at the night before, careful to point out I knew no one at it, or which street it was in. She told me about her sister's twenty-first, and rattled on about the social life she had, minding the sister's kids while she was away shopping in London. The girl clearly had me down as one of her own, telling me her brother was in the army in Germany, and this was confirmed when she discovered my name was Jeffrey. Thus we were becoming the best of friends when the bus hit the inevitable checkpoint.

Glancing out, I almost had a heart attack. Manning the check was the nail-thin officer from the incident before, standing like a grim pillar by a jeep. They had obviously upped roots and tried to widen the net. I began to take an undue interest in the wee lassie, as the kids fought among themselves, as the passengers sighed and frowned at the delay. I could tell she was weighing me up. She was out to take the kids to their granny's for a birthday treat, and here was this cowboy chatting her up and looking into her eyes like he'd known her all his life. She didn't know whether to be flattered or to get off at the next stop. And yer man was at university, too. She didn't pass any remarks at me taking the cigarettes out of the coat and letting it drop to the floor. I was answering her queries about life in academia, using my experience of Claire's friends, when the soldier passed us, walked on down the aisle, turned and came back. He spent a moment talking to the driver, then left. When the bus was on its way again, I fell silent. She asked me a question, but I didn't hear, for I was on the verge of collapse inside, physically and emotionally destroyed. Absent-mindedly I offered her a smoke, and she accepted. I lit it for her, hands trembling.

'Are you not having one?'

'I'm smoked out.'

'I'll tell granny you're smoking, Sadie.' The little boy was looking at her gravely.

'You'd better not.'

'I'll tell granny you have a boyfriend,' chimed the little girl. Sadie blushed, and I laughed. It was as if I wasn't really there. Reality was fractured, a broken mirror. I was back in the front room of Claire O'Brien's. I felt her in my arms, the warm softness and hardness of her body as she moaned beneath my hands, the smell of her clothes and skin flooded my head, her voice, small, precise, with a laugh sewn through it ... 'What if Joe comes in?'

'What did you say? Are you feeling all right, Jeffrey?'

There was some girl looking at me strangely through a thick fog, there was a kid laughing and telling me I was funny. We were moving up and down, around and around. I rubbed my face.

'Are we near the city centre?'

'Just any minute. You want to get home, Jeffrey. You need a good bed.'

Who the fuck is Jeffrey?

'I suppose so,' I answered, fighting back nausea.

I got off at the next stop, picking my leaden feet up and being careful how I put them down again. As the bus pulled away, a small golden-haired child was banging the window at me, but a bigger girl pulled her back into her seat, and glanced at me as if I owed her something. She looked confused, sullen. I walked on, hanging my coat over my shoulder, unaware of the drizzling rain. I got as far as a set of streets leading into the Falls, lost in a world of my own. Further down was yet another road-check. That way lay safety, emotional rescue.

I crossed the road and wandered on down into the centre of the hell I called home. In a café behind a damaged facade, beside a demolition site, I ordered tea and breakfast. The tea fell down my throat, welcome heat to my chilled insides, but I couldn't look at the food. I lapsed into a reverie in the heat of the cafe, and slipped towards unconsciousness.

Before I nodded off, I heard the whining voice of the radio newsreader recite the toll of the night's events. All I recognised and retained was the capture of two gunmen and the death of a third. Mathematics of disaster, sleepily ingested. Bricks, last of my band, was gone.

Born to the ghetto, growing to war. Superstition and legend on all sides. It was no warrior society when I was young. But it came to be. From poverty and myth, anger and pride. Working class and proud of it. Jesus, we had some strange roads to go down. Direct foreign rule supplanted that of our home-grown oppressors, and West Belfast changed, mutated. We lost our innocence. When I was a kid, the worst that could happen to you was a corrective clip round the earhole, a kick up the arse. But then the system collapsed at our slightest pressure, folded under its own weight, really. Law became that which was agreed upon, out of sight of the stranger.

My first blood-breaking operation, after months of being checked out, trained and vetted, had been strangely surgical, simple. The petrified criminal spread against the gable wall, pleading his innocence. Criminals were an avenue into the heartland, easily taken by the enemy; a conduit for information, for sowing dissent. Behavioural standards were molten in the heat of the conflict and poverty, and in the boiling void we spun, only the codes of revolt and the threads of our moral upbringing holding us to the earth. He folded, squealing in agony, and I walked smartly away, immediately distancing myself from the event. In that mutating, new morality good men strove for sainthood and the bad thrived. Corruption on all sides: pockets lined, financial alliances emerging among enemies; misuse of funds; police overtime, bribery, insurance fraud, building fraud, racketeering, laundering. Wartime taxation. For every bent Republican there were a hundred who sacrificed their security, pawned their future for belief.

Sitting in a greasy-spoon café, wiped out by my exertions, emotionally hammered on a sabbath morning; by no means a victim, but a simple, mathematical product, burning myself up in a society bound for purgatory. Could anyone tell me that it was all sentiment? That the reasons for our trauma were changing from economic, from strategic, into some warped, irrational craze to be considered right? The British effort, dressed as impartial policing of a fractious society – was it nothing more than a matter of saving face at any cost? Caught in a colonial trap of their own making, a mega-million commitment to retain a lump of grief-sodden turf as British as Finchley and as foreign as the dark side of Mars, trapped by yours truly and a few others who refused to see things their way. What a price – in life, in mental health – to torture and bully a half-million disaffected Catholics into accepting the impossibility of their freedom.

As I slept fitfully in the café, I was the grubby veto on a nation's rule over another, through all my delinquent actions frustrating what they prayed was reality. Tearing apart the tissues of my self, in hesitant sacrifice to things I felt greater than me. But the price for our merry little war was always to be paid on the nose.

My father and Betty McGinn, veteran of the storm, walked across the strewn debris of a Sunday morning's rage, picking their way around the boulders, the half-bricks, the rubble on the savaged pavements. Past a burnt Toyota coughing out black, poisonous fumes, past the sweating group of rioters who barely noticed them, up into the houses below the church which bore mute witness to the angry day. Up into the houses where people fretted and cursed, to the house I was born in, on past and around the other little streets, they hunted and searched, until they were sure they had arrived at the right address.

'You should be doing this yourself.' Betty's portly features were worried.

'They'll tell you what they won't tell me.'

'I'm sure ye're wrong.'

She beat with the door-knocker a forthright, authoritative tattoo. Bradley surreptitiously peered out from the parlour window, and finally came to answer the insistent knock.

'I thought that was you, Betty.'

'Do you know this man here?'

'Aye, I do, of course. What can I do for ye?' he asked my father, who hung back.

'He's looking for his young fella. The boy went missing last night.'

'What makes ye think I can find him?'

'His mother's in a bad way, Bradley.'

Bradley weighed up the situation. He didn't like getting

bearded on his own doorstep. On the other hand, Betty was a friend and a solid woman, and the ould fella was clearly upset. It was best handled diplomatically. He scanned the street, noting a couple of curious neighbours hanging over their gates, pretending not to notice.

'Come on in for a cup of tea, the pair of ye.'

In the parlour the air was rank with the smell of a fouled nappy. Toys were scattered all over the place, and two little boys were clambering over the furniture, trying to hide from the huge old woman who had entered.

'Sorry for the mess. Herself is away to mass with the two girls.'

'And ye've two more? I just remember the wee girls.'

'There's another one about somewhere. I only have to look at her and she gets pregnant.'

'It's the only thing keeps a man busy, Bradley. It's well for ye.'

There was a cumbersome silence, as Betty half-expected my father to speak up. He was standing in the middle of the room, weakly smiling at the youngest child who gazed at him over the sofa.

Betty began. 'We need to know if the young lad's safe, Bradley. He was out with the wee fella that was killed.'

'And ye think I might know about it?'

'For God's sake, Bradley, ye're talking to friends.'

Bradley looked at my father, but their eyes didn't meet. Yet he could feel the older man's despair, his anger.

'Do you mind if I talk to Betty alone?'

My father looked directly at him, his antipathy unhidden.

'I'll be outside.'

When he left, Bradley rounded on the woman.

'Ye can't be bringing everyone to my house, Betty. There's ways and means, ye know.'

'Him and me goes back a long ways, son. He was in the front of it when you were in nappies, like that wee one. There's no need to be shy with him.'

'Them days are long gone, Betty. From what his young fella

says, he's gone soft on the Brits.'

'So ye know the young fella?'

'I told ye I did.'

'And he was out last night?'

Bradley looked out through the curtains to where my father was standing, his head bowed.

'He was out last night. I would have sent word to his house if we had word. I've already been to the Driscolls' this morning. Do you think if I knew where he was I wouldn't send word? I know how hard it is, but ye know as much as I do.'

'How much do you know? You can tell me, can't ye?'

'The Brits haven't got him. They got the other lads, but it looks as if he got away. Or he's lying somewhere and hasn't been found. We had boys on the go all morning. Myself included. The thing is, no matter what, he can't come back here for a while. There are Brits all over the town after him, and we have to assume they know who they're looking for.'

'Ye're sure no one's heard from him?'

'Not a dicky bird, Betty. The minute there's any news, I'll get word to you. But ye're only wasting yer time hunting for him. If he has got out he'll be over the border as soon as he can get there.'

Betty released a long, ancient sigh. 'That won't be much use to his father.'

'It's a hard life, Betty. Will you tell Billy I was asking?'

'I will. Are ye telling me everything?'

'I have no reason to hold back on ye. Tell yer man not to be going to the peelers or anything stupid like that. Things have a way of working out.'

'There's no end to it, Bradley, is there?'

'There'll be an end to it someday, love. There has to be.'

When she was gone, Bradley grabbed his eldest son and rolled about on the sofa, poking and boxing him till he squealed with delight. The other boy joined in, and the three of them rolled about on the floor. Catching his breath, his thoughts went back to his days down the Falls Road. Big Billy McGinn was the man to look up to then. It was only a few years ago, for heaven's sake. Big Billy and his wife. She cut a trim figure then, and he still had both arms. Bradley remembered their son's funeral. One of the first to cop it, on the barricades. Po-faced little bastard, too serious by half. Death all over him. Glory boy. Not that you would say that to many. Hero of the revolution and all. There were songs about him, a club named after him. There were ould fellas from the South at that funeral. Names you read in the footnotes of the history books. Thousands at the send-off. Wee McGinn had died before he had lived. Bradley looked to the kitchen, where the two boys were running amok. He felt suddenly cold. Betty was right. There was no end to it. No end to the funerals. Spinkey Driscoll in the morgue. Bricks and the other wee gobshite inside, getting seven sorts of shite knocked out of them by now, dare say. And the other eejit missing in action. Fuck the songs they'll be singing tonight. He growled at the two boys, who had begun to squabble, and he went out to put on the spuds for lunch. If he didn't have them started by the time mass was over, the wife would kill him.

'Ye can't sleep here. De ye hear me? This is a café, not a doss-house.'

The sharp voice filtered through my aching head and a finger prodded into my shoulder. I leered up at the old man kitted out in apron and greasy, bright red shirt. I checked my temper.

'Can I use your jacks before I go?'

'I suppose ye can. Out the back, to the left. Don't be fallin' asleep out there.'

I went through the grotty kitchen and followed his directions to a ramshackle closet with a bowl, a sink and an ample supply of newspapers. After a painful bowel action, I splashed my face in the sink, roughly sousing myself with water to get the tiredness out of me. I doused my armpits and the back of my neck, fixed my hair as best I could, and was about to leave when I felt something in my jacket pocket. In the expanding, inside pocket was a square clip of ammunition which I'd completely forgotten about. I took it out and gazed at it in disbelief. One great big clip of trouble. Now it seemed like some alien piece of machinery, an artefact from another time and place. I rubbed it down vigorously with my coat, jumped up on the bowl, and lowered it into the cistern. It fell to the bottom with a gurgle. Replacing the cistern lid, I wiped my sleeve along it, until I was sure there were no dabs. I hurriedly cleaned around the sink and the walls I might have touched. By the time I left, the shithouse had never been cleaner.

Out in the street I looked around, unsure of where to go. I needed to be supplied, to be cared for. Somewhere therein a cocky, belligerent seed began to grow inside me, a kind of violent resignation which belied my actual condition. I was twenty-four hours without sleep. My nerves were ragged, my thinking numbed. My legs were in rebellion, each sinew protesting. I was sick, and downright tired in flesh and spirit. As I turned, hardly caring what was ahead, I saw a figure huddled in the cold, rocking gently forward, an island of distressed humanity in the broad, empty street.

'Dingus? Grey, ye wee fucker. Is that you?' Dingus stared up at my voice, distant, heavy eyes in a puffy, red face. A flow of green lava ran from nose to lip. He was far and away the most beautiful thing I had seen for some time. He came around a little, his baleful glare mellowed into recognition, then surprise.

'Have ye any odds on ye?'

'Hardly a penny.' I scrunched in beside him. 'What brought you down here?' He considered the question.

'I left Luby's last night. I remember getting a taxi, and that was it. I wasn't here all night, mind. There was this party up the road. Jesus knows how I found it. They threw me out sometime.'

'And ye've been here since?'

'Not at all. I slept in a phone box, most of the night. Had to light newspapers to keep warm.'

He did smell smoky, and a little faecal for that. But he was a sight for sore eyes, and I could feel my spirit rising.

'My feet are hurting something awful. Ye haven't any tablets on ye?'

'I've bugger all. How are ye getting home?'

'If ye give me a hand, we'll dander down and get a taxi. I've enough dollars for the two of us.'

'I've half a quid, myself, but it might be tricky. There's a heap of Brits down there I don't want to meet.'

'So what? They won't pull ye for ... hang on. What are you doing down here?'

When I didn't reply he began to figure it.

'You were farting about last night, is that it? You and the other glory-hunters.'

'It's heavy shit this time, Dinger.'

'How heavy's heavy?'

'Spinkey's gone for his tea.'

Dingus couldn't take it in at first. Then he did.

'Anyone else?'

'You won't be seeing Bricks for a while. He'll get the big twenty. Me and all, if they get their hands on me.'

'This sorta fucks up Friday nights, doesn't it?'

'It was Spinkey's turn to get the first round this week.'

'Bollocks. He'd do anything to get out of buying a drink.'

We sat in silence.

'Do you know anywhere I can go on this side of town?'

'I can think of a few places. You may not be welcome though.'

'I just need somewhere to stay, till I get a lift.'

'What you need is the express train to Dublin.'

'That can wait. Can ye get me in off the street?'

'There's somewhere I know. A squat. They're heavy into dope, mind. Will ye keep yer mouth shut?'

'I don't care if they're interfering with sheep so long as I get a Brit-free house for the day. I can get moving again after dark.'

'Help me up then. They won't be chuffed at us knocking

them up at this time o' the morning. But, sure what the hell.'

Dingus leaned heavily on me, and we hobbled away up the quiet centre of town, a peculiar pair of specimens in a sad landscape.

At one point a police Land Rover came by, but by then Dingus was going under his own steam, his injured foot swinging like a club. We must have barely passed inspection, for they drove on. Using Dingus's imprecise guidance, we caught a bus to the university and were ferried past the shop where Spinkey and myself had milled two people with a premature explosion in days gone by. It was now a boutique, the fine ladies' clothes masking its past. Strange feelings of *déjà vu.* Where was reality here? Off the main road, we hobbled and hauled, as his endurance gave out. We talked of the night before, in Luby's pub, of how he might have lost his crutch, of how Big George would never get off with Helen, and how Tommy would react if he found him trying. We laughed and gossiped like two old girls going to bingo, steering clear of Bricks, of Spinkey. When we came to a house with smashed, boarded windows and a rubble-filled porchway, he knocked loudly on the door, kept knocking until his knuckles were crimson. A sleepy, blonde-haired girl opened an upper window.

'We're looking for Tam,' shouted Dingus.

'He's not here.'

'Open the poxy door, woman dear. He's expecting us.'

She cursed under her breath and slammed down the window sash. Inside, we could hear the sound of oath-filled argument, and eventually she opened the front door and raced off, taking the steps two by two in her short nightie.

'Don't be embarrassed, love,' Dingus called after her. 'We're too cold to be looking up yer kite.'

The hallway was a minefield of bicycles and rubbish bags, heavy with the smell of decomposing food. Dingus pushed open the nearest door. Through the gloom I made out the shapes of two single mattresses on the floor. The room was cluttered with all manner of clothes and machine parts, books and upended furniture. It stank of stale clothes and grease, of sex and cooking. Dingus roused one of the sleepers and was directed to go forth and multiply, but eventually he got some answers and came back out to the hall, to where I had retreated.

'There's a room free upstairs. Come on.'

For all his enthusiasm, it took Dingus an age to negotiate the tricky stair-well, and longer yet to find the designated room. Each time he tried a door he received the unsolicited reply of 'Fuck off'. We found the empty room on the third floor. Despite his protestations, I took the armchair and let Dingus crash out on the bed.

In a short while my eyes closed. It wasn't sleep, more a drifting of the mind into its battered perceptions, a stroll into ugliness and painful, clashing bright colours. Pulsating lights, sinister shades, over and over the howl of a dog-obscene, meaty call, a summons to hell. When a hand touched my arm and shook it, I woke with a startled squeak and fell from the seat.

'Jesus, who are you?' A young woman, dressed in a housecoat, hair unkempt, stared in shock.

'I'm a friend of yer man on the bed.'

'Who's he then?'

'Dingus. Dingus Grey.'

She went over to the bed and shook the sleeping Dingus. He fought his way back to life.

'Wake up, you piss artist.'

'Is it yourself, Miss Hayes? Fine and well ye're looking.'

'Ye can cut that out. What are you doing here, you and yer head-banger mate.'

'We only called in to say "Hello", Eileen. Ye know how it is.'

'A social visit? What's he on?' She nodded in my direction.

'He's on nothing, are ye, Frankie?' I looked around to see who Frankie was, then realised he was indicating myself.

'I was passing on the landing when I heard this awful moaning and groaning. Do you always sleep like that, Frankie?'

'He was probably playing with himself, Eileen. Pass no

remarks.'

'I'd hate to hear him if he was getting serious with himself.'

'When's Tam due back, pet?'

'He's out all night with his druggie friends. Are you after chemicals from him?'

'I could do with something.'

'Is your mate after some as well? He looks a right druggie.'

'Frankie is a Guinness man, aren't ye, Frank?'

'That's right.'

'Get yourself back off the floor, there, Frankie. You'll get piles sitting there.' I rose from the floor, and couldn't help my eyes running up her stature. She was the first clean-looking, fresh-smelling being I'd come across in what seemed an age, and I couldn't take my eyes off her. She clearly noticed, for her blue eyes filled with distrust.

'I suppose ye can stay here till Tam gets back.'

'What's for dinner, Eileen?'

'You'll be lucky, ye cheeky skitter. If you want dinner, you can get up and make it yerself. And you may hurry, for the shops close at one.'

A memory came to me. 'Is there a phone I could use around here?'

'There's not one you can use, no.'

'Let him use the one in your room, Eileen. He's house-trained. May not look it, but he is.'

'I never let any of your druggies use it, Dingus. I'm the only one pays their bills in this house. And, for your information, I don't let strange men into my room.'

'That's why ye've such a bad temper.'

'I've no such thing, you cheeky so-and-so.'

'Let him use the phone, then.' She studied me for a moment, the bedroom door swinging between her fingers.

'You won't be phoning Australia then?'

'Local.'

She made her mind up. 'Just this once.'

I followed her up the stairs to the next floor, my eyes entranced at the motion of her small behind under the housecoat. In the context of this grim house, she was positively exotic. She took a heavy key from her pocket and opened the door into a spacious, well-lit room, most of which was taken up by a huge double bed. A flock of cuddly toys lay ranged across the bed-head, and the room was a neat, warm contrast to the rest of the dilapidated squat. It was the classic, single girl's room: pastel posters, fluffy slippers, closets with clothes spilling out.

'That's the phone.'

'How come it's not in the hall?'

'It was when I came here first. It was all flats then. The landlord got into trouble and the place went downhill. I'll be moving out myself before the year's up. Too many of you druggies about for my liking.'

'I'm not a druggie. I'm a dipso.'

There was no chance of me making the call in private. She was sitting at the end of the bed, watching me like a hawk. I got through to Bradley on the second go.

'Is that yerself?' he asked.

'It is indeed. How's it cutting?'

'Not too bad. Have you any holidays planned?'

'Do I need one?'

'Everyone does sometime. I'll let them all know you called.'

'Tell them I'm doing fine. Be seeing ye.'

It took less than a minute. The West Belfast phone system was the least secure in the world. Bradley's phone would be monitored as a matter of course, but it was good they knew I was still in the game.

'Can I make one more call, Eileen. A quick one.'

'Do you think I'm made of money?' I began to search for change. 'I was only joking. Make your call.'

She began to fold away her clothes. I got through to the club, a line certain to be tapped.

'Is Big George there?' Billy the barman recognised the voice immediately. Without responding, he went and dragged George off the pool table.

'Is that yourself in there?'

'It is, George. Do me a favour. Ye know the one I was with last night? Get in touch, say I'll ring tomorrow. OK?'

'Consider it done.' I hung up straight away.

'Thanks, Eileen. That's one I owe you.'

'Phoning your girlfriend?'

'I don't have one.'

I was on my way out the door. 'If you don't mind me saying so, Frankie, you need a bath. Ye smell of fireworks or something.'

'I wouldn't say no to a soak. Is there any hot water?'

'Loads of it. Here's a clean towel. Are you really not a druggie?'

'How often do you need to ask? I'm against the stuff. I leave it to Dingus.'

I had a good, brisk scrub-down in the bath across the way, and was stretching out for a snooze in the lukewarm water when she called out: 'What size of shirt do you take?'

'Fourteen in the neck. Why?'

'There's a clean shirt for you here when you're finished.'

After the bath I went back to her room, where she had a blue lumberjack shirt on the bed. I borrowed her hairbrush, and what with the fresh shirt and the feeling of relative hygiene, I began to feel like a human being again.

'Have you had something to eat today?'

I was wondering why I was getting the five-star treatment. At first meeting she had given all the signs of being a right targe. I had no illusions about my good looks, but she was making the running at this stage. From below came the booming sounds of a record player delivering huge slices of heavy metal to every room in the house.

'The undead have arisen.'

'I take it you don't get on with the neighbours?'

'Dopeheads, the lot of them. There's a wee girl died here a while ago. Overdosed on heroin. Heroin, I ask you? And that mate of yours is one of the worst of them.'

'Do you not get police raids?' I asked.

'Not for ages. They're too busy with the terrorists.'

'You'd be safer out of it.'

'Ach, it's handy for work, and I'm too lazy to move. I'll give it to the New Year, then get out. Where do you live?'

'Up near Dingus.'

'Is it as bad up there as they say?'

'Have you never been?'

'I'm a country girl. I'd be out of my depth up there.'

'Ye're not missing much.'

'I'm sure. How about food?'

'I'm not all that hungry.' I was sitting beside her, on the edge of the bed. 'I don't want to put you under pressure, but do you fancy going out for a drink some night, like? When ye're free ...'

'Are you always this fast?'

'Actually I'm very shy, but my tongue runs away with me the odd time.'

'When did you have in mind?'

I had guessed correctly. She was lonely, isolated, vulnerable, just the business. There was excitement in the corners of her eyes, the kind of delighted confusion I knew well in myself. If she had guessed this was just business, part of the game, I would have been out on my ear.

'What about tonight?'

'Aren't we the fast one? Where did you have in mind?'

'Your call. I'll have to organise some money first. Hang on there ...'

'Don't be waking Dingus up.'

There was a question in her eyes, a want. I reached out and stroked the side of her face. She exhaled, and came closer.

'This is madness,' she murmured.

We kissed, long and formal, finding each other, testing,

asking. I sat back and looked at her and she smiled.

'What are ye staring at?'

'I don't know. There's no label on it.'

'You must think me awful forward. I hardly know you.'

'That's most of the fun. It's when you get to know people the trouble starts.'

She gently took herself away from my touch. 'Well, let's prolong the moment, my boy. There's no point in rushing things, is there?'

'None whatsoever.'

'There's one thing you should know, Frankie. I'm no easy touch. If it's that ye're after ye can go downstairs. Ye'll be tripping over them.'

'Snob.'

'Too right. But I'm clean. Free of all germs.'

'You have a fine air of health about ye.'

'Is that meant to be flattery? You have a better air yourself since you had that bath. What were you two up to last night?'

'We were in the wars.'

'You sure looked like it. Do you want a nap?'

That was how we lay for the afternoon, talking around each other, stopping to hug and to laugh, to drift off to sleep. I lied like I'd never lied before. A *tour de force* of deceit. I lied till I believed it myself. I was an unemployed bricklayer called Frank Davis, from the quiet part of the badlands, who had no time for politics or religion, who had little or no family, few friends. I liked a laugh and a few drinks; no steady girlfriends; no commitments. It was what she wanted to hear. She was from a big family down the country. Too big. No room to breathe, so she moved out to the city, found her way into the civil service and into these flats, which had spiralled down into a cave of Neanderthals. What we had in common was what I made common; the years of practised lying ensured we had a lot of similar feelings, experiences. At four, I went to take a leak, exposing myself to the full brunt of the music blazing downstairs. I made my way to Dingus. He was lying awake on the filthy sheets, smoking.

'What have you been up to?'

'Nothing much. Talking, mostly.'

'Have you cracked that? The wicked bitch of the North? What was she saying about me?'

'She was saying you've been dabbling a bit.'

'Bitch.'

'You be careful, Dingus. There's boys up home don't know you as well as I do.'

'I never sell any, man. Never. Them's my rules. A man's entitled to do himself harm, in my book. You're no fucking saint yourself.'

'I'd never shop you, Dingus. But ye're setting yerself up for a fall. When was the last time you had a decent meal?'

'That's my look out. Don't forget who's doing who the favour here. It's me that put the roof over yer head. If ye're jumping that badger upstairs, you've me to thank for it. Ye'd be dining with the *federales* if it wasn't for me.'

'There's one more favour you can do for me. Scoot up the road and get me some money. Enough to keep the two of us going for a day or two.'

'I'm not sure it's a good idea you hanging about. Every Brit in the city will be on your case, man, going by what I heard on the radio.'

'Keep your voice down, ye blurt.'

'You might have swallowed all this Ireland shite, but I'm not getting into it. Mother fucking Ireland gave me nothing.'

'And you're the man who gives the Brits dog's abuse?'

'That's personal, between me and them.'

'It's dead safe, Dingus. You go to a man I tell ye, ask him for dollars and get a taxi back here. There's a score in it for you.'

'I don't need it. I'd do it for ye anyway. Yer a mucker. But you remember it. I'm fond of a bit of dope, but I never sell it. You're my witness.'

'I'm your witness. Now get yer hole up the road and bring back the readies, right, mucker?'

'Right.'

I gave him the details, and by the time I got back to Eileen he was struggling out the front door. He cut a poor figure for a courier. He was paranoid, hostile, completely unreliable. The more that he protested he didn't deal in dope, the less inclined I was to believe him. If he was ever caught at it, it would be a kneecapping at least. Criminality left him wide open to use by the enemy. He might end up in a ditch with a permanent headache. This was the only one left from the old gang, the last of the true muckers. Here was I, counting on the most erratic and open bastard I knew. Counting on his integrity, his discretion, on a precarious loyalty. And he couldn't count on himself. Eileen braved the decibels and went to the kitchen, returning with a tray of sandwiches and steaming tea. I wolfed it down, a savage hunger returning. She showed mock horror at my greed, and we laughed, spitting crumbs about, before cuddling up. At half past four there was a commotion downstairs, loud and angry voices rising up to us.

'That will be Tam and his gang back. They were out all last night. Wait until ye hear the carry-on now.'

On cue came the sound of rough horseplay and scattering furniture, drunken wails and laughter. There was a giggle on the landing, and a knock on the door.

'Eileen?'

'What?'

'Any chance of a shag?'

'Clear off, Tam,' she called out.

'Who's been in my room, Eileen? Who's been sleeping in my bed, then?'

'Dingus Grey, that's who.'

'That arsehole? Was he searching the room?' She got up and pulled the door open. Beyond was a long-haired son of Jesus with a foul complexion and grinning, bad teeth. A grebo, in the local parlance. He was rocking on his heels, a big beery smile on his be-whiskered lips.

'Didn't know you had company, darling. Right, fella? What about ye? Ye getting there, aye?'

'That's enough, Tam. Behave yourself.'

''S all right. Yer man knows I'm joking. Only a gag, chief. Right? No offence intended. Talkative bollocks, isn't he?'

'He's a mate of Dingus. Now clear off, Tam. Get back to your own floor.'

'Come on down for a few bevies, governor. Any friend of Dingus is a friend of Dingus, aye? Come on. We're having a party. Wine, women and song.'

'Out, Tam. Now.'

'Hang on till I talk to this man.' He sat on the bed and tried to roll a cigarette. 'What did you say you were called?'

'His name is Frankie.'

'I'm asking the main man here. Not you, slag.'

'Frankie is the name, like she said.' I didn't try to hide my feelings.

'Well, Frankie. What do ye reckon on Eileen here? No reply; wonder why? Isn't she the bee's knees, though? Thinks her piss is port wine, she does. Are ye a fighting man at all, Frankie? There's none of us fight over here, boy. No way, José. We fall out, we make up. That so, Eileen? Peace and love, and loads of Mary Jane.' He was rolling grass into the tobacco. Eileen went orange with anger. I winked to her and put a finger to my lips. Tam caught me and gave a knowing grin.

'Don't mind me. I'm not one for interrupting. If you two want to get on with it, I'll watch. I don't mind ye getting friendly.'

'That's plenty out of you, Tam. Take you and your joint out of here.'

'In a minute, girl. I want to talk to Frankie here. You don't look like a Frankie; have ye got a hanky? Hanky panky, Frankie?' He corpsed up laughing. 'Hanky panky, what? Is that a cracker or what?'

'It's a cracker.'

'Don't light that up in here, Tam. If you want to smoke that stuff, do it in your own place.'

'Fair enough, Eileen. You're one of the best. Come on down later, Frankie. Leave Snow White here. She doesn't know how to party, do you love?'

'I'll catch you later, Tam.'

'Aye. I like you, Frankie. There's something about ye.'

'Charisma, Tam. Big bundles of it.'

'Big bundles of shite.' He swayed over the bed, waving a finger in a threatening manner. 'You have cold eyes, Frankie. You have eyes that will get you in trouble. You a fightin' man, Frankie?'

'That's enough, Tam. You leave this minute.'

'I'm away, anyhow. Catch you later, Frankie?'

'Count on it, Tam.'

'Nice meeting ye, anyhow. See ye anon, what?'

'Whatever you say.'

When he'd gone, Eileen gave a sigh of relief.

'I'm sorry about that. He's not usually that high. God alone knows what they've been taking.'

'You don't have to apologise.'

In fact, I figured she was more relieved about what he didn't say. Intuition, if you like. I felt I'd witnessed the meeting of old lovers. There was a jealous tinge to Tam's goading, and she looked perplexed, in the way of one with a secret to hide.

She was putting on a show, a façade. If only she'd known it, there was no need for pretence. I didn't care if she was the paragon of virtue or the epitome of a tart. To me, she was simply another person to use, a tool in my survival. Not that I wasn't attracted to her. When faced with a woman of sounder intellect than myself, or one I really cared for, the result was often disaster; but I had a knack of being able to throw out a lot of quiet charm – bogus, but effective – and Eileen was the perfect subject for it. And she was attractive. It was easy to flirt and to woo when confronted with a pretty face and attractive figure. We kissed and fooled about some more; she gave me anecdotes about her family, about the farm she came from, and it was clear she missed them badly. When she got up to dress, I averted my eyes, and that pleased her. I wasn't about to jump on her bones and blow my plans. I was content to play her like a fish, drawing her in slowly. What I needed was a bed for the night, and that was more important than base carnality.

In West Belfast they were preparing to take Spinkey home. A small crowd had gathered on the access road to the hospital, a larger group had gathered at the mouth of the estate. Among them was Claire O'Brien, scouring the faces for a glimpse of me. Alongside her was my younger sister, who had been alone that afternoon when Claire had called. She had taken Claire into the house and told her of my disappearance, of what Daddy and Mummy were saying, how terrible it was for the Driscolls. They talked of me and of their respective families, shared experiences and grew friendly in their worry, till Bradley called and left a message for my father, a message which took away the undercurrent of dread and strain. Claire left then, cursing me in her heart. She had gone home to sarcastic Joe, who was drinking in the kitchen, but couldn't stand his attitude of 'told you so'. She took herself to her aunt's house, and there, in the quiet of the living room, she poured out her pain and betrayal, releasing the tensions of the morning and her fears about what was to come. Her hard practicality and unshakeable will gave way as she broke into sobs.

'They're all the same, love. Trouble, every one. What ye have to do is sort out how you feel, make yer mind up about this one. Have yez had relations yet?'

Claire was baffled, then nodded.

'Well, he must mean something to you, for I know what a good girl ye are. Now you go out and find this buckaroo, and get him away to hell out of here, out of all this carry-on. It's not good, you and Joseph up in that house all alone. He'll be like a lost sheep when you do get married. As it is, he can't lift a finger for himself. Now, he was down here yesterday giving out about this fella, saying he'd kill him sooner than let you go with him. You know what he's like when he gets a notion. That can't be right, Claire. It's time youse two led yer own lives. That's what I told him to his face. Laying down the law, at your age. You want to be up and making mistakes, and finding out about life, not suffocating around here.'

'But he lied to me! He told me he was doing nothing, he wasn't involved.'

'And what did ye want him to tell ye? "I'm going out the night, shooting soldiers?" Are you as thick as yer brother? You couldn't believe a one of them, not on a stack of bibles. Now, if you think he's worth it, and you're the only judge, get him to one side and tell him it's the war or you. If he loves you, he'll pack it in. If he doesn't, ye won't have lost anything.'

And thus Claire came to be at the removal of Spinkey's remains, searching for a man who didn't deserve her. She met up with my mother and sister, and was introduced to my Da. Mother felt she had to apologise to this wee girl for my waywardness. All day long, she had felt responsible, a point my father was quick to emphasise. Bradley's news had only made it worse in some ways. She was expecting me home at any moment, thinking I might spring to her side in the crowd, to smile and tell her there was nothing to worry about. Bradley said I was fine, but where was I, how was I? Who would make my tea? A plethora of recriminations weighed her down, and now she could barely speak to this shining girl who was supposed to come for Sunday dinner. All nature had gone astray. The storm had finally gutted the house and swept me away, and my mother felt she was to blame.

It was Spinkey's penultimate journey, the last homecoming. The naked hearse bore this son up the long road. Behind came his distraught family, his awestruck friends and neighbours, a few noted politicos and a clatter of nuns, rambling through West Belfast which sang a silent song of sorrow, heard only by the dead.

Propped against a wall, staring with doubting eyes, Dingus watched them pass. It was all so suddenly real to him. The waste. He couldn't get over the waste. In his catechism it was mortal sin. Life was for whoring about and getting high as often as you could. For someone to go out and invite death, this was sacrilege, taboo. He had entertained thoughts of picking up some money for me, then making whoopie. He figured I wouldn't mind too much. But this procession of idiocy brought him down. He would get the dollars, as he had said, then kiss me goodbye. Life was hard enough without getting in tow with overnight heroes. The circling helicopter, a vulture above the bones, underlined his thoughts. I was one piece of bad news Dingus could do without. As he was mulling over mortality, an old lady with a runt of a dog on a lead came past and stopped.

'Oh, God, son. Who's dead now?'

Dingus threw her an unsympathetic glance.

'At a rough guess, love, I'd say it's the eejit in the coffin.'

She hurried on, pulling her growling dog behind her.

He struggled on his smashed toe, and beat inward to the club. Once there he told Billy of his troubles. Billy summoned a young lad who was playing the fruit machine, and the boy left. He returned while Dingus was on a free pint. He went back to playing the machine, and ten minutes later a pair of guys came in and spoke to Billy. Dingus was rapidly escorted from the premises, protesting for time to drink up. They rushed him out to a car and took him to the rear of a block of flats some distance away. He was impatiently removed from the vehicle and taken to a set of garages. In the end garage, Mo was sitting on a work-bench. He was reading the *Sunday Times* by the light of a hurricane lamp.

As the door closed behind him, Dingus knew he had entered the underworld.

'Do you know me?' Mo spoke with deliberate menace.

'I don't,' Dingus lied.

'Would you know me again?'

'I've a bad head for faces. Never can remember them.'

'That can be to your advantage. Now, what have you to tell me, young chap?'

Night had fallen on West Belfast as Dingus told the day's events to a suspicious Mo. A cadaver was delivered to a broken home, followed into the house by people lost in thoughts of their own vulnerability and in thoughts of anger. The business of the clubs began to pick up, and the streets and roads, glazed with the afternoon rain, became the province of the patrolling troops. It was a quiet night, Sunday straining to be Monday. The streets were gathering their breath after the weekend exertions.

Down the country, a policeman's family crowded into a small farmhouse along with friends and neighbours, and a few dignitaries who called to shake hands, to extend the commiseration of government, of church, to the stoic father of the deceased, to his distraught mother.

Elsewhere, a lorry left a farmyard and pushed south, heading to the lip of the border. In a compartment beneath a load of timber lay a sickly man with a hot-water bottle pressed to his belly; he winced with every bump on the road. Morgan and O'Reilly had sat up all night with their comrades, a celebratory bottle of vodka passing between them. They'd lain low in the farmhouse, jealously protecting their trophy, basking in relief and success. Having slept away the day, they now saw him off, then left themselves, splitting into pairs. Morgan and another man took off on a motorbike. Later still, O'Reilly and his comrade drove away in a legitimately borrowed car. They were squeaky-clean, guns dumped, van and clothes removed for burning, every orifice washed and pinkly scrubbed. They would meet hours later in a city club, and one pair would pass the other without the slightest sign of recognition as they reintegrated into the social fabric.

When he had the house back to himself the farmer warmed his arse at the fire, glad to be rid of them, but a little lonely and bored at the same time. He set to planning the day ahead. He had work to catch up on, and a cow with a gammy leg in the top field that needed a vet. He fell to wondering how much the vet would charge him. Running a farm was a complicated and tight business, and he was a weekend behind.

CHAPTER FOUR

MY LUCK WAS draining away.

While Eileen got up, I went down to the front door to keep an eye out for Dingus. It was cold and miserable, the sort of Sunday night I liked to stay at home and watch the television, wind down before the week's work. It pleased my mother when I sat in of a Sunday, watching the box and indulging in endless cups of thick tea. I had a fair idea that those days were gone forever, eradicated in the turmoil of the previous twenty-four hours. What a difference a day makes.

'Will ye close that door?'

I was letting a draught run freely through the squat, and a middle-aged woman was giving out from the front room. She was standing in the hall now, a rotund figure in a woolly sweater, with a flow of straight, greasy hair hanging over her shoulders. She was squinting at me in the poor light.

'Who are you?'

'I'm a friend of Eileen upstairs.'

'I know you from somewhere, fella. Do you know Dingus Grey?'

'I've heard the name somewhere.'

'I went out with him the odd time. Here, you were with him one night. At a disco, yeah? You got off with that wee O'Brien one that works in Parker's. Do you remember?'

'No. Ye've the wrong man.'

'I have not. I never forget a face. If it's one thing about me ...'

'Ye've got the wrong man, missus. Now fucking drop it.'

I brushed past and made up the stairs, hand rubbing the lower part of my face. The bitch had me, all right. Now the night came back to me, sitting with Claire and her friends, while Dingus looked around for me, a hard-faced one on his arm. It was her OK, large as life and twice as nosy. Eileen spotted my jitters when I got back to the room.

'Don't worry. He'll turn up. I've enough to get a pint or two if he doesn't.'

'Sure. Who's the large girl downstairs; in her late thirties?'

'Jennifer Brennan? She's getting knocked up by all the fellows in that room. Different one every night, by all accounts. Mind you, when you see her go to work in the mornings you would think she was the Queen of Sheeba, done up to the nines.'

'Where does she work?' I could have guessed myself.

'I think it's Parker's factory. I wouldn't fancy working with her though. She must have every disease under the sun.'

'Cheer me up.'

'Are you going home tonight?'

'Would you mind me staying here?'

'Not at all. But ye're not on for sex. I'll tell you that now, so you don't get all frustrated later. I could only do it with someone I knew for ages.'

'I can live with that. I'm not into one-night stands myself.'

'Good. I knew you were no druggie. You look a bit rough on it, but ye're not like those ones. You sleep here tonight, but you behave yourself.'

'It's a deal.' Mission successful.

When she was out at the loo I did a swift reconnaissance of her dressing table to find out a bit more of where she was at. Beneath a collection of impossible underwear in the middle drawer was a plastic change bag filled with a set of grey tablets, and an envelope of cream-coloured powder. It all had the feel of non-prescription. I took one of the tablets and popped it into my pocket. Dingus might be able to put a name on it.

Ten minutes later the man himself arrived. He called from the hall below, and when I came down he muttered, 'There's someone outside to see you.' Dingus sounded distant, offended.

I approached the car warily. Inside was one of Mo's runners, a guy I knew.

'Jump in.'

'What's the story?' I stayed outside.

'Mo sent me to collect you. I'm to drop ye over the border tonight.'

'Forget it, Ronan. I'm stopping here tonight. Have ye any collateral?'

'I have. Listen, I can't force you to come, but this can't be a smart idea. The Brits have you down as Public Enemy Number One. Kidnapping and all sorts, from what we hear. Between looking for you and the fella out of the hospital, there's more aggro than there has been for months. We ought to get down near the border itself, drop you over in the morning.'

'What's this about the hospital?'

'Don't you listen to the news? While youse were cutting up rough some of the lads went in and liberated a top operator from the hospital. Head honcho in shit-kicker land. The Brits thought they had Joe Soap, volunteer, but yer man was top brass.'

I began to see things more clearly. I'd guessed we were some sort of diversion from the start. I was trying to remember Mo's yellow finger tracing on the road map. 'All the ammunition ...'

'I suppose they got away on the motorway?'

'That's it. Straight for the country and away.'

Straight? Fuck-all straight about it. Mo would have known that the peelers would fall on us, the motorway patrols bound to respond to a bombing so close. He would have counted on it. I could only admire the aplomb with which he had sent us out. Perfectly ruthless. Even Spinkey would have liked that, I thought bitterly. Sweet-talking, scheming bastard. I admired his style.

'Ronan, tell Mo for me that he is one dickhead.'

'Do you think I'm mad? Tell him yourself. What are you for doing, then?'

'I'll stop here tonight. Head for the border tomorrow. Did he send any ID?'

'One blank driver's licence was all he could get at short notice. Hundred quid cash, as requested. He had to put an IOU into the club for that. And he says he doesn't like the company ye're keeping. Reckons your messenger boy is a liability.'

'He was around when Mo wasn't. Is this motor clean? I'll hang on to it; when I get across I'll let you know where I drop it.'

'Is there any more I can do?'

'Just tell Mo "thanks". Tell him I've got the right hump with him. I haven't really, but it will get the old bastard going. He's getting too smart for his own good.'

'Ye'll need a photie for that licence, anyhow. Ye're probably right to leave it till then. The roads are too risky. Have ye nowhere better to stay, though? That looks a right dump.'

'It has its compensations.'

'Here's a wee something for you, then.'

He held out his hand and in it was a tiny, ladies' .22, a regular Saturday-night Special, for tucking down your boot.

'It's in case ye're attacked by a rhino, or something.'

I told him about the clip of ammunition I'd left in the café toilet and he promised to look into it. He gave me the car keys and strolled off to catch a bus.

On the stairs I met Eileen. She had been sitting on the bare wood, watching through the open door.

'It's not nice to keep a lady waiting.'

'Sure, am I not worth waiting for?'

As she said it, I felt a sudden surge of contempt and anger rising. I gave her the best smile I could rally, excused myself, and went into the bathroom. My breathing became strained, pulses began to lance my temples as tears cried out to rise, but my eyes wouldn't permit it. Looking in the mirror, all I could see was a stressed and haggard caricature of what I'd hoped to be.

Just a diversion in someone else's plans. Just another one carried away on the storm, I was sold on a dream of release, of freedom, of the kingdom on earth where none was king, where none were done down by dint of religion or culture. No queen had sanctioned my actions; no bishop's blessing here.

Technology and opportunity had failed to meet; the logistics of victory had escaped either side, and now there was only struggle, defiance, little victories and slight defeats, heroic rescues and the deaths of boys like Spinkey Driscoll. We took from the past, looked to the future and damned ourselves in the present. Now I was planning to seek anonymity in a southern state an hour's drive away, a land where people lived happily on the freedom bought by our oppression, with peace of mind paid for by my father's silence. Ireland, Mother Ireland: a duplicitous little sub-colony off the 'mainland', selling its trinkets like a reformed whore outside the markets, rosary beads and tax exemption for whoever was kind enough to invest. Still loving their myths: all our wars were merry, and spotlessly clean; never a civilian killed in the old days, never a mistake. The land of family values, run by politicians whose policies sent families to the dockside to wave goodbye to Daddy as he went to the English factories. Ignorance was bliss, but I'd run out of myths that night. The girl waiting patiently downstairs, secure in her innocence: what could I say to make her or anyone see? It was wrong, plain and simple. The price for normality was always going to be debasement; that was how the Irish allowed partition. Churlish to even think of it. Blame the Brits for everything. But it was ourselves, ourselves alone, that were the problem. Mammon had become God, and all else was a cynical nod to history. Ireland's only consuming wish was to disappear up the backside of European subsidy, wincing at the screams of daily life in the war zone. Suited, supercilious, pious, complacent bastards. The country didn't deserve us fighting for it. I heard my mind say it, and immediately the pain abated, becoming a dull seam in my chest as I grinned at myself in the mirror.

'It's only a fucking game,' I said to the jaded image. Whatever the outcome, whatever the politics, there was a job at hand. It was pointless to analyse. I'd learned that, time and time again. Action. Movement. You do what you can, think what you like. I was on the thankless edge of power, just a pissed-off worker in hell's factory, another ungrateful, malcontented Fenian with a chip on his shoulder. I couldn't afford grief or doubt. I had to call in all my wits, to get the hell out of this city. I could feel Mo's reproach and concern even from this distance. I sat on the edge of the bath and breathed deeply. I had to improvise till morning. Keep in with the crowd, hide in the middle, keep everyone sweet, then walk away, drive slowly, casually, to the border. It was the only plan I felt comfortable with: a few drinks and a good night's sleep was what the doctor ordered.

Eileen rapped on the bathroom door.

'Are you coming or not, Frankie?'

When I emerged she was leaning back against the landing wall, her expression stuck between a thought and a frown.

'Sorry for keeping ye. Man's gotta do what a man's gotta do.'

She pushed herself away from the wall and strode down the stairs. I took a deep breath and followed.

Six men sat around two formica-topped tables, supping coffee from plastic beakers. They discussed the day's events, and progress made. Sundays were a long, unpopular shift. The money was good, but there were families to be taken care of, and golf rounds had been missed, drink left untouched. To cap it all, they had been working all-out, to little result.

'How far have we got with O'Hare?'

'He's giving us the big freeze.'

'It'll take another day or two for him to open up.'

'The other wee prick is putting himself in the frame, but he knows a lot more than he's cracking on.'

'A cunning little bastard for it all.'

'Slippery as a buttered eel.'

'Has he given us anything on Mo at all?'

'Nah. He's scared shitless.'

'Mo must be slipping, using eejits like that. We'll have all we need out of him tonight. I don't know how much will go down on paper, though.'

'I'll want a decent statement from him.'

'Ye'll have it, even if I have to write it myself.'

'What about the hospital?'

'No joy. My guess is they went in blind. They didn't need to know.'

'But the other fella might know. He was in charge.'

'He might. But then again, we haven't got him, have we?'

'How come he was in charge and we never got to hear about it? That worries me, that does.'

'Bolt from the blue. Going on his previous, ye couldn't have worked it out. Attempted murder and kidnapping? I would never have twigged him. He never showed any bottle when he was in here.'

'Mr Co-operative. Nice fella. We should have beat the shite out of him the last time he was pulled.'

'I didn't hear that remark. We've been badly caught out on all sides. The important thing is to learn from this. Take none of the scum at face value. Remember it.'

'There's no altar boys left, is there?'

'The Brits want their arses kicked for letting him away. He should have been blown away first thing.'

'Easier said than done. It's a hard call when there's a citizen in the way. Do you think yer wee man would have shot him?'

'I was there this morning when they brought him home. You want to see the state of his wife. The bastard gave her an awful hammering. The kids were up the wall as well.'

'The swine was desperate. He would have wasted his dear old granny by the sounds of it.'

'Are we sure we have the right man?'

'It can be nobody else. He's the only one fits the bill.'

'Fair enough, gentlemen. Far as I can see, there's little chance of us getting a clear result on the hospital job. Even if we do, the prisoner will be over the border. Now, assuming the lads who did it are local as well, we have a chance. That's why I want ye to concentrate on the quare fella. If he does know the unit involved, that will give us Constable Patterson's killer. I'd be pleased with that. The quare fella is priority one. I don't like wee turds running around scaring the ratepayers, holding women and childer at gunpoint. This is one bad wee get, and I want him. Rustle up your sources, lads. It's possible he's still in the city. He sounds stupid enough for it. Jesse fucking James. After the day, he probably thinks he's bullet-proof. Descriptions out to all patrols, including recent photographs, house raids tonight, friends and likely relations. Pull in everyone who ever heard him fart. If possible, let's get him alive, but make sure it's known he's dangerous. The longer this boy is at large, the colder it all gets; understand?'

'What about Mo, sir? Any chance of pulling him in?'

'Any chance of finding him?'

'What's the point of pulling him in when we've nothing on him?'

'He enjoys being pulled. It keeps him on his toes.'

'He's a priority target, but the next time he crosses our door I want enough shit to bury him for a lifetime. Last night showed us one thing. He's pushed for staff if he has to use his own driver for operations. They got lucky, but it was still only a draw. One dead each; they have their man out of hospital, but we have two to work on. Let's get rid of this idea that Mo is something special. He's a pimple on the arse of humanity, and we're squeezing him. If we get this other piece of trash, we have a right chance of bursting him. Get working on it. First sign of development, let me know.'

When the briefing broke up, Inspector Harry Grange looked down at the file on the formica table. His eyes were red from tiredness and tobacco fumes. He shook his head. The longer he was in the job, the more despondent he became. It never got easier, a murder a week to deal with. Here was a boy in front of him, no older than his own son, running about beating up women, creating pandemonium. For what? Pie in the bloody sky. How the hell did you get the gall to go running about with an automatic rifle letting loose on other people? What sort of ignorance brought it on? How the hell were they raised? This wee bollocks had no morals, no scruples. No fucking rulebook at all. Putting a gun to a married man's head, willing to leave a widow just to save his own miserable hide. Grange had long come to terms with the horror of war. But he couldn't figure out the ruthlessness of the scum he was fighting, the sheer wickedness. Their ability to drag themselves to ever lower levels always surprised him. Scum. He closed the folder, tucked it under his arm, and went off to the interrogation rooms for the evening sessions.

In the cells below, filled with swamp heat and smelling of sweat, Ten-to-One lay on his bed, doubled up with pain. Each bone in his body rang with its specific note of agony, and his head was terrified.

Two doors away, unaware of his presence, Bricks O'Hare was perched on the side of his bed. He was staring at the Judas hole in the door, and a faint smile was playing on his lips. As he thought of his predicament, he was pleased. Things could be much worse. He was still alive and in decent fettle. For Bricks, being captured was a career move. He'd always known it would come to this, or worse, and now he had joined the big boys, the ones who had done their time for Ireland and for the left. Inwardly, he was in turmoil, but it wasn't total displeasure. He had played the game, and now the secret was to assert your dignity and correctness in front of the enemy. Now he prepared himself for even greater resistance to the pressure ahead. He had said damn all: he was a captured combatant, and sought no favours from the State, realising it could only take full vengeance if he condemned himself. Talking would do no good, but would earn him the opprobrium of his future comrades in jail. He was on a sixteen-to-twenty stretch, whatever way the cookie crumbled. Rather than co-operate, he chose to lose himself in the world of the mind, in concentration, meditation, breathing exercises. He was counteracting the heat, the searing light, the timelessness of the cells, the threats and promises. For Bricks, the future was taken care of, and like a monk he lived minute by minute in a world of his own construction, where he felt the enemy would not reach him.

As for myself, I was no patriot. I was just handy, merely happened to be there. I hadn't been about to lie down forever, to be walked over. Hope frustrated became a deadly virtue in me. It engendered sacrifice and sanctified my pain, but I shied from martyrdom. Nevertheless, I would not be found wanting in the eyes of my generation. I had to follow what I presumed was my conscience. I wanted to be able to walk in my own streets with easy pride, knowing I was paying my dues. Now I was in blood to my neck. Christ, I had the sour taste of killing, of blasting civilians apart. But therein was the cost of the game, the entrance fee. Inhumanity was the concept we used to cloak actions which were all too human.

Pride and bloody ego. That was the root of my trouble. I hated being lied to. I hated being a victim, even by proxy. Everywhere else in Europe was the ballot box, the media, the open debate, all providing some measure of fairness, some means to change. No matter how we voted, the cursed border put the boundary to our march and perpetuated our humiliation. We were governed by coercion, not consensus. Concussion, not consent. Bricks and his like, me and mine, we grew up fast and flaming hard, admiring the martial potential in each other, laughing in the midst of offal, clinging to the family, to the community, for endorsement of our sanity in a world that didn't want to know.

We fought a war between television programmes, between weddings and funerals, between dates and football matches.

And now I had a bed for the night, a pistol in my pocket and money in hand. I would be just another face in the hundreds of students milling in the bars and clubs of the university area, walking out with a girl on my arm. The horrors of the night before were pushed back, to be dealt with when I finally achieved sanctuary, to be dealt with when I was fit. I had long since learned to compartmentalise my life, my feelings. I could show one face, one personality to one person, be totally changed for another. There were a dozen more within. You dealt with one problem at a time, one set of emotions. It was to preserve the secret life.

To this strange and lonely girl, with her drawer of drugs and her act of convent girl purity, I was Frankie-Nice-Fella. A rough character with a good feel to him. To Dingus, I was the friend he never knew, mystery man. To Mo's messenger, Ronan, I was a hard man he might admire, a fledgeling legend he was proud to meet, a man of war. To Claire O'Brien I was the duplicitous wee swine she had fallen in love with, who had brought her nothing but trouble and tears. I had a face and a story for all of them; each had a part of the whole, but none had access to the others' perceptions. Her brother, Joe, had a fair intuition, a recognition of me in his own bad days. Unknown to me, he had determined to take the wheels off my wagon at the earliest opportunity.

Eileen was surprised at my sudden acquisition of a red Fiesta.

'Is it yours?'

'My cousin's. But he lets me use it when he's away at weekends.'

'Right.' If she suspected anything, she didn't show it. Dingus came out of the house with a half-downed bottle of milk in his hand. He wiped his mouth with his sleeve, to Eileen's disgust.

'Where are you going, then?'

'I was taking this young lady out for a drink. Are ye coming?'

'I'd better.' He indicated the house. 'Is that yer one Jennifer I hear in there?'

'She's there all right, Dingus,' said Eileen. 'Go in and say hello.'

'My arse I will. She's an indiscretion, that one.'

'One of your many!'

'That's not nice, Miss Hayes. She is a very generous and kind-hearted class of person behind that rough exterior.'

'Let's not hang about. We're wasting drinking time.'

Eileen got into the back seat, observing a kind of false propriety. She didn't want Dingus to feel excluded, or that there was something going on between us. For his part, Dingus was revelling in the situation. He had enough to hang me, and knew her a lot better than I did.

It was a jolly jaunt to the Tropical Hotel: a barely sensible renegade on the run, a festering junkie, and the Lady Bountiful of the squatters in the back seat. By the time we got to the bar, I was well able for a drink.

Big George lumbered up the path to Claire O'Brien's house. She answered the door, anticipation on her face giving way to disappointment.

'I'm sorry to bother ye, love. I have a wee message for ye. Yer man phoned the day. He says he's a bit tied up, but he'll get in touch as soon as he can.'

'What's that supposed to mean? Is he all right?'

'Aye. He's all right. He was kinda worried you might be worried, if ye know what I mean.'

'You tell him to catch himself on. I want nothing to do with him. You can tell him that.'

'I'm only the messenger boy, love. Sure, I'm only doing what I was asked.'

'I'm sorry, George. Where is he?'

'No idea, love. He phoned me at the club. All he said was "tell her I'll ring tomorra".'

'I suppose I should be grateful. Do you want to come in for a cup of tea, George?'

'I have to be running, love. I've someone to see up the road, like.'

'Is that your woman Helen you were with last night?'

'Jesus, don't say that or ye'll have me killed. Sure, she's a married woman, like. I only walked her home last night. Do it for anyone.'

'I was only joking, George. The colour of you! I know you're only friends.'

'That's it. Friends, like. I'll see ye when I see ye.'

'Thanks, George.'

'Don't mention it.' He stopped half-way down the path. 'Don't mention anything.'

'Your secret is safe with me, George.'

In the living room she turned on the television. The news touched briefly on the weekend's attrition. A part-time soldier killed in Tyrone, the body of a Catholic found by the shores of a lough. The search continued for the escapee from the hospital. Spinkey got a mention as a gunman shot near by. A breathless little litany of hardship and terror, it was only marginally more violent than previous weekends of that year. If the 'glamorous' aspects of the hospital incident hadn't attracted the reporter's interest, the other snippets would hardly have been relayed to a Britain grown tired of the conflict. Watching it, her depression and anger increased in rhythm with the unfolding reports. I would phone her tomorrow. Should she be grateful? God's gift to women. Conniving bastard. Evil little sod. She was well rid of me.

Claire O'Brien never gave herself freely to anyone. She had a good feeling about herself; not smugness or over-confidence, but a calm appraisal of her own worth, of how others valued and liked her, a pride in her control of emotions and body. She had a way with her, an understated grace, a gentleness and warmth which conveyed itself to all, and whilst she knew this, she didn't need to work at it. It was a gift. She knew how fallible she could be, how vulnerable. But she had a confidence and style I would have killed for, and now she had been betrayed, not for the first time, by a smile and a laugh.

For her, taking life was a sin. A sin against life itself, leaving God out of it. Life was sacred, and to be treated as such. Like most women at that time there were two things she hated: violence and the British army. She detested their presence, which had created more grief than it would ever prevent. Yet she saw no morality in the struggle, saw it for what it was – a filthy exercise in power politics which sucked people in and spat them out. She aspired to neutrality, having seen the consequences on her own family as Joe had become more and more involved; the sacrifices that were made in her own home had left their mark. As a child, she had comforted her mother, a woman driven mad and old by a son's beliefs. When the Stickies had called their war off, she had been relieved. Only a child, she had known the politics involved, and had vowed to stay clear of the likes of me. But she had given herself in a flood of tenderness and warmth, a rush of love. In a few short weeks, she had fallen for a liar, a conman. We'd had a right few laughs and, beneath the reams of deceit, she felt that I loved her, was sure of it. Now that trust was looking foolish, and she had only the memory of last night's touch to tell her if she had been wrong or right, if there was anything in me for her. Damn Joe. He was right, again. She always picked the worst, when she deserved the best. She would never take a man seriously again. They were good for a laugh and a hug, but no more. In the grip of indecision and emptiness, she felt soft tears roll down her cheeks. She sucked in her breath, forced her eyes to stop. She would play the fool no more. From now on she would live for herself, and to hell with the rest of the world.

Joe came home early that night and was surprised to find the downstairs deserted. She usually sat in and listened to records on a Sunday night, or had girlfriends over. It was another disruption and worry to him, and he softly cursed my memory. Quietly opening the bedroom door, he peeked in, schoolboy-shy. She was lying in the dark, barely asleep, lost in deep, dark thoughts. He gently closed the door and went back downstairs. In the pantry, he prised off a section of the skirting board about ten inches long. Behind it was a hollow in the wall, dug years before.

It was empty now, but Joe took the revolver from his pocket and lowered it into the crevice, where it sat snugly, as if having come home. He replaced the board and covered the spot with tins and baking trays. Joe O'Brien lit up a smoke, and thought.

A few streets away my younger brothers were quietly and busily going through my effects. They checked every nook in the house lest something be stashed. As they ferreted away, my father went out to get drunk, my mother cried her way to sleep, as my sister stroked her hair.

In Spinkey's house the wake continued. The two *Fianna* boys who stood guard on the coffin were relieved, replaced by two equally stern young men. People came and went, viewed and prayed, drank tots of whiskey or tea from best china, talked and told stories, watching each other come and go, reacquainting, meeting anew. Bricks's family were in heavy attendance, using the greater grief of their neighbours to cloak their own distress. Occasionally a mobile patrol of Brits would pass, studiously surveying the depressed house, watching for faces that might be noted down for later action. The mourners coming and going in the drizzle ignored them as one might a turd on the pavement.

In the Tropical Hotel we had standing-room only. The bar was crowded with students, ringing with broad country accents and the braying tones of the middle classes. It was a notable contrast to the Falls. People here seemed bigger, healthier, more intense in some ways. The women were more exotic, fresher. Jealousy and inferiority, of course. I always fancied I had the brains to study. I'd been pretty sharp at school, nothing exceptional, but always in the top half-dozen. Laziness and disillusionment had driven me from study, and I was fated to regret it. Under different circumstances, had I made other choices, followed self-interest, I could have been one of these dry-witted, confident boys at the bar, bound for better things away from the war, surveying the good-looking women with their tight jeans and sharp minds. Yeah. I could have been a contender.

'Fucking bunch of parasitic wankers. Using my fucking tax money to subsidise the sprogs of the upper classes.'

Dingus had two pints in him and was off on a freewheel. He had some poor lug cornered against the wall and was giving him a lesson in civics.

'Ye come up here to the city with shit on yer boots and think ye know it fucking all. Using my money to get a trade so ye can shove it up the workers. Ye should be strung up by the bollocks, every last one of ye that has a bollocks. Education, my arse. Ye know nathing about life, nathing. All ye know is books, and books is nathing, de ye hear? Nathing.'

Dingus was completely without prejudice: he would get up anyone's nostrils, irrespective of title or faith. The young student who had been silly enough to listen to him was looking for a place to hide.

'It doesn't take much to get him going, does it?' said Eileen.

'Crack on he's not with us. There's no harm in him, really.'

'Tell that to those big football players in the corner. I hope he doesn't start about football.'

A group of tall blokes in the corner were giving Dingus the bad looks. Within minutes, he was over talking to them, offering to buy a round, and getting on great. He was a sly wee get in his cups, seldom pushing it too far. I was praying he stood off politics, or more especially his pet subject, goading the Brits. Sure as hell, before the night was out he was showing everybody his war wounds. I took to giving Eileen Hayes the full-attention treatment, thinking of my billet for the night. I hung on to her every word, asked questions and looked intently into her eyes which were slowly stirring to the drink and the crack. At the right, quiet moment, I put my arm around her and she slid up to me, the public breakthrough. Dingus caught my eye, and raised a glass, a big drunken grin on his face. When Eileen asked me what I was laughing at, I told her it was because I felt good, and asked her what she was doing next weekend.

'We could go for a spin in the country if I have the car.'

'I'd like that. Any particular part?'

'We'll get into the car and go where the notion takes us.'

'That would be great.' Looking into her face, I almost believed it possible myself.

'Are ye all right, Eileen my old flower?'

It was a slurred, offensive voice filled with sarcasm. Tam, Prince of Shiteheads, was here. He had fractionally straightened up from the afternoon's matinee he'd put on in her bedroom, but looked as repulsive and hitable as he had then. 'Any chance of a leg-over?'

'Oh, Jesus. What are you doing here? You never come out of yer coffin on a Sunday night.'

'I'm looking for me old mate, Dingus. Is this the boyfriend?'

'You met Frankie this afternoon.'

'You the quiet one? I remember now. I'm not sure I like you.'

'Cut it out, Tam. Dingus is over in the corner.'

'Nice shirt, Frankie. I used to have one like that.'

'I gave it to him, Tam. Now, don't stir the shit. We're out for a drink, with no trouble.'

'Cat got your tongue, Frankie?'

'Ye're doing enough talking for both of us, wee fella. Just carry on talking. Let me know if you decide to do anything else.'

'Pushing your luck, Frankie boy. That's my woman ye have there.'

'Did ye win her in a raffle or what?'

'I'll have your teeth in a raffle if ye keep it up.'

'If ye didn't win it, and ye didn't buy it, then ye don't own it. Now fuck off.'

'What's the crack, lads?' Dingus had put himself between us, his back to me. 'Come on, Tam, I'll get ye a drink.'

'I'm down the other end with Jennifer and her mates. You can come down if ye like, but yer mate here – he's not welcome.'

'That fella? Sure I hardly know him. You go down and I'll be along. No need for trouble on the sabbath, is there?'

Tam spun on his heel and pushed back through the attentive

crowd of drinkers, who rapidly went back to their pints. Eileen was crushed against the wall, paring a fingernail, looking at me shyly. Dingus winked at me, and went over to his new-found mates.

'I don't know what to say. I never thought he'd act like that.'

'Forget it. He's a mouthpiece.'

'I've been forgetting about him for months.'

'Was it serious?'

'It was for him. I don't know how it came about. One minute we were friends, then we were more than friends. It was all a big mistake.'

'It often is. Don't let it get you down.'

'Can we go now?'

'What are you worried about?'

'I don't want to get you into trouble. He has loads of mates over here.'

'I'm surprised he has any mates, with an attitude like that. We're going to have a few more jars, and then we can go.'

'I get worried sometimes. When I'm alone. He takes it too seriously. I get afraid of what he'll do. Did ye see the temper on him? There's badness in him, real badness.'

'You won't be alone tonight.'

'I can handle him. It's just if he caught me off guard, and him high. He wouldn't stop at killing me. I know him too well.'

'You can't live in fear, Eileen. Give in to fear, you might as well be dead.'

The games people play. I thought it was my charm. I was the guinea-pig, someone to test the water; provoke a reaction. The dope in her drawer, the bullshit, the coyness of it all. The truth was she was using me, as much as I her. His frigging shirt on my back and all. Man, why wasn't I on my way out of this city. Did I need this shit?

'Eileen, I like you. I've enjoyed the afternoon. The crack was ninety. If we're going to be friends, build some kind of relationship, I can't have you running scared of a prick like that.

If he gives you any hassle, get Dingus or myself. I'll leave you my phone number in the morning, you can get me any time. I'm only an hour away if you need a friend. Understand? Now drink up and give me a kiss. Speeches are over for the night.'

'God, I like you, too, Frankie. Just remember, this doesn't change anything. You're not on a promise, mister. Just a bed for the night.'

'There'll be other nights.'

'You do fancy yourself. What makes you think there will be?'

'It must be something about the way ye're undressing me with yer eyes.'

'Away out of that with ye. It's that I've left my glasses at home.'

'Yeah! Let's get the drinks in.'

Dingus intervened and called a pint for me. He had his manky socks off, and was showing his bashed toes to a captive audience in the corner. He rapidly had a group of interested piss artists assembled to inspect his rotting digits, all swapping loud stories of disease, capped by a male psychiatric nurse who began to relate some darkly humorous experiences of his own in graphic mime. As the drink flowed, the crack got mighty, and Eileen pressed closer. Out in the toilets, Dingus talked low.

'Are you on the job tonight?'

'Looks like it.'

'Keep the door locked. That Tam fella isn't to be taken lightly. He's used a knife, the odd time.'

'I thought he was a mate of yours?'

'I thought you were. He has his uses, but I wouldn't trust him.'

'What's the story with yer woman. The truth, now.'

'She was his wench all right.'

'Ye could have told me.'

'What's it to me? It's your dick, not mine. She used to do a lot of dope. Since she quit she's been a right pain in the ass. No fun at all.'

'Were you in there?'

'Once, when she was out of her head. Listen, she's a nice girl.'

'Here. Check this out.' I gave him the tablet I'd taken from Eileen's drawer.

'It's a Benny or suchlike.' Without hesitation, he swallowed it dry. 'Soon tell ye what it does for ye.'

'Ye're an animal, Dingus.'

'Listen. I've been thinking. This business with Spinkey ...'

'Forget it.'

'Forget nothing. After the night, we go our separate ways. Nothing personal, old sport, but ye're too heavy for me. I saw them taking him home tonight. It fair put the mockers on me, man. There's no need for that carry-on.'

'You've been more than a friend, Dingus. We'll cool it after the night. I'll be away for a long holiday tomorrow, anyway.'

'Best thing. Fuck, I'm getting a buzz from that gear.'

'It could be her suppository or something.'

When we got back outside the bar was clearing. Tam and chubby Jennifer were poised at Eileen's side. Jennifer looked past Dingus and shot visual knives at me. As we approached, they moved off. Dingus walked on down to their company.

'Are you ready to go?'

'What's the hurry?'

'I thought you and Dingus were lost. Were you having a good laugh?'

'Bit of a one. Why?'

'What was he saying about me?'

'More to the point, what did Jennifer say to get you upset?'

'She says you have a girl up the road. She says ye're taking the piss.'

'And you believe her?'

'Should I? She says yer name isn't Frank, either.'

'What is it then? I'll get my birth certificate changed.'

'She can't remember what it is, but it isn't Frankie Davis.'

'She's full of crap. I asked did you believe her? If you do, I might as well blow.'

'I don't want ye to.'

'Look. Let's take things easy here. What's important is we like each other. I don't see this as a one night stand, I told you. Eileen, I think we can be good for each other, good friends and more. We've all the time in the world to get to know each other. I've no reason to lie about my name or anything else.'

'There's a lot I haven't told you.'

'What I do know is ye're a very attractive, warm person. I reckon you've had it rough, but we all have, sometime. Let's just have a giggle and get to know one another. See where it takes us.'

'I hope you aren't lying.'

'I can stay at your place?'

'You can, of course. As long as you stay by the rules and behave yourself.'

'Scout's honour. I just want to be near you.'

Dingus was in trouble with the management. They hadn't like his exhibition of mangled toes, and were less impressed on discovering his friendship with Tam and his ill-dressed cronies. Now he had taken a wobble and knocked over a girl's drink. Her boyfriend was up in arms and a barman came over, but Dingus was unrepentantly laughing. *In loco parentis*, I intervened, doing my sober drunk routine. Jennifer left on the arm of one of Tam's fragrant mates. We flung back a final short, under the steely gaze of the barman, and left by the side door, herself and myself dragging a stupefied Dingus between us. We deposited him in the rear seat of the car. As he slumped down I heard the rapid approach of steps behind. The Tam fella was standing with his back to the wind, like some Old Testament prophet, fresh returned from the desert. He had a wild stare on him and was breathing heavily with anger.

'Can I help you?' It was the old stand-off story. Hold me back or I'll hit him. Any kind of fighting man would never give me the chance. He could have come from behind, but here he was, heaving on the spot, two bedraggled mates some way behind, shuffling, almost embarrassed as he stood fuming. He was falling at the last fence, I thought. While I'm not one for fisticuffs, I had enough liquid fortification and suppressed stress within me to tear him to pieces if need be. I was on a ridiculous high.

'You're not staying at the flats tonight, chief.'

'I didn't realise you owned the place, Tam. Get in the car, Eileen.'

She got in, and I made to leave. He stepped forward, and I turned, flexed to have a go as he was just in range. It became clear I wouldn't have to.

'Listen, man. That's my girl you have there. Why don't you clear off?'

'She's big enough to make her own mind up, Tam. Let's say you and me talk about it?'

'There's nothing to talk about. Just you get out of the picture.' He was an inch off tears.

'I don't want to fight with you, Tam. And you certainly don't want to fight with me.'

I was too close to him. When you get to optimum range you should attack. I had the comfort of Ronan's pop gun in my pocket, and my thumb flicked the dinky safety catch off. A piece of tin, made no doubt in Hong Kong, but plenty to scare this fool with. He moved to push me and I stepped back, freeing the pistol from my pocket. He didn't notice it, blinded by frustration and confused thinking. Under the foul clothes and offensive language, he was a big baby, with the same emotions and problems as the rest of us. There would be no trouble.

'Has Dingus said anything to you, Tam?'

'Like what?'

'Like not to mess with me? He should have told you to steer clear of me, if you value yer kneecaps.'

'Hard man, eh?'

'A lot harder than you'll ever be, Tam. Now run on home. You'll feel better in the morning.'

I was sure that had taken care of it. Street diplomacy, fuelled by drink, but it would have the desired effect. I returned the gun to my pocket and moved to the car. That's when he jumped me, a flailing fist sinking into my neck, spinning me forward over the car door. Eileen screamed as he landed on me, all jabbing angles and suffocating weight. He was pulling to get my arm up my back and had a forearm around my throat, fingers scrabbing my right ear.

Fighting for breath, I managed to dig him in the ribs with my elbow and shifted most of his weight over to the right side. His hand was now clamped on my face, and he was grunting in my ear. He raised himself to land a blow and I got a positive elbow to his stomach which lifted him fully off my body. I scrambled out from under him, and found him back on his feet, kicking. My left hand went to shield my face, and my knuckles got a bootful of venom. Putting weight on my left foot, I dived for safety, hectically springing out of range, but he was fast and back into me before I could regain my stance and turn. A pummelling fist flashed into my face and a swift, long kick found my thigh. He backed off a step, squaring up with his fists making small circles in the air, winding himself up. From the corner of my eye, I caught sight of his mates. One of them was arguing with Eileen, the other nervously keeping watch for police. I began to see my predicament.

'Come on, hard man. Do your stuff.'

There was no option but to move forward. The piece in my pocket was practically useless now, for he would have me before I retrieved it. I threw a futile kick at his balls, which fell short by a mile, and he was in punching; hard-knuckled, pounding punches which stung the strength out of my right arm, numbing it, shocking my chin-bone and rattling the side of my head. I drove my head hard into his chest and flicked it back up, catching his chin and momentarily driving him back, but his foot came in seeking my groin, stabbing and burning the side of my thighs. In desperation, I grabbed him high around the waist and lifted him in a crush, squeezing for dear life, till his breathing became ragged. He could only pound on my back and drive his knees up into my crotch, but I held tight, using my extra poundage to meld him to me in a vice which was bursting my own brain and sending dull pains up my arms. He struggled to bring us to the ground, but I was fighting as for life itself, and knew I had to keep him on his feet, struggling and straining. He yanked at my hair but couldn't get a grip on the short roots, and with a last summoning of strength I put every muscle into the grip, squeezing the very life out of him, finally throwing him away in a release which sent him sprawling to the ground a yard away. As he rose, I charged, and delivered a foot clear into his left eye, which sent him rolling, and a second kick which crashed into the back of his head seemed to stop him in his tracks. I was moving in for another go, when his mate came in on top of me. I had no strength left to fight him, but he held off, slabbering and restraining, palms upraised. He was trying to call a halt, but by then Tam was on his feet, and back tearing in. He caught me with a swipe to the head, and I felt a tooth tumble onto my tongue in a blood sauce. He got a second poke in before his mate dragged him off, and I simply folded into a shop doorway, crawling in a defeated bundle into the wet tiles, searching belatedly for the gun. I heard a scream, and got an earful of obscenities directed at me, but I was in too bad a way to make sense of it all. I had the feeling I was losing blood. Vitality seemed to be pouring down my legs in a warm, interminable flow, and my insides were filled with burning pain.

How long I lay there, I cannot say. It was probably no more than minutes, but it felt like a lifetime. It sounds corny, but for a moment I was with Spinkey. He was beside me, grinning craftily, like a fox that got the chicken, and he was chuckling at my plight. I even laughed myself. He seemed so real, so healthy, but strangely different. In the dark of the doorway, he was shining, not ethereal, but a natural light was around him, sunlight, as if we were young and going off to school on a summer's day. As I opened my mouth to speak to him, someone hauled me up by the arm, pulled me from the doorway and helped me out onto the street. I wanted to go back to the doorway, to my old friend, but they wouldn't let me. Rather, they shoved me into the car. I couldn't take my eyes off the porch, even as I agreed to drive, and turned the ignition. A girl's hand helped me steer and a pair of voices kept talking to me. I was answering in monosyllables and noises. As my mind cleared I followed the instructions; the road was clear, but unrecognisable, and we came to Eileen's house.

She asked me if I was all right. I was still trying to put her face in the scheme of things, but played along with her. Why shouldn't I be all right? Slowly it dawned on me that I was bleeding. My lip was cut. My gums were grotesquely raw, like liver in my mouth, my arms and coldly wet legs were pulsating. Gradually it came back to me. In the rear seat Dingus was sound asleep, snoring. The girl was looking at me, trembling with concern.

'They won't be back for another hour. You can't stay here tonight, Frankie.'

She had an angry weal on her temple, and her eyes were surrounded by glowing flesh. She was calling me Frankie. No one gets my name right.

'Did you see Spinkey tonight?'

'What? Who's he?' She looked at me as if I had two heads.

'Forget it. Who hit you?'

'Who do you think hit me? Are you being smart?'

'Tam, was it?'

'They've gone to a party, but when he gets back I don't want you here. He'll kill you, I swear.'

'I think I've died already. Is Dingus all right?'

'He had no part in it. He wouldn't help you in a fit. Jesus, Frankie, if I had know this was going to happen ... he's a madman.'

'I should have kept my mouth shut.'

'It was him that started it.'

'What was it about, anyway?' I was acting the goat at this stage.

I kept thinking of Spinkey, of Bricks. Visitations from beyond. Would I see Bricks on this side of the great divide? I needed someone to talk to, needed a friend badly, and all I had was this mixed-up, game-playing woman, who didn't know me from Adam, and a kipping drunk in the rear seat.

'Do you want the bad news?'

'I haven't had the good news yet.'

'The good news is I got ye home in one piece. The bad news is, I've pissed myself.'

'You what? Jesus, Frankie, that puts the tin hat on it.'

'Help me inside till I get cleaned up, will ye?'

'I want no more trouble tonight, understand?'

'Ye'll have trouble holding yer breath if I don't get me legs under a running tap. Now get me inside and cut out the cackle.'

Inside, I put the catch on the bathroom door and stripped painfully off to survey the damage. My left sock was sopping wet, and I rinsed it first, as if decorum and scent came before my physical injuries. Apart from the odd welt and bruise, my lower body was remarkably unaffected. The insides of my thighs were raw, and would play up later, but my ribs were clear. It was the head that was the problem. The last blow had been a peach, virtually paralysing the right side of my face. I might have banged the other side going down, for it felt no better. Fortunately my eyes had escaped severe punishment, but my lips were gashed and my nose tender. It could have been worse. I could have been hit by a steamroller. Abruptly, I felt sick, and threw up a healthy feed of drink into the toilet bowl, mixed with strands of bonded blood from my mouth. It did me the world of good. I washed my mouth out, rolled rings of water down my legs to remove the urine and ease the burning skin, soaked my neck and shivered as the cold water went down my back.

There was a knock on the door.

'Are you all right?'

'Why wouldn't I be?' My voice sounded odd to me, slurred and watery.

'Can I come in? I have something for ye.'

'Just a minute.'

I chucked my damp trousers and underwear in the bath and ran some water over them. When I let her in I had the famous shirt wrapped around me as best I could to protect my modesty. She had a pair of jeans in her hand.

'Are those Tam's?'

'I'm afraid so. They might not fit you.'

'I'm not sure I want to wear them. If he goes that mad over a shirt, what's he liable to do over a pair of jeans?'

'Ye'll have to wear them if you're going home.'

There was a mellowness about her. The excitement had gone.

'What's it like to have two men fighting over ye?'

'It's very flattering. I wish it hadn't happened, that's all. I should have told you what he was like.'

'You told me. I didn't listen. You're worth fighting over.'

'Will ye make a habit of it?'

She was standing in the bathroom, a dreamy look on her face, and a sway to her body. She turned and locked the door. I kissed her politely on the mouth, not knowing what reception it would get. She came closer, and my arms went around her, the shirt hitting the floor. She firmly brushed my arms aside and stroked my face, my chest, then lower, tracing circles on my legs, then up. She didn't let me touch her, but gently, smoothly stroked and kneaded, her eyes closed, head rolling back, until I began to relax and play the game, giving her control and shifting to let her grip increase and the pleasure multiply until I came fast and quiet onto her clothes, head wrung with alternating currents of pleasure and pain. She kissed me deeply.

'Ye're a mess.'

'I was trying to clean up.'

'Now I'll have to clean up, ye messer.'

'Can I stay tonight?'

'If ye're quiet.'

'You won't hear boo out of me.'

When she had left I sat on the side of the bath trying to regain my mind. Try as I might, my brains refused to function as I wished them to. I wanted to be scared or angry, to get up and do something constructive. There was no safety for me here. It was as if I were inviting trouble. But inside I was calcified, as dead as the cold enamel beneath me. Tired, I dressed as best I could, leaving my trousers and underwear to dry over the bath. I went slowly to her room. She was already beneath the covers, wearing her housecoat over a nightdress.

'Will you be warm enough?'

'Lock that door tight and get into bed. Straight to sleep ... nurse's orders.'

'What about Dingus?'

'He's down in Tam's room. If anybody knocks on the door tonight, just ignore it. I can have who I like in my room.'

'And ye like me?'

'I'm not sure. Do you think I do that with everybody?'

'No. It was nice.'

'It's all you'll get tonight, mister. Now get into bed.'

In the dark I cradled her and pretended to sleep. Each move brought protest from my tender and broken regions, and soon my mind was swooping off to the frontiers of agony. She tried to talk to me, but I played possum, afraid to speak. Pretending sleep, I soon fell into it, thinking I was still pretending, and Monday crept up on Sunday and quietly deposed it.

Monday came in West Belfast with a steely grey shawl wrapped around its shoulders as it coughed and shrugged itself to life. Taxis, cars and vans formed a casual, yawning stream which grew to a torrent, joined by the crowds of workers heading to factory and office.

Claire O'Brien woke to join them, another wrapped-up girl in the stream, lost in her own thoughts. She had spent a hard night tossing in a fitful sleep, dodging the swarm of black thoughts racing through her dreams, and now she hurried on to work, to get in early and immerse herself in toil, that she might find relief.

Bradley was half-way through his rounds when he called into the timber-yard and told the foreman I'd be gone for a while. He was an old soldier himself and knew not to ask any questions. Bradley then stopped off at Murphey's café, where Mo was resting up. Over tea and toast they discussed the night's raids and totted up the damage. The raids were only starting, and the damage was minimal, with none of Mo's actives being scooped.

The raid at my house had proved fruitless, but seven men had been lifted in and around the estate. Three of them were Bricks's associates, all of them non-movement. A couple of people who knew me, the others friends of Ten-to-One; an information trawl carried out in the early hours, rather Eastern Bloc, if you were to experience it. They raided when the community was at its most disabled, between four thirty and five thirty in the morning, hours of deep sleep and least fuss. None of those arrested were later charged, but the swoops would continue in the days ahead. These swoops were what kept the revolution going in its darkest hours. They caused immense discomfort and turned many a man to resistance. While they provided the British war machine with a valuable picture of the nationalist areas, they gave the revolution a reciprocal boost.

By nine o'clock Mo had a clear and not unsatisfactory picture of the night's plunder. There was no structural or material damage to his people. The week's plans could go ahead. Mo was more concerned about my presence in the city.

'Get Ronan to take another run over to this kip. Tell him to make sure the boy gets on the road to Dublin. We should have done more to get rid of him last night.'

'According to Ronan he's in no hurry. It might be no bad thing if he stopped over. From what I hear, they're going bananas looking for the escaped prisoner, the country boy. They should be easing off the roadblocks after the day.'

'It depends. They're still smarting from it. It's the Lone Ranger that worries me. He never was the great one for following orders to the letter. I've plans for him, though.'

'Border-wise? Has he the bottle for it?'

'He got himself out of a nice jam this weekend, and he did it well. I hand him that. He has a good head, and now we see how far he can go. He may be blown out in the city, but the boys down the country might use him.'

'His ould fella was round at my house yesterday morning. With Betty McGinn no less. The charge of the geriatric brigade.'

'I heard his father was sympathetic once. Before my time, I'm afraid. If it happens again, tell them we aren't running a lost and found office. Make sure the blackguard is out of town today, and we must have the Fiesta back before Thursday. Make sure he knows that.'

'If that's all, I'll be leaving ye.'

As Bradley carried on with his rounds he met Big George and wee Barry on their way to work. He had heard George was knocking up Tommy's wife.

'Ye're late today, boys. Were ye out with ould bad women last night?'

'I can only talk for myself, Bradley. George might have been, but not me.'

'Is that right? Ye'll be getting married, George, by the sounds of it. Ye'll have to wait for the divorce first, from what I hear.'

'You hear too fucking much, Bradley. Ye must have ears like Dumbo the fucking elephant.'

'Aye. And I mean to keep them separated with me head.'

'You get on and deliver yer juice, Bradley. It's all ye're good for.'

Bradley laughed aloud. 'Christ, George, this true love hasn't done yer temper any good.'

'On yer float, ye slagging bastard.'

'Have a nice day, boys.'

As he drove along, a British duck squad came bobbing down past him. The stocky corporal at the front called, 'All right, Milky?'

'Powerful, captain, sir. Never better.' They walked on urgently past him.

It was the same most mornings. Same corporal, same greeting, same charade. Politely letting him know they knew. That Brit was good at his job. He would just as politely have blown Bradley away, if it had been allowed.

As they walked on, Bradley noticed the tail-end gunner on the right side of the patrol was taking six steps with his eyes to the front, just one facing backwards. The corporal ought to pick him up on that. He was the eyes in the back of their collective head, and wasn't making a great job of it. Tut, tut, old bean. Do ye think this is Salisbury fucking Plain, or what? That could get you killed, thought Bradley, as he placed a crate of empties on his float.

At home, mother packed brothers one and two off to school. No one had slept much in our house, just rested, apprehensively awaiting the arrival of the British search-party. Even my old man, drunk as a newt, was unable to snore it off. If anything, drink had exacerbated his fretting, and he was fully dressed beneath the blankets when the Brits landed in, thumping the door in the early morning. Time was when they would have put a sledge-hammer through the door as a starter, but they were growing diplomatic. There was no hope that I'd be there, and the raid was a formality, the kid brothers having had plenty of time to make the house politically antiseptic, as my old man always wished it to be. (My father had once copped me with a clip of 9mm ammunition and a yard of Cordex in my room. After that, and the thrashing I got, I never kept gear in the house for more than a few hours.)

By the time the Brits had confirmed the inevitable, my old dear had gone into a fainting spell, the old fella had gone into a slagging match with a Scottish trooper, and the two brothers were sitting smirking at the good job they had done. Only my little sis got through it with anything approaching dignity, being tiredly resigned to having to pick up the pieces when the invasion ended. This wasn't the first time, wouldn't be the last. It was the least dramatic and destructive sortie to date at our place. The floorboards remained unlifted, and no overall damage was done to the house's integrity. Under the circumstances, the Brits were almost gentlemanly.

They could hardly lift the two young cubs, and the old man didn't look to be much of an intelligence asset, so they mounted up and tore off through the knots of assembled, glowering neighbours who had come to stand witness. If a Brit fed a dog, a crowd would gather to see if it had been poisoned. If the dog enjoyed the treatment, they'd mark it down as a collaborator.

My father and his long suffering wife set about reorganising the house, she and my sister putting ornaments and fixtures back into place, he manfully answering the concerned queries from the neighbours. All the time they flashed recriminating glances at one another. They had long ago fallen out of love, and now went through the motions for the sake of ourselves, to protect their identity in the community, to ensure their place in Catholic heaven.

My parents were of farming stock and had gravitated to the city just before the Second World War, my father following the work. They were the inheritors of nothing save the faith and the music, and that was what they wished to leave us. Divorce was not a consideration. Marriage guidance or such would be shameful. They were indivisible after the sacrament, destined to walk together unto death, or to drive each other there. As children came and further enhanced their poverty, the marriage deteriorated. I do not know, nor care to guess, the process by which it decayed, but by the time the sister appeared, they no longer slept together, and communicated with each other in gruff, elemental words that spoke of lovelessness and fatigue. Before me, there were three miscarriages, a family secret. Hard, good people, whom I sorely tested.

Our house always seemed to waver between open marital

warfare and guarded truce, but mine was not a particularly unhappy childhood; it was par for the course around our way, where society was poor and tough, matriarchal and masculine in contradictory doses. The roles of man and wife were set in stone, the Church policing the bedroom where the State couldn't reach. Children were a blessed burden, heightening your plight, increasing your woe.

The ghetto was an abattoir for sensitivity and compassion. Men grew up thinking women rare, treating them with outward charm and secret contempt, hiding our ignorance and fear in a panoply of duplicity and show. The woman reigned in the home, but her daughter was the hunted species, a carnal cipher. One dared not take them as friends, as confidantes, as actual people. Claire was the first woman I'd approached in a sensible, respectful fashion.

I'd always liked to keep a low profile, generating a public persona as a quiet drone who enjoyed a pint of a Friday night. It had worked well for me. For a year and a half I kept Bricks and Spinkey under control and out of the cells. We were a *ménage à trois*, and while many guessed at our individual sympathies, few would put us together as a unit. Perhaps foolishly, I had an unshakable belief in hiding in sight. We made a habit of drinking in the same pubs on the same nights, being open about our friendship. Friday nights in Archer's were religiously observed. We looked out for each other. Call it what you will, *ésprit de corps* or criminal covenant. We were mates. No victims of society, in the classical sense, and no debts to pay it either. We would have died rather than call our fight a crime.

The fly boys, the ephemeral ones, the glory boys evaporated with the years. They demanded respect by the very fact of membership, by the size of their reputations, which were often false. Joey O'Brien was of this ilk. If they never shot a Brit, they were good men to tell you how to. Then there were the other ones, the occasional head-banger, the die-for-Ireland merchants, the flag wavers. They were the guys who scared the life out of their own side. The ghetto has a way of revenging itself on those larger than its limitations. Often over the years they became shadows on the walls of bars, greasy marks on the wallpaper of time, without respect, without friends. For most of us, the movement tamed our ego. Armed and outlawed, we weren't about to parade our beliefs and connections around the streets, and any flag wavers became quickly subdued in action. Glory soon wears off. Blood will strip it.

As my old dear was nervously making breakfast across town, I was waking up to a bruise-filled morning, wondering where I was and what I'd done to deserve flagellation to the bone. Eileen was rummaging about for clothes and presented me with a cheering profile of her lace-clothed buttocks. I could detect her smell all over the bedclothes: warm, sweet and sour smell of the female awakening. I had a fleeting vision of me standing cold-footed and naked on a linoleum floor, being milked and worked into delirium. When I saw her sombre face, it all came back to me.

'Good morning. Fine and well ye're looking.'

It wasn't going to be easy. She glared at me through a swollen, vacant face.

'Did you hear that racket last night?'

'I didn't hear a thing. Slept like a log.'

'Tam was up battering the door. I'm surprised it stayed on its hinges.'

'I'm well pissed off with Tam boy.'

'What am I going to do with this eye? It's like a beetroot.'

I held out my hand. She looked at it, but turned away.

'This will be all the talk at work.'

'It's not so noticeable. You'll get away with it.'

'You can stop being nice now. You've had your bed for the night.'

'What's that to do with anything?'

'That's all you wanted, wasn't it? Somewhere to bunk up and maybe get your creature comforts?'

'Maybe. Why take it out on me? I didn't hit ye.'

'If you weren't here it wouldn't have happened.'

'That's one way of looking at it. Do you want me to go?'

She was on the edge of the bed, holding back tears.

'Do what you like. I've work to go to.'

I creaked myself over towards her and put a hand on hers. She turned to me. The eye was well blacked and detracted a great deal from her appearance. She was pouting.

'Can we still be friends?'

'I slept with you, didn't I?'

'Sounds like I did the sleeping.'

'Good job, too. You had your hands all over me last night.'

'I should have warned you. I've more hands than an octopus.'

'It's well you were hurt, or I would have kicked you out on the floor.'

'Would you, now?'

'I would, too.' We kissed, slow and warm.

'You could use some toothpaste, boy.'

'I could use a wheelchair.'

'Is it really sore?'

'A sore thing is a sore thing.'

'At least it will take the friskiness out of you.'

'Take more than a hiding for that.' She broke away.

'I've work to get to. Let yourself out.'

'Fair dues.'

'I'll see you tonight?'

'About nine o'clock.'

'Come earlier.'

'What about Tam?'

'I'll have a word with him on the way out. He'll listen when he's sober. But you'll have to call it quits. If you come over here, we can't have fighting all the time.'

'Far as I'm concerned, the best man won. He made his point. Is it all over between you two?'

'What do you think? Would you be here if I wanted him?'

‘I’m not exactly a prize catch, am I?’

‘You’re worth two of him. Because he beat you doesn’t make him the better man. Just an animal. When ye’re leaving, be quiet when you pass his room. Nine o’clock at the latest. Do you promise?’

‘Scout’s honour.’

‘I’m not sure about them scouts.’ She stopped in the doorway.

‘I will see you tonight, won’t I?’

‘Believe it. Don’t work too hard.’

When she was gone, I once more nosed through her belongings. The bag of loose tablets was missing, but the powder remained. Further investigation turned up a set of photos of herself and Tam dearest on the beach. Eileen and myself would have been well matched. She was a chancer like me. I doubt if she believed the guff I’d told her. Living on hope. There was nothing dishonest in the little operation she’d performed in the bathroom though. Tender and sudden, but how much of it was penance? She had used me as a sounding board, to confirm her value in Tam’s eyes. I was an accident, an available body. Jesus, now she wanted the whole works. And I’d played her. I had no more intention of turning up tonight than I had of turning myself in. I retrieved my clothes from the bathroom. The trousers were still redolent of my little accident the night before, but I wasn’t about to wear Tam’s cast-offs. Eventually I found my original shirt, and doddled down the stairs. I made a sharp left into Tam’s room.

He was alone, sitting propped up on the pillows, smoking his first cigarette of the day, and I could see him tighten at my entry.

‘I didn’t hear you knock.’

‘I’m sorry, bwana. You pack a mean punch.’

‘She says I’m to be sorry to ye. I was out of order.’

‘Do ye feel sorry?’

‘I’m sorry ye’re not dead.’

‘I feel like I ought to be.’

‘Well. If that’s all we have in common, you can close the door on the way out.'

'Fair's fair, Tam. Just one wee thing.'

I took the .22 from my pocket and pointed it at his head. He sat bolt upright in the bed, his hands up and quivering like a black-and-white minstrel. Behind the straggling hair his face drained of what little colour there was in it. He began jibbering and swearing, now on his knees among the bedclothes, his eyes fixed on my hand, trying to judge the direction of my shot, which seemed committed to ending up in his face.

'I could a done you last night, Tammy boy. I could a put one in your lousy head an' saved myself a beating. You won't be so lucky next time. Is that clear to ye?'

'It's clear, it's clear.'

'Go back to sleep, Tam. You want to look after yourself. Oh, I'll be back tonight around nine. I don't want to see you here then, or ever again for that matter.'

'I'll be gone. Is that the end of it?'

'It is for me. Be seeing ye, Tam.'

Dingus was in the kitchen, which stank of dope.

'I'm off now, Dingus.'

'Was there a fight last night?'

'Bit of a one.'

He smiled to himself, dreamily.

'I'll see ye when I see ye.' I turned to go.

'Hold on. I'll get a lift off ye.'

'Best not, Dinger. Like we were saying last night, best go our own ways.'

'Don't be like that, man. Have a drop of vodka before ye go.'

'I'll be seeing ye, mucker.'

Dingus was slipping off the cliff. If I'd seen it, chances are I would have let him go. I had my own troubles. As it was, he was clinging by a finger-tip, and no one saw it. He was dopey Dingus, gargler and piss artist extraordinaire. He always survived. An institution among his friends and peers. But he didn't have any friends. He had me. Vodka and dope in the cradle of the day, the boy about to drown, and I didn't see it. I was watching for myself, and didn't see the tiredness in his expression. What I saw was Dingus being Dingus in a Dingus way.

The car smelt of piss for some reason, but I drove on, machismo restored, wounds feeling better and the prospect of getting to safety in front of me. Oblivious to all but my own needs, and my lucky touch. It was a good morning to be up and about.

CHAPTER FIVE

IT WAS TEN by the time Joey O'Brien woke. He stretched himself on the bed and jumped up to shake off the languor and the remote lust which piled up on him of a morning. He was in his shorts at the kitchen sink when the whine of Rolls Royce engines filtered in off the street and the door was roughly knocked.

Only rent men and peelers had that knock. There was a soldier standing in the back garden, looking at him in a non-committal way. Joey nodded to him, holding his fear and surprise within, more curious than alarmed. The thumping at the front door grew louder. He grabbed a pair of jeans and took his tea and a sandwich to the door. On the step was a Brit, a wee bear of a man, standing alongside a plain-clothes peeler whom he knew only too well. Out on the street were a pair of armoured Rovers, and he craned his head past the intruders to see the top of the road blocked off by a Saracen. Undoubtedly they had the other end sealed as well. The peeler smiled at him in recognition.

'Long time no see, Joe.'

'Not fucking long enough, Harry. I thought you'd be dead by now.'

The policeman's smile, thin at best, wore off.

'We are authorised to search this house, Mr O'Brien. We would appreciate your co-operation.'

'Ye had better come in before someone shoots ye.'

Five of them were in through the door before he'd offered the invite. Joey's head went into overdrive, computing the possibilities. The only thing of any use to them was the shooter in the pantry. Only one guy knew he had it, and he could never be taken for a tout. This was either lucky-dip time or something more sinister. He flopped over the cushions on the sofa, flicked through a few old newspapers on the kitchen table, then went out to the back garden, where he spoke to the young Brit who was covering the door. The soldier took out a smoke and offered it to him as they chuckled and spoke. Upstairs, he found the sergeant and his pet policeman hunting through the bedrooms in a desultory manner. Joey picked up on the relaxed style of the invasion. The Branchman came into his bedroom and looked around.

'Where have you the guns, Joe?'

'Buried in the back garden, Harry. It could do with a bit of digging if ye have the time.'

'Who's living with ye now?'

'That's none of your fucking business.'

'Mind the language, Joe. I'm only doing my job. We were told you had an arsenal in here.'

'Well, you were told wrong, Harry boy. Do ye not know we're political now?'

'I saw ye were up for the council a while ago. You'd make a good councillor, Joe. Is it a sister ye have?'

'What if I have?'

'Ye can come with us and have a yarn up in the barracks or ye can answer me civilly. It makes no odds to me.'

'The sister is the only one that stays here.'

'That's the idea. That's all I was asking. Is she working?'

'There's nobody works up here, Harry. Don't ye know we're all on the dole.'

'All doing the double, ye mean.'

The Brit was standing in the doorway.

'Nothing here, inspector.'

'In that case, we'll be off. Sorry to have got ye out of bed, Joe.'

'That's fair enough, Harry. Sure, ye're only doing yer job.'

'You've got fierce sarcastic over the years, Joe. Ye want to mellow out a wee bit. Ye'll get so sharp ye'll cut yerself.'

In the front room the young Brit and the peeler were mumbling to themselves. The trooper was staring up at the Sacred Heart picture over the fireplace, staring in a fascinated way, as if it were the first one he'd seen. Joe felt a rising of the old anger within, and fought to subdue it. In a minute they were saddled up and gone. The whole operation had taken barely a quarter of an hour. A flying visit.

Standing in the doorway, Joey felt the sweat drying on his bare back in the late autumn draughts, and crammed his hands into his jeans pockets to stop the shaking. For a while he nodded and joked with the neighbours who were out in force, curious as to the score. When they were assured that all was well, they drifted back to their cleaning and shopping. It was a ruffle in the ghetto's grey dress, nothing more than a cheeky piece of fishing on the part of the State, a petty, misdirected incursion. Joey closed the front door and went to the pantry. The old hiding place had been well tested down the years, and even a full scale demolition raid would probably have missed it. This had been a gentlemanly affair. Harry the Hat just calling for a chat. Fat chance. All the old suspicions came back. He raced through the bedrooms, looking here, looking there. Downstairs, he scoured and probed. Nothing planted, nothing missing. Just as he predicted. A single, solitary reason. It was me they were after, Claire's lover boy. And now they had Claire on the player's list, they would be back. If not that night, then another. When they got a bite, they never let go. Once you were on the files, you were never off them. Joey felt his temper redirecting itself, and his anger now focused on his young sister.

When he left the house that morning it was with a revolver in his waistband and a sense of purposeful anger he hadn't felt in years. The neighbours watched him go, and remembered who he was. Sticky Joe, hard man. They wondered who was in trouble.

At the gates of the local barracks Inspector Harry Grange talked to two detectives who were waiting for him.

'The house is clean. Only the two beds slept in from what I could tell.'

'Maybe he was shacked up with her?'

'In a good Catholic house like that? With mad Joe next door? Anyhow, here's a picture of her that slipped into my pocket. That looks like the quare fella with her.'

'That's him, all right.'

It was a photo taken at a party. Her mate, Angela, had gone snap-happy that night. I was always camera shy, but that night the drink was in and the wit out. Claire inveigled and slagged me into posing with her. It was the time we were getting close, when we both started to feel there might be more to it than a laugh and a hug, when contented silences settled into our talk and the need to impress had gone. Around the time we began to feel there was no hurry, that we could see each other the next evening, without having to ask or plan, without any fear of rejection. It had been barely a month before, me with a big drunken grin and an arm around her, the snap now doing the rounds of the circle of policemen.

'She's a fine looking girl.'

'She'd be a bit skinny for you, Albert.'

'Word is she works in Parker's factory. Want us to dander down and ask her about the company she's keeping?'

'Go down and keep an eye on her,' said Grange. 'Keep a distance, though. The man himself might turn up, although it's unlikely. I keep getting the feeling he's still in town. If he is, I want the bastard.'

Downtown, I was tying up the loose ends of a bloody weekend, preparing to leave town. I had parked the car well beyond the controlled zone, away off on a loyalist side-street, and had sat for a while, taking stock. There was no good reason for me to be in town; a thousand reasons why I shouldn't be. Gradually it dawned on me that the sense of almost euphoric invincibility was something of a shock-induced illusion, a compensatory fantasy put up by the mind to block out the pain, the dread. While I sat there, my body ached with fatigue and assault, my brains scrambling and unscrambling, thoughts rushing to the edge of unreality and back again. Spinkey was dead. Spinkey would be at work by now. The police were looking for me. The police hadn't heard of me. In and out, around and around, from the strangest dreamy thoughts to the most mundane observation.

I must have sat there for an hour before I settled down, before I wrenched myself into reality, forced myself out and on. At the first clothes shop I came to I got some new gear, unfussily selecting a pair of black trousers and a sweatshirt plus underwear. I changed in the shop and dumped my stained clothes in the nearest litter bin. In a chemist's shop near by, I used their booth to get a set of passport snaps, choosing the one snap that looked least like me. Disposing of the others, I proceeded to knock up a reasonably decent driving licence using gum and fountain pen. It was never going to get me into Buckingham Palace, but would almost certainly get me past a road-check.

When I rang Claire at work it was after twelve. I'd a good, greasy breakfast in me, looked considerably sharper than I'd done since the Saturday night, had a few quid in my pocket and a passable piece of identification. If I was still a bit tremulous inside, I could at least be fairly confident.

Reception patched me through, and when she answered the phone I couldn't recognise her voice.

'How are you?'

'I'm not talking to you.'

'I can't blame you. Will you let me talk?'

'There's nothing for you to say. Look, I'm busy. Goodbye.'

Thus goes the world. Nothing cruel, nothing hard. Polite, efficient. Hanging on the phone, crushed and fearful, I felt hard done by. It's impossible to see yourself through the eyes of another at the best of times, and I felt I'd had more than my fair share of grief and pain that weekend without her heaping on more. At that moment, she became the only one I cared for, the only one I wanted to see, to hold.

I had done nothing wrong, nothing seriously wrong anyway. What the hell had she to be upset about, put against myself? It took me three calls and a series of long waits before I got her back on the phone.

'Listen. We can't leave it like this.'

'I said I'm busy.'

'If I told you I love you?'

'You don't know what the word means.'

'Lunchtime in Rockley's bar. I'll wait for you.'

'You can wait, but I won't be there.'

'Then I'll wait. I must see you before I go away.'

'Goodbye.'

None of us are the people we set out to be. We all end up becoming the people we laughed at, like a glove turning inside out, so slowly over the years.

I needed her, needed her desperately, needed her to understand, to accept. I needed a face that would look at me as I looked at myself. That would see some good beneath the fear and the lies, something of value beneath the terror. I needed my own worth confirmed, that day more than ever, and she was all that was left to me.

The only others were in jail or dead, or up the Falls Road beyond my reach. *Sans* friend, *sans* family. Endlessly selfish, possibly mad. Who could I talk to other than her; from whom receive the answers I needed to the questions I dared not ask myself?

I went back to the car, wrapped the tiny handgun in a plastic bag and stuffed it down the upholstery in the back so that it rested behind the rear seat, hidden but available. I walked back into the city centre, cautiously watching for police patrols.

Not for the first time that week I thought of my father. He must believe I was free and safe. Of that I was glad. He must have been through much of this himself, must have been ducking and diving through the city as a young married man. What on earth had he told my mother? She was the model of Catholic womanhood, seemed to be the wee, quiet family woman, and I couldn't see her putting up with his antics. How had the old bugger managed it? He must have been a bigger liar than I was; and she must have known, must have suspected.

For it all, I never had heard him say one seditious remark, or utter a patriotic phrase. When he had driven me from the house, his face had been flushed with disappointment and impotence as much as anger. Having done his best to raise me clear of the war, he had taken my call to arms as a personal failure, the ultimate rebuke for his sacrifice and efforts. It must have been no joke raising a family, grabbing work where he could, cutting the cloth to fit. He had been tight-fisted and cute, running his family on the old adage, 'save a match, buy a car'. Behind it all was a man who had once been a dreamer. Certainly one who had believed, who had had hopes. In those days of the '56-62 campaign, he had been one in a thousand, working against the wishes and mood of the Catholic people, who had still had faith in evolution, in their elders and betters.

Perhaps he and I were more alike than I cared to admit. At that moment, entering the dark warmth of Rockley's pub, I felt a yearning to sit the old man down and beat the truth out of him, demand to know what he knew, how it had gone with him, even to become what he was, to think as he thought. Just then I longed to be with him, for once to listen, plead or threaten: father, father ... tell me what you believed in and why; why did you change, for I need advice, guidance, to survive in a town which militates against survival. And if nothing were forthcoming, I would settle for comfort, for love, or what passed for it in my fevered heart.

Two peelers sat in a car facing Parker's factory, one yawning, the other studying the card for that afternoon's jump racing. Propped on the dashboard was the photograph of myself and Claire O'Brien. As lunchtime approached the stream of workers leaving the factory gates began to gather strength. Both men studied the passing faces more keenly.

'There she is. Beside that wee podgy one.'

Claire was standing at the gates talking to Jennifer Brennan, the girl who'd almost sussed me out the night before. In fact it was Jennifer who was doing all the talking, and Claire was listening with a dry intensity, determined not to get any angrier or more tearful. The policemen studied the pair from afar, until Jennifer rambled off, calling back, 'I just thought you should know.'

Claire stood transfixed at the roadside, her features blank and pale as she struggled to decide. After what seemed an age to the watching policemen, she gave a deep sigh, tucked her hair down into the collar of her coat, turned the collar up, and walked up, then over the street, taking the narrow lane that led out to the broad avenue where old Rockley's pub stood.

Behind her came the equestrian-minded officer, strolling and reading his paper, keeping her carefully in view.

She was half-way down the lane when she met Joe coming towards her. In the shadows of the tall buildings he seemed misplaced, out of time and function, like some animal let loose from the zoo and nonchalantly padding the streets. She immediately knew there was something going on, but felt inexplicably thrilled. The only time they ran across each other was in the gritty context of the ravaged and embittered streets of the war zone. Suddenly, here he was: big brother, out for a stroll?

'All right, wee girl?'

'What brings you down here?'

'I was coming to see you. Are ye skiving off work?'

'Going for my lunch. What are you really doing here?'

'I came down to see if you were all right.'

'Why shouldn't I be? There's nothing wrong, is there?'

'We had a bit of a house-search this morning.'

'A house-search? Our house?'

'Like the good old days. Where's your boyfriend?'

'I haven't got one, Joe. Not since Saturday night, anyhow.'

'Have you given him the shove?'

'That's it. I've given him the shove.'

They stood in the laneway, a wealth of silent fear and anger between them, neither of them yielding to it.

'You're in over yer head, Claire.'

'I don't know what you're saying, Joe. I'm away for lunch.'

'Are you asking your mate along?'

'I told you, we're finished.'

'I mean that piece of trash that's following ye.'

She was confused, wondering what twist he was putting on things now, but she followed his glance to the young fellow at the mouth of the lane, sorting through his newspaper. Like them, he was stationary in the path of the shoppers and office girls.

'Do you know him?'

'Not personally. I can tell you he's police though. I'm never wrong about some things.'

'What's going on, Joe. What are you up to?'

'I'm keeping you out of the shit. They weren't after me, pet, and they didn't drop in out of the blue. They're after lover boy, and they reckon you know where he is.'

'Oh my God. What are you saying?'

'Where is he, Claire? If he's still in town he's for the high jump. I want you well away from him. Now, you tell me and do it quick.'

'Will you go and see him? Will you give him a message from me?'

'I'll do that. Now, where is he?'

'He's in Rockley's. Joe, don't fight with him, for my sake. Tell him I'm finished with him. Tell him to take care of himself. Will you promise me, Joseph?'

'If ye're finished with him, then there'll be no point in fighting. Get yourself back to work, and go to Auntie's house tonight. Stay there for a few days.'

'Promise me, Joe.'

'I only want him out of town. Now, you get going, and take that ugly bastard with you.'

The policeman had seen a photo of Joe O'Brien at the morning briefing. He looked twice as nasty in real life. As the girl passed him, heading back the way she had come, he opted to follow her. Joe was staring down the lane, straight at him, unflinching aggression in his stance. There was no point in following him. If anyone hated the Provos more than the cops, it was Joey O'Brien and his mob. No, he would settle for an easy afternoon keeping tabs on his wee sister. As she walked past, head down and rapid, he fancied he heard her snuffle. He waited until she had cleared the lane, folded his paper and walked to the top of the lane himself. He could feel O'Brien's eyes in his back. Out in the street, his comrade picked him up in the car.

'Well?'

'She met big brother down the lane. Neither of them is too pleased with life.'

'She was crying a bit when she came back out. Do ye think he warned her off?'

'You can be sure of it. Whatever Harry Grange says, this is a waste of time. But we may as well hang about and see does she get us anywhere.'

'We've finally got her works number monitored. If the wee prick rings, we'll get a fix on him.'

'Maybe he's rung already. Strikes me this boy is always one step ahead.'

'They always start that way. Thing is, they never stay ahead. We always catch up in the long run.'

The young detective looked at the photograph on the dashboard.

'Yeah. He's a length ahead, but we're coming up on the rails.'

His companion looked at him strangely. 'Something like that, I guess. Are you sure you didn't apply to join the Mounties? Ye're more into horses than anything else.'

Rockley's was a draughty great box of a place, full of vulgar Victoriana and journalists about as old and even more vulgar; a garish labyrinth of twisted, gilded pillars and high, moulded ceilings. The barmen wore looks of solemn, informed servility to match their aprons and arthritis: butlers to the city merchants and the semi-famous – solicitors, local television personalities and visiting English financiers who wanted to drink in the 'real' city, a relic of supposedly better times. Antiseptic and safe, frequented by enough 'characters' to keep the circus going, it was without the animals. Its one advantage was that it was always busy, morning to night, and a man could get lost in it. There was also no shortage of conversation, as I found out. I had barely ordered a pint when I was buttonholed by an old wastrel who insisted on giving me a science lesson. The weather had never been the same since they sent up 'them saddle-ites', no, sir. And had I noticed the rain these days: not like it was years ago; a lot dirtier, more acid.

'What do you think, young fella?'

'You could be right, ould hand.'

I was waiting for her, feeling sick with expectancy every time the door opened. I had no idea what to say to her, what to tell her. I was in the habit of lying about my feelings, a habit far too useful and much too ingrained to be easily overthrown in a moment of weakness. I'd never given love much thought: women were for fun. For the most part the girls I knew understood that, and they approached men in the same way. They were even more ruthless in the pursuit of a laugh and a bit of experience. But this girl was really different, really under my skin. I knew that if she came, she would bring some answers with her, in her eyes, on her mouth, in her smile or her frown. Salvation? Was I after that?

Internally, I was ripped into bloody fillets, the shock and torment now absorbed, the bravado draining away, insecurity sneaking in to replace it in the heart. I knew it was vital to get out, to head southwards. But if she came, that would be something. Something to hang on to, to remember. Something to come back for, to work towards. Something for myself, not for a country or a cause. Not for some thought, for an abstraction, not for the future generations, but for me. And if she didn't come? Shrug it off. Pretend it didn't matter. In a week she would be an issue, in a month a memory, in a year another forgotten face, a name you struggle to remember, a faint, dying feeling in the heart.

Perhaps.

Looking over the shoulder of my drunken meteorologist friend, I almost fell off my stool as Joey O'Brien elbowed through the crowd of drinkers towards me, a queer, ugly smile on his face.

A lorry crossed the border at nine o'clock that morning, through the main, direct route heavily policed by the British army. It was ostensibly no different from a hundred others that had crossed in the misty morning, and after an elementary check it was ushered on to the southern side to run through the dark forests of Louth. An hour later it parked on the edge of a sprawling, provincial town. A group of men welcomed the driver. On the quiet road they went to the rear of the vehicle, prised up the false floor and gently helped the injured man out of his compartment. He was parched and plainly ill, kitten-weak and rambling. Within the hour he was in a private room at the local hospital, a man at his bedside holding vigil. He was kept in the hospital for almost three weeks, the guard on his bedside maintained by a chain of youths, hard-looking boys, many with northern accents. The nurses grew to ask no questions of these men, who invariably claimed to be cousins of the patient.

In the North, his escape and disappearance had become history by the same afternoon; events more important and bloody had eclipsed the affair. A landmine had killed three soldiers and a civilian in Fermanagh on that Monday morning. By evening the pretence of searching for him had been given up; police and troop resources began to dissipate into other lines of enquiry, other priorities.

'Are ye buying any drink?'

'What will it be, Joe?'

'A pint of Black Label. The Guinness doesn't look too healthy.'

'Were you just passing?'

'Aye. Just passing. I didn't think you would be around. Is it not time for your winter holidays?'

'I'm on my way, Joe. Is it anything to you?'

'Nah, not really. Our one gave me a message for ye. Do ye know the Flyover bar?'

'I know it to walk past.'

'She'll be in there after work. 'Bout half-five.'

'What made her pick it?'

'It's a quiet wee spot. Ye can talk in there, get yourselves sorted out.'

'I don't follow ye, Joe. What's to be sorted out?'

'I can't say in here. The walls have ears.'

'Don't take this the wrong way, Joe. Who's fucking leg are you trying to pull? Do you think I'm walking into some Sticky pub on me todd, at your say-so?'

'I'm only giving ye the message. Strikes me you should be grateful. Ye're not exactly the safest man to be standing beside at the minute.'

'There's no one asked ye to stand there.'

'Ye're right. I'll leave the pint for now. Just a wee word to the wise, fella. Every tout in the city drinks in this place. You're not using what's left of yer brains.'

He was speaking loud, too loud and deliberately so. Even those who didn't want to hear couldn't help it. Psychological warfare.

'You head on, Joe. I'll be out after ye.'

'Will I tell her you'll be there?'

'I'll be outside the Flyover at half-five dead. Tell her that. If she isn't there, I'll be on my way.'

'You should have been on yer way last week, sunshine. It would have saved everybody a lot of grief.'

'I'll be seeing ye, Joe.'

'You will and all.'

He was gone in a trice. With his leaving, there was a chill in the air. More than a draught from the swinging-shut door. A chill inside myself, a long cold breath running through the pit of my stomach, then creeping its way around and up my spine. We were well met, Joe and I. Cut from the same brutish mould. Don't start it, but don't back down when it starts. He was obviously affected by something, and when guys like Joe get upset they take it to the end. The question was, how far down the road was he? If some guy was messing my sister about the way I was messing his, I would be going cuckoo as well. The difference was the degree to which I would take things. Women were the property of the family, and for all its matriarchal qualities the family was run for the benefit of males. Male pride and arrogance governed the family, and while a female member remained single she had the right to paternal or fraternal protection until she was safely got up the aisle, whether she wanted to be protected or not. I would go quite some way to protect my sister; I was sure Joe would go the whole hog. The evening appointment stank of a set-up. I wasn't certain, but it was a fair bet he had in mind an abrupt ending to the romance.

I tried to ring her at work to double check. The engaged signal was all I got. I left the pub at almost two o'clock and walked to where I'd left the car. I didn't see him in the doorway on the other side of the street, face deep in a newspaper. If there had been fewer people about he would have risked a shot there and then, to hell with the consequences. As it was, he had done his best. Claire had been told on the phone that her message had been delivered, that I was shot down in flames and had left. He told her not to talk to me on the phone if I rang, not that she needed much prompting. If I did turn up at the Flyover, so much the better. He could take care of me there, discreetly, permanently. If I didn't show, I'd have broken for the border. Either way, it was a fair morning's work for Joey O'Brien.

In a house down the Falls Road, Mo was sipping a cup of tea and dreamily watching the woman of the house sitting across from him as she knitted a grey woollen scarf for her youngest. He had known and fancied her for years, but there was too much history and friendship between them for anything to start. Too much respect, too many risks. Her husband had long been his friend, often his only friend. Non-movement, but sympathetic, he and his wife had regularly put themselves in jeopardy, hiding him when no others could, in days more dangerous than these. Good people, not loyal to a cause, but fanatical in their adherence to West Belfast itself, to all its diverse peoples. They would never dream of turning anyone from the door.

Months before, a British soldier had been injured in an ambush outside, on a lazy summer evening. Even as the shooting was going on she had rushed to the fallen boy, using her apron as a tourniquet, dressing his shocked body in a child's blanket. Not even the hardest voice in the street was raised against her. Decent, Christian people who didn't go along with killing, but who knew that the blame was not on the area or its people. When Mo knocked on the door, he was always received, regardless of the time or the danger.

Now she was knitting away, the needles clacking in unison, her reading glasses gradually slipping down her nose, revealing her intent brown eyes. Occasionally she would brush back her locks and take in a breath, looking up at him, smiling. He would stir himself and smile back, then pretend to resume reading the book he held loosely in his hand. Mo had had little or no home life since the advent of the conflict. He relished little moments like these, small pretences which fed his need for conformity. Until the fall of night, he was the man of the house, relaxed and native to the place, a surrogate father and husband in his own deeply buried fantasy. By the very definition of his vocation, Mo was a man acquainted with hundreds, but known to few. He held all but a tiny few at bay, seldom lowering the drawbridge to allow in those to whom he would be committed. He entertained no hope of settling down, of opting for himself over his beliefs. He could never hold down a regular civilian life and carry out the duties of command as well. Others could, but Mo knew only the war. He was married to the army, a ruthless and unsentimental guerrilla; thoroughly unscrupulous, totally pragmatic; a bedrock revolutionary devoted to the overthrow of the State.

He shrugged off the growing feeling of contentment and checked his watch. As he did so, the key turned in the front door. Bradley entered, looking tired and cold. As he warmed his red hands at the fire, the woman left her knitting and retired to the kitchen to put the kettle on. She pulled the kitchen door shut behind her. Mo's gaze had followed her every movement, and he was now staring at the closed door.

'Ronan went over to see if yer wee man went south.'

'Did he?'

'Looks like he's gone all right. We may have a problem, though. Are you listening?'

'I'm listening.'

'Turns out the door's open, so Ronan goes in and checks things out. Yer man's only put a gun to the head of some character living there.'

'Would you mind saying that slowly?'

'He's had a run in over some girl and pulls out the shooter. Seems it was just a frightener.'

'Nobody hurt?'

'Just yer man's feelings. The cops aren't involved. Ronan has yer man's name and his whereabouts. He won't be running to complain if he knows what's good for him. That other fella, Dingus Grey? He was lying over there doped out of his brains.'

'I'm getting fed up wet nursing the wee bastard. Does he think this is a bloody game, or something?'

'What I'm thinking is, he's taken the operation badly. Maybe he's gone off his head.'

'You can never tell. I should never have let him out of my sight. Has he any access to dumps?'

'He knows about the one over behind the roundabout. Will I move it?'

'Do, just in case. We won't even know if the bugger is picked up.'

Mo massaged his brow. He looked older than his age, greyer, like a man nearing the end of his best years.

'Do you ever ask yourself is it worth all the aggravation, Bradley?'

'Only every morning when I get up.'

'We still go on, though.'

'We have to go on. Sure we'd miss the crack if we didn't.'

Mo gave a grudging smile. The crack. Where would an Irishman be without the crack? That's why the Brits were on a loser. They didn't understand the crack. It wasn't in a quip, a skit or a joke. Not in a pantomime, nor a dance. It was in the air, when two or more were gathered in its name. It was the ability to laugh at a funeral, to giggle at the thought of being alive; anarchy and devilment, the native appreciation of the absurd, the hopeless; the way we arranged our lives in a ritual invitation to disaster. Mo's agitation subsided with a long breath.

'Yer man can't do much harm. I'll be down South next week. Give him a good bollocking and see what ails him. In the mean time, we have this funeral to organise ...'

Joey O'Brien arrived at the Flyover and ordered whiskey. In the dimly lit lounge he conversed with old friends and comrades. He joined in a game of darts, and began to drink heavily. By evening he was well plied with Scotch and Guinness, and his friends noticed he was much better company than usual.

Claire O'Brien asked her boss for an early departure from work. He showed concern at her nervousness and discomfort. She was a good steady worker, popular and efficient, but all day she had been preoccupied, annoyed at something. Taking early leave was out of character, so, realising it was important to her, he rapidly agreed. Gazing from his office window, he watched her slim, thoughtful form leave through the gates, small and strangely pathetic in the falling darkness.

My young brother bunked school that day and joined a score-strong body of teenagers on the waste ground down the road. From a blocked-up, burnt-out house they retrieved a cardboard box containing a dozen crudely manufactured petrol bombs. My father arrived at the school to find him missing, and spent the afternoon scouring the streets and laneways, anger and fear pounding in his heart. There was no end to it. The young lads were going the way of their brother, heading to hell in a handcart, and there was nothing he could do to prevent it. The kid brother got home in time for supper and a clout on the ear. He smelt of petrol and sweat, and provoked an almighty row in the house, my father seething and obscene in his temper, my mother frantically seeking some middle ground, some peace, my sister threatening to up and leave, stricken by the awfulness and the repetition of it all, the relentless arguing, the potential for horror that ran through our lives. My other brother smirked knowingly and held his tongue. When he looked at my father it was a look flecked with condescension and contempt. Did the old bastard not know there was a war going on?

Relentless, unremitting. The times that were in it. None could leave the past when it held such unresolved puzzles and unsettling horrors. An ambush in the ghetto. Earlier days, again. A single shot from an old Yankee Garant. A flat boom from out the window had sent the pigeons wheeling off the roofs, skittering in panic through the blue skies.

We had clambered down the stairs, piled out into the small back-yard, across the alley and in through another house, dispersing in the street beyond. I had walked briskly up to a waiting motorbike, stepped on to the back of it, rifle awkwardly clasped to my side beneath a black Derby coat. Some streets away, and into a friendly shop. Through a huddle of shoppers, out the back. Rifle passed on and away, ferried to a distant dump.

When they had gathered their senses, they had stormed the house by the front door, finding a terrified, elderly couple tied up in a back bedroom. My first and only clean shot. The result of a dozen less successful operations. We had listened eagerly to the news bulletins, and when he had been confirmed dead there were eager smiles all round. That night Mo had greeted me with a handshake and a smile. I had joined the club. Spinkey and myself went to Casey's and got quietly drunk. No one saw the excited grins we gave each other. A lad came in selling the movement paper. We waved him on and carried on drinking, later weaving our way home in good spirits. When I read his name in the next day's newspaper I felt sad. He was some mother's son, as my own mum would say. I didn't feel regret or remorse, the criminal option. Just a passing sadness at the thought of his destroyed family.

Tough. He had been a serving soldier of an occupying army. Had the operation gone wrong, he would have toasted my demise as I did his. There was nothing personal in it. We could have been friends: same age, similar background. Instead he had walked in uniform on my streets, I had lain in hiding to kill him from the shadows of a summer day. I felt no pride or joy in his passing; just a strong sense of achievement at having broken the ice, lost my virginity. I had done a good job. It was a final loss of innocence, the putting away of childish things, and there was a fragment of redemption in it. The piece of me that was dead inside was massaged by the feeling of having struck a decisive blow. Those thousand little indignities and offences were salved and paid for in a moment. He toted a gun in the streets of my people for a few hundred quid a month, immune to argument or wisdom, and he had perished on those streets. He had been doing his duty, I mine. His armed, oppressive presence on my turf had been the only mandate I required, his occupation my election.

The afternoon came and went with a sweet rapidity that saved me from going mad. To get off the streets, I joined the afternoon queue at the cinema and filed in to watch the show, the darkness hiding my mounting anxiety. I sat in vacant indifference as the screen flashed out scenes of cinematic bloodshed and images of alienation in the big city, De Niro playing the embittered and vengeful loser running on his own pain and delusion.

My mind was flinging itself against the padded walls of my consciousness, images of my own life pounding in my head, begging me to scream and thrash. Spinkey lying in a damp gutter, his head a floppy, disconnected shell, stove in and pummelled by the high velocity round. That first soldier, seeming to rise off the ground then crumple, to lie in his own gore. Two shattered corpses in the carnage of a bomb blast, flesh splayed and ripped into bloody joints of burnt meat in the firestorm. I watched two girls in the seats in front: engrossed faces lit by the screen, their features melted into the half dark. Life in the midst of death. Behind them sat a man they would run from, a man who had trodden the road to the suburbs of hell.

I had never enjoyed killing, nor had I been repulsed by it. It was the only way to assert resistance, to deny the enemy. My soldiering had been formed on the streets, the product of the failing, total war that filled the graveyards and prison camps with the best men, leaving gaps to be filled in by men like myself, men secretly unsure of the outcome, certain to carry out orders to a point, but doubtful to stay the distance. I was a five-furlong soldier in a four-mile war.

My stamina and heart lay with Spinkey in his coffin.

As I sat in the theatre I could feel my will draining away, like blood itself seeping from my heart. I began to feel that for me it was over, that I'd paid my dues, done my bit. History was surely requited. It had my sanity as a deposit for the future; it had my balls and my soul as hostage, the best years of my life. It had my humour, my potency. It had sucked me dry, and left me here, arid and dismayed, drifting in an outback of doubt and ugliness, waiting to be taken, to be seized by the enemy I had been born to face.

At five o'clock I dragged myself out onto the streets to join the throng of homegoing shoppers and workers in the uninviting city, all of them with their day done, the long night ahead.

On to the Falls Road and up. Fatalism stamped all over me, uncaring fatalism. Driving patiently in the one long stream winding out of the bowels of the city. At any point on the road I could have recalled a bitter tale. Of how so and so had fallen here. Of how this man had been shot here from a passing Unionist car; how another fella died in that corner in a feud; and that was where a woman lost her legs when an ambush went wrong. Each street corner had a tragedy appended, each door a secret and every passing face a tale to tell. War stories.

The Flyover was off the peaceline, that silver border within a border that stood testimony to our progress. A dingy little bar nestling in a row of shops standing off the main road, it had got its name from an attack on the local barracks, when a flurry of Mk.6 mortars had been fired from behind it. It had developed into a Sticky pub – that is, a haunt for the 'Official' IRA – and although I had often been in it, the underlying currents were of violence and antipathy to my sort. For a dozen reasons of history and the struggle for power, the Sticky/Provo factor constituted the most rancorous and volatile of all relationships. They hated and distrusted us with a fervour reserved for one's own, and the feelings were entirely mutual.

I drove past the place and parked the car out of sight. Then I took up position across the road and studied the building.

Five thirty came and passed, with no sign of her at the front door. If she was inside, I was in no mood to find out, love or no love. I wasn't even sure why I'd come.

Joey O'Brien was sitting on a stool, deeply drunk and lost in thought. The barman winked at him, and nodded to me as I walked in. Only a couple of sullen old boozers remained from the afternoon. At least he wasn't mob-handed; it would be man to man.

'Get this boy a pint, Charlie. This is a man I've a lot of time for. This is a man out to make history, Charlie. Do you know the sort? Boy thinks he can change the world.' Charlie pretended he didn't hear a word. He served me a pint of lager, and a whiskey for Joe.

'Put that on the slate, Charlie. I'll fix you up later. Do you know this man, Charlie? This is a friend of my family. One of the lads. This is a man much in demand, right? A good socialist and a Republican. One of the People's Army, no less!' Charlie had made himself scarce and the two old guys made ready to jump ship; it wasn't the sort of talk a Christian wanted to hear. Joey looked at me through heavy, soused eyes which gripped my own and held them. It was a gangster act from a poor film, and I was determined to stare him out.

'I've been sitting down here trying to figure out what to do with you, son. The way I see it, there's only one way to get you out of the picture.'

'You should take your chances, Joe. Every other fucker is out to get me.'

'The Brits can join the queue, son. I have you here. Why did you come? Are ye stupid as well as daft?'

'That about sums it, Joe. What are ye planning?'

'I was planning to get ye up here for a drink and a chat. Maybe blow your head off, afterwards.'

'I guessed that was it.'

'Ye still came? That's a brave man speaking.'

'Maybe it's a tired man, Joe. I've been running all weekend. I'm fed up running. I'm no hard man, Joe, but if you want pistols at ten paces I'll give it to ye.'

'What is it ye want? Really want? I've never known what I wanted, not for myself. I've never been a happy man. All I have is Claire, that's all that's left for me. Can you see how important she is to me? Can you imagine?'

'I can see it, Joe. What I don't see is what's holding you back. I expected a bullet in the head outside.'

'I'm going soft in my old age. I drink too much. It dulls the edges, puts ye to thinking, stops ye doing. You'll find it out if ye're operating as long as I was. If ye see as much crack. Ye get to the way of thinking there might be a better way, when there isn't. Are ye civilised?'

'I'm house trained, if that's what ye mean.'

'Are ye willing to reach a civilised agreement. A gentleman's agreement?'

'I'd have to see the terms and conditions. I wouldn't agree to anything I couldn't stand over.'

'Spoken like a man of honour. If it wasn't for the cunt ye're making of my family, I might even have liked you. The terms are, you walk out of here and don't look back; you have nothing more to do with Claire.'

'What's in it for me?'

'Ye don't get carried out of here, ye don't get major surgery, and ye don't get buried. Now there's a bonus for ye.'

'It's a bit one-sided, isn't it? Can I have a last word with your one before this agreement comes into place?'

'She won't entertain ye. No shit. She told me this morning.'

'Did you believe her?'

'If I thought there was no way she'd see you again, I would leave it at that. Strikes me she's open to persuasion, and that's why we're here. I want it straight in your pathetic head, sonny. The fun's over. Ye're a non-runner as far as she's concerned. Do I have to spell it out for ye?'

'Where is she, Joe? Is she at home?'

Suppressed rage released, he rounded on me.

'Steer fucking clear of her, do you hear? I've been more than patient with you, ye bastard. Now take yerself out of here and don't turn back or ye're dead.'

He had the shooter out, hanging at his side. His face was a mask of hatred and reckless temper; the beer glass had landed on Charlie's side of the bar with a crash. The barman looked on, open-mouthed, and the two old boys hustled one another out the door.

It wasn't bravery, by any means. I was shit scared, but I was fed up as well. Fed up with all the macho crap, the posturing, the play-acting, the lies and the death. I was fed up being frightened, fed up coming second-best; fed up with the unholy, miserable mess my life was becoming. And I was fed up with shit talk from the likes of O'Brien. In him I saw my future self, the bitterness, the self-pity and self-seeking behind the guise of family concern. He wasn't concerned with Claire. He was frightened for his miserable, whingeing self, imagining being unloved, living out his days alone to the sound of his own trumpet being blown over the glory that never was. I was fed up with the pain and wrestling with the submerged doubt, pushing myself to believe, to sink the awful reality into the seas of history, fed up putting things down to experience.

It was a thunderous kick to the balls I gave him. One of those sweetly connecting kicks which drive an apocalypse of suffering up into the heart and out through the mouth, carrying the very life out of the recipient. When he doubled I swung an angry right to the side of his face. It was unnecessary. He was bound for his knees when it found him, and his head went out and into the bar with an unhealthy crunch. In a second, I had his gun. He hadn't even taken the safety off. As he fought to gain his breath he tried to rise, halting when his left eye came into line with the barrel.

'You had yer chance, Joe. Now, where is she?'

'In her aunt's house.'

'Ye're in the wrong game, Joe. Out of yer depth. A year ago, you would have nailed me. There's only one agreement now, Joe. I'm going to see her, and whatever she decides, it's fair with me. You are out of the picture, Joe. Do you agree?'

He nodded.

'Let's hear ye say it, boy.'

'I agree.'

I didn't hang about. Having emptied the shooter and left both it and its load on the bar, I took off. Trying to start the car, I found my fingers playing an invisible piano, and a voice was whispering in my head, calling me 'mad, mad bloody fool'.

Weaving in and out of the estate, I drove down through the little back-streets, past the desolate waste grounds, the clearance areas for the great redevelopment, the houses and the rubble staring out at me. I was exactly where I shouldn't have been, plum in the centre of the revolution, where life was at its cheapest and most precious. In my childhood these streets had been nothing but a giant, red playground where we skipped and ran, full of mischief and exuberance, annoying the old people, amusing ourselves at their expense, little princes. Now there was no joy, no innocence, no safety. My second night on the run, gone mad and careless, no purpose save some foggy notion driving me on.

She was the last good thing I remembered. It was she who had held me in the dark, excitement-scented room where we had made love, before Spinkey had been sent into the gutter, gurgling his last, before the brutal flight from the dreadful truth. Seeking survival or death, I had found my way back into danger, stripped of any sense, bereft of logic, into the streets where better men had fallen. I had gone past the line marking indifference to best interests, indifference to life itself, where the mind snaps and the will has been played out like an old mine, exhausted and scarred by plundering. The spiritual gravity within had gone. I was floating over the city, drifting over its slashed belly, numb to all save the illogical need for some salvation, some sense or reason.

My father could have given me some answers. He must have known. The Northern world was a wilderness. The preaching, the caring and the charity, were an illusion. God had been executed and buried on a hillside at dead of night; human values remained, convenient rules to hide the ugly truth, the unmystical reality. The causes we leaned towards gave false answers to our questions. It was the limbo of the world, where the lost souls gouged and chewed each other in profane confusion. A society where the dog catcher was king, where the best were barking mad; a wilderness marked by lies and evasions, hypocrisy and sadism, by the disdain of the cunning. We had fought all the wrong battles, shot all the wrong people, and to our shame we had failed to hang the priests and the rulers, content to attack our own mirror-images. And for that we had driven ourselves mad or to the wall, had plunged into wells of clotted blood to destroy those who could destroy us, all ignorant of the other's desires, of their confusions and mistrusts; we had ploughed through flesh to achieve our fallow dreams of redemption. Blood on all our hands, none more than the hands of our rulers and our intelligentsia; on the hands of the stranger who had brought his ugliness to our land; on the wringing hands of the sin-eaters who condemned what they could not control, the hands of the media and the union bosses oiled with corruption, the hands of us all. Prod and Fenian alike, walking in a dreamworld of slender hope, where the stranger mocked our suffering by his detachment, and furnished us with reasons and weapons. We banged our heads against the wall of treacherous time, while the bloated Hibernians of the South and the sneering Queens of Whitehall condemned us from the safety of their superior 'morality'.

My father saw it for the game of cowboys that it was. That was why he had turned his back on the clarion call of West Belfast, why he sneered with anger at the constitutionalist calls for 'justice'. Justice meant war; freedom meant total war. One implied the other. Freedom? We had been sold into captivity by the Papish mandarins of Dublin, by the whiskey-sellers and altar-lickers of the North. Britain had only provided the cannon.

History found the liars and the spineless out: the Dublin effete, the Holy, Catholic and political Church, the merchants of the North. Only West Belfast cared about patriotism, about brotherhood. The rest was conspiracy, of silence, of violence, designed to do down the workers of all these islands. For your country you were to keep your head down and your Fenian nose clean, to prostrate yourself and let the industrialists, the pulpiteers, the politicos get on with it. My father had grown old and cynical, grown away from hope. When he saw all the flags and the old canards reappear, he guessed the price we would pay.

I had fought, for not to fight was to run. The community demanded its tribute, called you from every corner, from every alley and weeping wall. I had made my decision to fight for it, for its people, to respond to the pain and hatred of those around me, to resist on their behalf and on my own, to assuage the anger and humiliation that grew within, to soothe the hurt and redeem myself. I chose to stand with men and women who had raised their heads and said, 'No more, ever again.' So that I too could hold my head up, could look myself in the mirror, straight in the eye and say that I was alive.

Now I was adrift. Defeated by the sheer horror and distress at what I was becoming, I had reached the end of my belief. All I had was an emptiness inside and an obscure longing for something to fill it with, something personal, something good, to give me the will to go on, the will that these wet streets had robbed from me, these tortured, thirsty streets.

When I knocked on her auntie's door, a cheeky-looking rascal answered, a little boy of about five years old with the eyes of an angel fallen.

'Who are you? Have you come from the pub?'

'No, I haven't. I'm a friend of yer cousin Claire. Is she in?'

'You look drunk.'

'Kevin, who is it?'

She came to the door, slowly, hesitantly. It was as if she wanted to run. She looked pale and fretful, drained of blood, her life. She took the child by the hand, gripping it tightly.

'He looks drunk, Claire. Doesn't he look drunk?'

'Don't be cheeky, Kevin. Run in to yer mother. Go on, or I'll spank you.'

The child twisted his face up at me to have one departing glance. He scrutinised me, then, bored with the silence between us, he ran back into the house.

'I didn't expect to see you.'

'I thought I'd better call. I was talking to Joe. He said you were here.'

'Did he tell you I didn't want to see you?'

'He did indeed.'

'Well, then.'

'Don't close the door. Please. I want to say I'm sorry.'

'You've nothing to be sorry for. Look, I told you if anything like this happened you were on your own. I didn't tell lies.'

'I only tell them when I have to.'

'Do you have any idea what you've done? Do you know how stupid I feel? I was at your house yesterday. Your mother is off her head with worry. Your poor father is fit to be tied. You can't do that to other people's lives. Just you go away, now.'

'If I didn't care I wouldn't be here.'

'It's a bit late caring now. You've only ever cared for yourself, mister. Look at the state of you. I feel sorry for you, hard man. Do you get a thrill out of messing people about?'

'I love you, and that's the truth.'

'You wouldn't know the truth if it ran over you. You lied to me from start to finish. And now that wee fella is dead, and you can't bring him back. You're only sorry for yourself.'

'Spinkey knew what he was doing. I don't feel sorry about that. I'm only worried if I've lost you.'

'You never had me to lose. The fella I was going with was somebody else. I believed him when he said he wasn't up to anything. I feel for that fella. You're just a ghost of him. It is all over. Goodbye.'

'The fella you were going with was me. You'd better believe that. He didn't tell you anything because he didn't want you worrying. Same as he didn't tell his Ma or his Da, nor put it in the newspapers. If you shut that door, girl, ye're shutting out the only one who'll ever love you well. Would I be here in this state if I didn't feel for you? What did you expect of me? What do you want me to say now? I can't change what's happened. But I want to change me. Do you understand? Don't shut me out, Claire. Ye're all I have. There's no more left in me, only what I feel for you.'

'I thought I was getting to know you.'

'I never lied to you about how I felt.'

'How can I trust anything you say?'

'I lied because I had to lie. I don't any more.'

'If you had been straight with me, at least I could have made my mind up. You used me. You made me look like a fool. You stayed over in Jennifer Brennan's last night. I was sitting here crying my eyes out like an idiot, and you were off with some bit of skirt over there. How big a fool do you take me for?' Her aunt came out to the door.

'Are you all right, Claire?'

'I'm all right. This boy is just leaving.'

'How'ye, son. Cold night, isn't it?'

'It is, yeah.'

'Will ye not take him in off the doorstep, Claire? That's not a night for standing out talking.'

'He's going now, auntie.'

'Right ye are then. You know best. Nice to meet ye, son. I've heard a lot about ye.'

'Auntie!'

'Right, right. I'm away inside. If ye change yer mind, come in.'

When she left, Claire made to close the door a third time.

'Whatever Jennifer said about last night is a load of rubbish. There was nothing going on between yer woman and me. I had to stay somewhere, and that's where I landed up. She's a friend of Dingus Grey's, and he was there every minute. Yer woman has it in for me because I had a row with her boyfriend.'

'You never stop, do ye? It just keeps coming out of ye.'

'That's not fair. I'm not leaving this doorstep till you believe me. I've screwed everything up this weekend, every damn thing. I'm not proud of myself, granted. There's not much to be proud of. I've told you lies, I've wrecked my mother and father. I'm everything you say, and more. But I swear, I feel for you more than anything else in the world, like I've never felt for anyone, like I'll never feel again for anyone. I don't want us to throw it away. Do you see that?'

'How could I ever trust you? Look at our Joe. He's never changed, not in years. There's still a badness in him. You can't wash it out like a tea-stain or something. Do you not see I want nothing to do with it?'

'Neither do I. Not anymore.'

'If only I could believe that.'

'I'm off to the South tonight. I won't be back, ever. I've been running about like a blue-arsed fly all weekend, trying to figure it out. I've nothing left to give, Claire. Even if I wanted to, I'd be no use to anyone. I'm a mental wreck. Look at the state of me, girl. I just want out and away from it.'

'Is it as easy as that?'

'No one can make you fight, Claire. All I'm fighting for is you. If we don't mean anything to each other, than there's no hope for me.'

'Emotional blackmail. You never know when to quit.'

'Can you say you don't love me?'

'Would I be listening to this if I didn't?'

'I love you, believe me.'

'I wouldn't go so far as to believe you. What's to be done about it?'

'Will you come to Dublin?'

'God, no. What would I do there? It's too far, too dear. Would you like it across the water?'

'England might not be a good idea. I've seen enough of the Brits to do me a lifetime.'

'I'm making a big mistake even entertaining you. I should have nothing to do with you.'

'It might be the best move you ever make.'

'Don't push your luck. You're back on probation again. That's all it is. There's no more second chances. You're out of the fight from this minute. Is that understood?'

'They probably wouldn't have me back.'

'Is it understood?'

'I understand.'

'You may come in for a cup of tea, then. You look like you could do with a bite to eat.'

She put her hand out and barred the way.

'Whatever you think, I'm not going to forgive you as easy as that. I wish I could run down the path, but for now I'll take you at face value. There won't be any more chances. And it's you that will be missing out, not me.'

I kissed her gently on the mouth. She held my hand as she did the child's. I was too tired to say anything, but walked behind her into the kitchen.

They had shadowed her from work, expecting her to lead them up the Falls Road. When had she turned off into the enclave where her aunt lived, they could only follow and leave. All strategy in the conflict was based on percentages. The chances of mounting surveillance in that area at that time were less than zero. They operated on sufferance in these streets, a closed community where the police were considered a terrorist organisation, where the writ of the revolution was respected. Retiring to the local barracks, they organised low-key monitoring of the area and the roads leading in. At six fifteen, a soldier reported the entry of a red Fiesta, driven by a man answering my description. They checked out the car's provenance and found it was registered to a man on the south side of town. A further inquiry ascertained his description, which contradicted mine. By half-six, they had their suspicious car, and a fair suspicion as to the driver.

The young constable was chewing a hamburger at his desk when Harry Grange arrived.

'Have you heard the latest, Harry?'

'About this suspect vehicle?'

'No. There's some wee lad attacked the fort a while ago.'

'Anyone hurt?'

'Three soldiers taken to hospital with their balls laughed off. Yer man was chucking rocks at the front gate and him bollock naked. Scared the life out of the Brits.'

'Is this their new tactics? Scare us with the size of their lashes?'

'Naked terrorism, Harry. Naked terrorism.'

'They're all mad, ye know. Never met one that wasn't.'

'Maybe it's just a flash in the pan.'

'What's the story of this character in the Fiesta?'

'Sounds like our man, all right. The minute he comes out of wherever he is, the Brits will lift him and have a look at him. It's all in hand.'

'It's good to know we weren't dealing with a Mastermind champion here. What would bring him back here, do you think?'

'It's what you said, Harry. They're all mad in the head. In-breeding does it.'

'You might have a point there. I'll wait till ten or so, then I'm away home. Let's see does he raise his head.'

After a feed of liver and beans, which I couldn't refuse, myself and her aunt got down to talking. She quizzed me on my relations and neighbours, throwing her hands up in delight when she recognised a relationship or an incident from long ago. The little chap, Kevin, engaged me in fixing one of his birthday presents, a battery car with a broken wheel. His Da was working these two years in England and the kid loved male company in the house, even if it was this apparition of a man whom he figured to be drunk, but was merely tired and stunned. Claire moved silently around the kitchen, sometimes stopping to look at me blankly as she did the clearing and the dishes. Her aunt was more interested in me than she was, probing away and forming her opinions in the canny way of the real city woman, reading between the lines. As she and Claire held a conference in the kitchen, and the young lad curled on the sofa for a nap, I allowed my eyes to close. In the heat and homeliness I slipped away into sleep, and when they returned after their low confab, they found us both pegged out in front of the droning television set. Claire stood in the doorway, looking long and hard at me.

She turned to her smiling aunt and shook her head.

'What am I going to do?'

A man once said that it's easy to train men to use guns, but it's hard to tell them not to use them. In his day Joey O'Brien had been a popular local hero. Then both Provos and Officials had supplied local defence against the Orange activists, armed and ruthless resistance to the British army. When the Sticks had downed tools, Joey had taken the announcement for politicking, and by the time he had realised that the ceasefire was really that, a ceasefire, it had been too late to remonstrate or switch allegiances.

Years of standing on the sidelines watching the Provies and the Brits making all the going had turned him sour and soft, and now he had come to this. Faced down and caught dead drunk by a little swine, the same puke who had usurped his place in his sister's feelings, who posed such a threat to her happiness.

In the bathroom at home he nursed his testicles. He had taken some knocks on his day, but this was a hammer blow. They stared up at him, like two angry old bald men, accusing him. In the kitchen he drank a beer and stared at his reflection in a kettle. When the temper and shame left him, he got dressed in his best suit, brushed his teeth and conspired to look sober. He stowed away his gun, and left the house with a few bits and pieces he had thrown into a canvas bag. At the top of the road he caught a bus which left him near his aunt's house.

When I woke, she was standing by the bedside in the dark. I could muzzily remember being taken upstairs and flopping down and into sleep.

'Where am I?'

'You're sleeping in my bed. You can't stay here, you know.'

'Has it been long?'

'About an hour. I can't go with you.'

'I haven't much to offer you.'

'It's not only that. It'll never work between us.'

'I love you, though. That must count for something.'

'We'll see. Sleep for another while. Have you somewhere to stay?'

'I'll get on the road, shortly.'

'You're not fit to drive. Not tonight.'

'I'm only catching up on my sleep. I'll be all right.'

She stroked my hair until I relapsed.

What was the sum of my dreams? What was my normality? The killer in me resting, buried under waves of exhaustion, of dread, of confusion.

We had been waiting inside the garage for an hour before Bradley called over and gave us an address. Bricks couldn't drive then, so I took the wheel. We were a while finding the right door. I was surprised to find Mo there. The flat was lit by a tilly lamp glowing on a scuffed coffee table. Mo told us what was to be done. I was surprised they needed us: they ought to have taken care of it themselves; he was one of their own. It was as if Mo were testing me, studying my reactions beneath a fine mesh of smoky net which crossed the stifling air. I tried to look unconcerned.

The gun was in a pillow-case, lying on the sofa. I stuffed the case into my shirt and was walked down the long landing past the broken flats and back down the trying flights of stairs. At the rear of the flats, three men were waiting. They nodded solemnly to us. One of them passed the cigarettes. I politely declined. From behind a stinking rubbish skip, they produced him. He was a small, blonde man, trussed up with hay rope - yellow, brittle rope, but it held him. Out on the road, traffic was darting up and down a stone's throw away, but here we were shielded by walls and bushes which were somehow growing on the inhospitable ground. They forced him back down to his knees.

Bricks came to me and whispered, 'Do ye want me to do it?'

I looked at him, and said, 'No. It's my job.'

As the three men took up position at the wall corners, one came up to me. 'Make sure you do it clean.'

I nodded. They had pulled a dark cap over his head.

From beneath it I could hear a man breathing in a laboured, sickly train of gasps. I took the shooter from its sheath and nudged off the safety. My hand was suddenly trembling. There arose the sound of whimpering, a sound so low and plaintive it may have been prayer. I reached out and shoved the hood back over his ear, exposing the temple, and tried to remember the training and the lectures, the pale face of a man older than he should have been factually telling us the best way to do it, in the back of a van bouncing over the Armagh hills on the way home. An afterthought. More war stories.

An irate voice came from behind. 'Will you fucking hurry up?'

I scooped his hair back over the ear and pressed the muzzle tight to his temple, then drew the gun straight back to within an inch of the chosen spot, and fired. He jerked, rose and collapsed as if hit by a massive electrical bolt, a great shocked gasp rending the air. His flailing legs caught my own and almost brought me down. I felt like running away, running and never stopping till I was on board a boat, but somehow I was rooted there, fascinated at this writhing sack of clothes which refused to be still. Almost instinctively I stood over him and put the gun back down to the bloody hood and fired, twice. On the second shot he stopped moving.

Bricks caught my sleeve. 'Let's go.'

We marched back into the flats and took the stairs ten at a time. I stopped as we neared base, breathless and ill, the sort of illness you got as a child, when you'd been spun around the room too much by a boisterous uncle.

Bricks murmured admiringly, 'He didn't feel a thing, did he?'

At times like that you don't want to disagree.

Mo had the look of a funeral director on his face, meeting the relatives of the deceased and about to distastefully mention money.

'How did it go?'

'I gave him a couple extra to help him on his way.'

'Fair enough. It always is a messy business.'

One of the look-outs came in. The shots had gone unnoticed.

A thousand people had gone deaf. More than half knew what those shots represented. One of their own dispatched. City justice.

Mo dropped the gravity of his expression.

'I don't know about you chaps, but I'm starving. Does anyone fancy a Chinese?'

When he mentioned it, my initial revulsion turned quickly to a feeling of total hunger. I could have eaten a horse that night.

When I awoke from an unbalanced, difficult sleep, I found myself lying alongside a soapy-smelling kid who had entangled himself in my face and arms. I prised him off, and soothed him back to repose. Sliding from the bed, I checked my watch. It was nine thirty-five. There were mumbling voices downstairs. When I reached the kitchen door, I froze. Joey boy. My heart began to pound. The car, with the gun in it, was parked down the street, a good twenty doors away. I had a sudden vision of the Clan O'Brien having lured me into a trap, now about to set upon me as one. I went inside to find him seated and drinking a cup of tea, not one apparent bother on him.

'All right, Joe.'

'Ah! Here's Sleeping Beauty now,' said his aunt.

Joe was mulling over his words.

'I'm all right. What about yerself?'

'Never better. I needed that wee rest.'

'I hear ye've some travelling ahead of ye. The rest will do ye good.'

'Yeah. I have to be off.'

'No real hurry. I suppose I should congratulate you.'

'I told Joe about us getting married,' said Claire, now looking bright-eyed and bushy tailed. She had made herself up and was obviously trying to pass this confrontation off as a family party. It was the first I'd heard of marriage, but this was no time to be cheeky.

'Yeah,' I said. 'We wanted you to be the first to know.'

'Ye'll make half a lovely couple, anyhow.'

'You'll be getting hitched next, Joseph,' chipped in his aunt.

'Not after what happened me the night, Auntie. I lost my entrance tickets.'

'I'm sorry about that, Joe. I got a bit carried away.'

'What are you two talking about?'

'Nothing, Sis.'

'Me and Joe had a bit of a fall-out earlier. It's all behind us now, isn't that right, Joe?' He didn't answer.

'I came with a bit of news myself. I'm away down to Cork to live for a while. There's a mate of mine can fix me up with work.'

The two ladies went into the scullery, clearly leaving us to chat. After a while, it was he who broke the silence.

'I haven't forgotten, and I never forgive.'

'Neither have I. Guns scare me, Joe. There's nothing between us that needs a gun.'

'I just wonder about that.'

'I'm getting out, Joe, away out as far as I can.'

'Ye're taking my sister with ye. I was planning on getting out and leaving ye to it, anyway. She's a fool herself. Ye beat me to the punch for the second time tonight.'

'She has a mind of her own, Joe. It's her decision.'

'I'm glad I won't be at the wedding.'

'You'll be giving her away, Joe. And ye'll enjoy it.'

'We'll see.'

'How come you've changed your tune, Joe? I wouldn't take you for it.'

'I haven't. I've changed my tune about myself, is all. A while ago you wouldn't have come out of that pub alive. But if I'd taken care of you, she would never forgive me. Then there would be a next one, and a one after that. That's what saved you, that and a few whiskeys too many. From what I can see, she's set on you. It broke me up to see her this weekend. I'll never like you, fella, and I'll never trust you. Nor your sort. But if I get too involved, it'll only make matters worse.'

'I do love her, Joe.'

'You and me are too alike. We only love ourselves, back of it all. Keep yer nose clean and use some brains for a change. Maybe things will work out for ye.'

'If you don't mind me saying so, ye're being very reasonable about all this.'

'Not so reasonable that if there's a next time I won't kill ye stone dead. You believe that, boy.'

'You've nothing to worry about. I'll get sorted down South and send for her. If you want, I can give you a lift to Dublin tonight.'

'Me sit in a car with you? I fancy keeping the head where it is. These bastards will kill you on sight, boy. There's a Brit was shot in that wee escapade yez pulled the other night. He died in hospital tonight. You count yerself lucky if you make the border.'

'How long will you be in Cork?'

'Six or seven months should get me a few quid together. Then I'll take a run back and open a wee business. I have the shop picked and all.'

'What line of business?'

'Flowers. I always loved the smell of flower shops. Warm, friendly smell, like ye don't get anywhere else.'

Joe the florist. I can't say how much of it was fertiliser, but Spinkey sure would have laughed to see Sticky Joe pouring his heart out to me. I thought of him then. He would laugh no more, gone for his tea. Joe was right. You can only go so far before the burden cripples you. You can't live it for other people.

'Have you two been getting along? I thought you would be at each other's throats by now.' Claire had returned. She sat on the edge of his chair and put an arm around him.

'We were getting on OK,' I said, quietly.

'Me and the wee lad have been having a man to man. Are you sure you want to marry him? I think he's a bit of a chancer.'

'It takes one to know one, big brother. Has he asked you to be best man yet?'

'I'm thinking whether I'll go. Let's just see.'

There wasn't the trace of a conspiratorial smile on her face. She had seized the initiative. It gladdened me. That was how it was to be, it was in the air. From now she made the decisions. She would take me on, but on her conditions, under her terms. I wasn't to be trusted with her future, and that was fine by me. I didn't even trust myself. In the absurdity of the situation I found a sense of rebirth. Now there was all to play for, and if it meant playing happy families with Joey O'Brien, then so be it.

Joe rose, having decided it was time he was gone. He had a lift organised with a mate who was heading south on overnight business.

'If you children will excuse me, it's time I was off.'

'I'll be heading shortly myself, Joe. Are you sure I can't drop you anywhere?'

'You get yourself out of the area in one piece, son. And from now on you do the right thing, or you answer to me.'

'No fears, Joe.'

No fears. For the first time in two nights, no fears. Regaining the feeling of humanity, the fear of the weekend softening into a confused and happy state. As he left, behind his back she put her warm hand in mine and stole a kiss. Her aunt spotted it from the corner of her eye, and smiled.

It was seven minutes past ten as Joey O'Brien left the house. His distracted thoughts were interrupted by the sight of two young boys checking out a strange car in the street. They were seeing if there was anything worth stealing in the vehicle. Joey reverted to his role of potential councillor and challenged them, causing them to walk away.

He smiled to himself. There was life in the old dog yet. As he came to the vehicle, he noticed a smashed tail light, and called out to the sulking youths, 'Did youse do that?'

One small boy squared up to him from the safety of the far

side of the street. 'Fuck off, mister. We was nowhere near it.'

Joe stood there looking for broken glass, a canvas bag in his hand.

I was getting ready to leave the house. We had agreed I would write, that she would join me as soon as she could get someone to mind the house, that everything would be worked out. She was holding my hand in the darkened hallway, reluctant to face the parting moment. Between us was a future, a crack in the prison walls of our birth through which we might squeeze. My heart was throbbing and my mouth dry. It was hard to hope, to reconcile the possibility of a new beginning with what had gone before. I was using her like a crowbar to lift off the weight which was suffocating me. Maybe she was my way out. But I felt I loved her, and that was as good as knowing, for when the shot rang out I grabbed her and put myself between her and the door, each of us looking at the other in panic, not comprehending anything in the crack of the SLR so close to us.

'They've come for me.'

'Oh, God.'

'Quick son. You get out the back. I'll take a look outside and see what that's about.'

'You don't move, Auntie.'

Then the thump at the door and a shout. A civilian. The door half opened. An old man, breathless, disbelieving. 'Claire, love. I think your Joe's been shot.'

The stunned moment that is a lifetime. She threw herself out to the street, into the rushing people racing from their homes. Young girls running, dispatched to find siblings, young men running for action. She among them, a distressed, pained expression, the look of an animal before the kill. And I was walking in a dream behind, watching her race ahead through the onlookers collected in a knot some ten feet from the Fiesta.

Suddenly a furious cry. A screeching Land Rover stopped at the car, but I couldn't run, or go back, drawn forward to the cluster beyond, heart pounding, tears welling in my eyes. At the edge of the excited crowd a hand reached out and grabbed me. It took me a moment to recognise Bradley in the jostling. They were pushing and shoving to have a peek at the central attraction, from where a full-blooded, lengthy scream erupted. I shrugged him off and pushed into the middle.

She was cradling Joe in her arms. A woman was trying to talk her into rising, but she was oblivious to all but the agony. Her keening was submerged in an angry roar as the Brits on the fringe moved in to claim the body, to secure a path for an ambulance. There was scuffling and cursing and one angry screech as they were repulsed and forced from the middle. Bradley had me by the cuff and was frantically pulling at me. As I bent to help her, to offer what poor love was in me, she looked up at me. There was a blank, glaring hatred in her eyes. She no longer knew me, or knew me as her nemesis. As she held his bloody corpse, as he released his last wind in a thin rattle, she stared at me in recognition. 'Get away from me! Get away! Get away!'

In a small, poorly cared for house, I spent a sleepless night. I sat stock still on a chair, staring into a fireplace. A bulky woman moved quietly about, circumspectly putting coal on the fire, clearing the table. Several times she offered me tea, and I shook my head. The man of the house sat up most of the night, talking to me, talking to himself. He was a huge man with an empty sleeve where an arm had once been. He told me stories of his son – simple, innocent, endless stories speaking as if I should know the boy. But I barely listened and could not respond. Bradley came in several times, and when he looked at me there was anger in him, and mockery.

When the sun came up, the one-armed man rose from his chair. He smelt of sweat and age as he brushed past me. Staleness. He went stiffly up the stairs. As dawn broke and the room became grey, I got up and switched off the light. On the mantelpiece was a photograph of a young man, in a gold frame too rich for the image within. It was a snap hived off a greater photograph, probably a group photograph of some post-training unit in far off days. A young, proud man in serious stance, dressed in webbing and jumper, with a beret on his head. A head full of ideals, full of grave intent and dedication. He seemed vaguely familiar, not facially dissimilar to myself, if he had relaxed. I was studying the photograph when Ronan came in. He looked at me as if I owed him money, as if I had somehow let him down.

'What took you back here?'

'I had someone to see.'

'That's what I heard. They reckon that bullet was for you.'

'Probably.'

'Are you not worried?'

'What's there to be worried about?'

'You can worry about Mo for a start. He's not best pleased with you. If ye're ready we'll go up and see him.'

I was in no mood to argue. I followed him to the car. We drove through deserted streets, in a land I no longer recognised. There were no patrols, no furious crowds. No dangers, no comforts, nothing but the dull aching in me. In a house in the shadow of a chapel, on a cold iron-grey morning, I met Mo. He was warming himself on the twin bars of a tiny heater. We talked in low, clear tones as the residents slept upstairs and Ronan kept watch from the parlour window.

'I won't ask you what you are doing here. Suffice to say you should be somewhere else, and I should be catching up on my sleep.'

'I've no apology to make, Maurice. Put it down to experience.'

'I put it down to disregarding orders, chap. And I don't need cheek from ye.'

'So court-martial me.'

'I have the feeling that won't get us far. How do you feel?'

'I feel like death warmed up.'

'From what we can gather they had you under some type of surveillance. O'Brien was in the same house, correct?'

'That's it.'

'Chances are it was just an excitable Brit. Over-zealous.'

'I'm beyond caring.'

'Has it got you that bad?'

'It's been a rough few days.'

'I can imagine. We are ... concerned about you.'

'You needn't be.'

'What do you want to do?'

'I'm handing in my notice, Mo.'

'I talked you out of it once before.'

'I'm no good to man or beast. There's no way I'll operate again. That's the last word on it.'

'I'll be sorry to lose you. You're washed up in this area anyway. If you like, I can get you introduced along the border.'

'Can you see me in wellingtons? I'm a city boy. Listen, it's much deeper than that.'

'You and I both know you never leave. Not really. If it's any comfort, I have an idea of how deep it is. But someday you may feel different. Don't be a stranger, chap. Someday you'll look back and be glad, be proud. Do you hear me? Otherwise it's just waste, waste. Do you see that?'

'All I see at the minute is death.'

'You won't always see that. We had some crack as well in our day.'

'We had some crack, all right. For me it's over. I've done my bit, Mo.'

'There's no one will say any different, believe me. Get ready to leave around ten. I'm taking a nap now; I suggest you do the same. Ronan will run you over the border. That's what he should have done on Sunday. We wouldn't have had all this shit to worry about.'

I couldn't sleep, as the house was quickly awake. There was frying bacon, curious children, uncertain looks and polite conversation. I left Mo sleeping in the house, and we drove down into the estate. We parked up at Ronan's house at ten past ten or so. He asked me in.

'We'd best wait till the funeral is over.'

'What funeral?'

He looked at me strangely.

'Spinkey Driscoll's fucking funeral. You want to wise up, wee man.'

It hadn't occurred to me. From his back bedroom we had a view of the cortège. We waited in the quiet of the room until the hearse slid into view.

'There's the lads.'

From the facing street came a guard of honour, led by the crow-black girls of the *Cumann*, flanked by six boys of *Na Fianna Éirinn*, followed by the battle-dressed, hooded men of the Republic, the stateless soldiers of the rearguard. They fell in at the sides and the rear of the hearse. My father and old Driscoll, with two other elderly men, awkwardly transferred the coffin to the guard, as Bradley spoke low orders from beneath his hood. As the funeral moved on I saw my father grip his neighbour's arm, and him so small and old, so beaten and depressed.

My mother and Spinkey's followed, his Ma so weak, so distraught. They were all there behind. Big George and Barry, Helen and Brenda, looking so blamelessly sexual in her black. (Spinkey finally got to step out with her.) Tommy, Toto, the boys from the club, murmuring to each other and smoking, all so serious, so manly, so stoical and so slightly embarrassed, and behind, the growing throng of neighbours and friends, the rolling mass of the risen people of these barren bands of streets – the Republicans, the nationalists, the committed and the unsure, the religious, the indifferent. A host of wonder-filled, silent children and a phalanx of hard-nosed, hard-dressed boys with an unending potential for revenge and vindication.

He had been a warling, one of their own, one of them all. There were none here to condemn or to damn, but the streets were filled by all who saw a bit of their own agonised dreams in his death. West Belfast raised him and taught him, and brought him the dreams which took us down a cold road on a silent early morning.

'Don't be a stranger,' said Mo. How could I be a stranger, ever, to these people and their simple ambitions. A while after the procession, we left.

Ronan gave up talking to me as the journey progressed. I could only look at the skeletal trees and the corpulent, green fields, and sigh at the bumpy roads which took us the back way into the sullen county of Louth, beyond which was a life I barely wanted.

POSTSCRIPT

As Spinkey was buried, and as I left the city, police comrades lowered Constable Patterson into his grave. In a tiny postcard village he was buried amongst his own.

Toss O'Reilly stood trial for his killing in the hospital raid, but was cleared of the charge when statements credited to him failed to stand up in court. Nevertheless, he was found guilty on associated charges and received a ten-year sentence. Bricks O'Hare spent three years on the blanket protest in Long Kesh, joining the first hunger strike as a volunteer in the prison war. I had no direct contact with him during the twelve years he served, but I heard he disappeared upon release. Ten-to-One received an eight-year term, some of which he spent on the blanket. He drives a taxi in Dublin now.

Two years after his death the inquest into Joey O'Brien heard that he had approached a stolen car and made to drive it off. The soldier who had dispatched him stated that he had called on the deceased to stop; that the deceased had reached into a canvas bag and brought out a handgun; that he had fired a single shot at the deceased, and that the handgun had been ferried off by terrorist sympathisers who had gathered at the scene. For the police, Inspector Grange, first on the scene, had found nothing to disprove the soldier's account; indeed, a small-calibre weapon had been discovered hidden in the deceased's car, lending weight to the military version of events. An open verdict was returned.

Dingus made so many visits to the mental hospital after his naked assault on the local army post that there was talk of installing a revolving door for him. Each time he appeared he was functionally worse, until one night in winter he died, having lain stupefied with drink in a pool of water that froze. They had to break him off the ground to fit him into the umpteenth ambulance of his career. Those who didn't know blamed the Brits and his running battle for his madness. But Dingus had always been too free for us all.

A universe away, in time, in place, I'm in a tiny bed-sit in the middle of London, wondering at the strength of the condensation on the window-pane. It is early morning.

A long time elapsed before I dragged myself home, for my mother's wake. The funeral was unadvertised, practically secret, to allow me the chance to stand by her graveside. Afterwards I took a moment to walk among the graves of fallen revolutionaries, to pause over the names I knew. My father stared at me from the huddle of waiting relatives. There were no words between us, and when I returned again it was to bury him, the ultimate civilian in a city gone insane.

The hunger strikes had ravaged West Belfast and solidified its terrible destiny. Mo turned up for the funeral, to my surprise. He was a lot brighter and younger than I remembered him. The Long War was agreeing with him, and I was tickled by the irony of his newly and easily won seat on the city council. New phases, new ways: same struggle.

The young man asks if it would be all right to put some music on. I tell him to keep it low. I've spent years keeping the neighbours happy, no matter where I lived. Years staying nameless, staying blameless. He puts in a cassette and returns to the table as a slow ballad runs around the little room, just beneath my thoughts.

Claire O'Brien weighed heavily for years, the unyielding anchor tying me to those days. She once asked my sister to get me to write, perhaps trying to lay the ghost, but I never can.

The kid at the table is humming unconsciously to the tune as he deftly tapes the last coach bolt on to the package. Satisfied, he looks up at me, just a little puzzled.

'Are you sure about this seven-second fuse bit?'

I can't help but grin. He thinks my old legs won't carry me. Jesus, I'm over thirty. To him, I'm past it.

'Any longer and there'd be no fun in it.'

He shrugs his shoulders. You can't put a price on inexperience. He has the simplicity and the eagerness which eluded me all those years ago. His is a black-and-white world, and he has yet to lose. You have to experience loss, you have to keep paying the entrance fee. For the show goes interminably on, the revues and tableaux unfolding, time whiling itself away to some promised climax that refuses to come.

That weekend was my making. It stripped me of all save the few inherited truths which could not be dissolved, which itched and throbbed in my abandoned heart and slowly, insistently drew me back, always back, to the central pride at my root.

The young man thinks he is history's master. I am its slave.

The music expires, the room grows chilly. The youth is becoming impatient, nervous, anxious to hide it.

'Tell me,' says he, 'what time will we be back at?'

'Is it important?' He is standing by the door, a carrier bag at his side, like a puppy anxious for release.

'I just want back for eleven. Yer one, Anne Diamond, is on the television. I never miss her show.'

Christ, there's no end to the eejits. Looking out at the alien nothingness I feel my destiny forever being retraced, as what goes around comes around, and I'm happily trapped in the circle of my days, duty bound to spiral through mad mornings to the last.

Outside, a car horn sounds, and puts to flight the baying memories, the empty introspection, summoning us to our inescapable vocation.